Praise for

ALL THE LONELY PEOPLE

"…a tender and heartfelt journey through grief. With The Beatles' music woven into the fabric of the story, and an unforgettable romance, this is one book you won't want to put down until the end."

—Sonia Hartl (*Have a Little Faith in Me*, Page Street and *Heartbreak for Hire*, Gallery Books)

"…touching, poignant, beautifully-written, fast-paced, irresistibly romantic and funny. Oh my gosh, funny. You can read this in any mood and it will lift you up. Don't miss this one! Jen Marie Hawkins is a fresh, beguiling new voice in must-read YA."

—Elly Blake, NYT Bestselling author of the Frostblood series

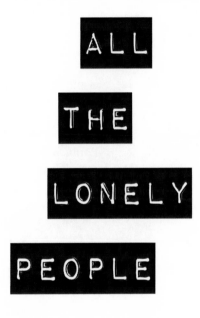

ALL THE LONELY PEOPLE

Jen Marie Hawkins

OWL HOLLOW PRESS

Owl Hollow Press, LLC, Springville, UT 84663

All the Lonely People

Library of Congress Cataloging-in-Publication Data
All the Lonely People / J.M. Hawkins — First edition.

Summary:
When Jo lost her father three years earlier under mysterious circumstances, he began appearing in her dreams, beckoning her to London where he'd been the lead singer of an internationally acclaimed Beatles cover band. Armed with an atlas of Britain's supernatural ley lines and a tenuous friendship, she sets out with a new friend to uncover the truth and discover what they've grown to mean to each other.

ISBN 978-1-945654-78-7 (paperback)
ISBN 978-1-945654-79-4 (e-book)
LCCN 2021940777

Cover design by Jen Marie Hawkins. Image via Shutterstock.

For my boys,
Jonathan and Jackson.
You are both
my best and brightest dreams
come to life.

*"A dream you dream alone
is only a dream.
A dream you dream together
is reality."*

—John Lennon

CHAPTER ONE

: Across the Universe :

BEYOND THE INTERNATIONAL arrivals gate at Heathrow, welcome-to-London fanfare swirls like confetti that's meant for someone else. Fellow passengers move past me toward families and friends and people holding signs with their names on them.

Only Pop's memory has shown up to greet me.

He flickers like a hologram in my periphery, parting a sea of people with guitar riffs. A playful grin stretches through his wild, penny-red beard. He opens his mouth and sings off-key: *Jojo was a girl who thought she was a loner.* It's on purpose— the changed lyrics and the fact it's off-key—because *of course* it's on purpose. Pop had pipes, and he regularly threw himself on the altar of humiliation to make me smile.

See, *that* is the Pop I remember. He wasn't a die-in-a-hotel-room-with-a-needle-in-his-arm kind of guy. And I've come here to prove that.

Floor-to-ceiling glass stretches up one side of the terminal, dumping buckets of gray evening light inside. Pop always went on and on about the silver sky, and I get it now. *Poof.* The past tense in my head makes him disappear. He fades into the secret letter folded in my wallet.

A near-constant pain reverberates along my solar plexus. I try to ignore it, but it has the tinny, extended frequency of a crashed cymbal. Even when the song is over, the residue lingers.

I hobble over and take a seat in a chair next to baggage claim, and while I wait, tilt my phone's viewfinder until my feet fill the camera screen.

Right foot: tucked snug-as-a-bug in a red ballet flat. Left foot: bare. *Click.*

Caption: shoe theft at twenty-thousand feet

My left shoe was missing when I woke up on the tarmac. It vanished at some point after I'd fallen asleep. I'd waited until the man-spreader beside me started snoring before I closed my eyes; he had a certain vibe from the moment he harrumphed into the aisle seat and trapped me in. My suspicion was confirmed when he rubbernecked the romance novel Lexie let me borrow for the flight. I always skip to the good parts, and he caught me, as evidenced by his sleazy eyebrow wiggle.

After that, he insisted on calling me *little lady* while hogging my armrest and regaling me on the success of his *biz-niss in Chah-lutt.* Frankly, he's the kind of Southerner that makes the rest of us look bad. Everyone knows the type. It wasn't what he said, but how he said it, all leering and obnoxious. Former Auburn football coach meets Foghorn Leghorn.

When I woke up, he was gone, along with my shoe.

I knew I wouldn't find it. Two weeks ago, before I found out I'd be coming here, I dreamed I was standing shoeless in an airport. This odd little psychic dream phenomenon has been happening on and off for three years: I dream it, and then it happens.

Sometimes the details vary a smidge. I'm only missing one shoe; in the dream, I was missing both. And I'm standing on plain gray tile instead of gleaming white marble. I guess my sixth sense assumes European airports are fancier and shoe thieves are more thorough.

There have been times, though, that I've relived a dream exactly as it happened while I slept. The first time was right after Pop died. Mama and I had gone to the grocery store one Saturday afternoon, and while I was waiting on her to finish checking out, Pop's voice whispered: *You want some gum?* A slant of sunlight broke in through the storefront and bathed the gumball machine in an otherworldly glow. I went to it. Without putting a quarter in, I reached up and turned the handle. It cranked one, two, three times, and then the whole thing poured out in my hands. A few smaller kids ran over and picked up the ones that slipped through my fingers—red and blue and purple hitting the floor in a chorus of pops and tinkles.

I knew I'd leave the store with my pockets full of gumballs before I ever touched the knob that day, because I'd dreamed it the night before. Pop stood on the edge of my periphery, giving me a thumbs-up. When I turned, he was gone.

There have been many of these dreams, but there's one in particular that I'm desperate to make a reality. The dreams are the *real* reason I've come here, but nobody else knows that. On paper, I'm here to make college visits and skip a senior year elective. I can't go around telling folks that Pop is sending me winks and nudges and beckoning me to the UK, through psychic dreams, to clear his name. People (like me) who have daily medication regimens know which things to keep zipped up. Faking normal is imperative. Faking normal is how I got my psychiatrist to sign off on five weeks between sessions so I could make this trip.

There's one other suspicion I can't tell anyone about—a less likely one—so I just need to disprove it: What if Pop is still somewhere in the UK, alive? And the urn in my carry-on bag is full of dust instead of his remains?

CHAPTER

TWO

: Her Majesty :

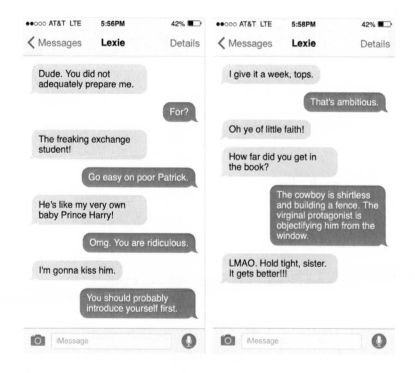

Lexie

Dude. You did not adequately prepare me.

For?

The freaking exchange student!

Go easy on poor Patrick.

He's like my very own baby Prince Harry!

Omg. You are ridiculous.

I'm gonna kiss him.

You should probably introduce yourself first.

Lexie

I give it a week, tops.

That's ambitious.

Oh ye of little faith!

How far did you get in the book?

The cowboy is shirtless and building a fence. The virginal protagonist is objectifying him from the window.

LMAO. Hold tight, sister. It gets better!!!

I'M SURROUNDED BY shoes.

There are shiny oxfords and beige stilettos. Casual loafers and laced athletics. I guess the things you don't have yourself are more noticeable when other folks do have them.

Passengers scramble to identify and collect their zippered clones. I wait for my own, a red Samsonite covered in sewn-on patches Pop brought me from his Walrus Gumboot world tour. It overflows with more thrifted clothes than I can wear in five weeks. And plenty of shoes, thank the stars.

I field a few disapproving glances as the crowd thins. My toes curl under, and I stare a hole through the curtain at the end of the conveyor. My phone blares *Her Majesty* from my back pocket and makes me jump. Heads turn as I scramble to answer it. All of my ringtones were chosen to showcase my status as Beatles Fan™. But as I stand here absorbing the side-eyes, I realize my credibility isn't quite landing.

I answer the FaceTime call before it stops ringing. "Hey."

Mama's frantic face appears. If the antidepressants hadn't dulled my ability to read auras, I'd bet hers has turned from pale pink to ink black. I concentrate for a moment. Squint my eyes. Stare hard just past her—but no. Still nothing. It's been two days since my last dose. Might take a little longer.

"Josie Michelle Bryant!" she hollers. "You promised you'd call the minute you arrived! Flight tracker says you landed forty-six minutes ago!"

She's louder than the ringtone. I rapid-fire the volume button down.

"Don't have a fit, Mama. I had a slight technical difficulty."

I pan the camera to my feet and back again. Her pencil-thin eyebrows make a V on her forehead. "Where's your shoe?"

"Someone must've picked it up by accident." I say this a little louder than necessary for the benefit of the gawkers. "I woke up on the plane and it was gone."

I know better than to mention Foghorn Leghorn. She'll go broke hiring a security detail to follow me if she thinks perverts are stealing my shoes.

"You're walking around *He-frow* barefoot?" I hear our exchange student snicker in the background before his grinning face appears next to Mama on the screen. Though he's standing in my country and I'm standing in his, Patrick's accent jars me. Pop didn't speak that way. You would've never known he was born in Liverpool except when he was drinking. Twenty-five years in the states all but erased it. "People are going to stare."

I laugh. "They're way ahead of you."

Mom cuts in. "I find it interesting that you texted Dylan when you landed, but you couldn't do the same for me."

I roll my eyes so hard I see my brain. The only thing that irritates me more than Mama knowing things about me I didn't tell her myself, is Dylan—boyfriend extraordinaire—being a suck-up.

"He called me the minute he heard from you." Her smile borders on taunting.

Dylan likes to cover his bases. We're both pretty sure the only reason Mama finally agreed to this trip is because she's figured out we've been sleeping together, and she's not ready to make me confess it to the church just yet. Putting an ocean between us is easier.

"I texted him but then had to look for my shoe…" I lose my train of thought as more bags disappear from the conveyor; there's still no sign of mine. Another flight crowds in, and the carousel's obscured. I stand on my tippy toes. "Then it took a while in customs," I continue, searching, "and… Look, can I call you back?"

She huffs that *okay-fine-whatever* huff.

The background swirls and Patrick takes the phone.

"Wait, love." I met Patrick all of twenty-four hours ago, but he already feels familiar in a way I can't explain. "My brother is coming to meet you to ride the tube back. So you don't get lost between stops."

I haven't even been gone a day, and Mama has already lost faith in me to take a train from point A to point C. I siphon a deep breath, filling my lungs with all the things I want to say. Like that I'm seventeen years old and will be off to college in a year. She can't micromanage me then. But the jet lag is setting in. My will slips away like the empty conveyor belt. Where my luggage is supposed to be.

"Fine." I exhale the unspoken words. "Where should I look for him?"

"I gave Henry your mobile number," Patrick says. "He'll text if he can't locate you."

I've only seen photos of Patrick's *bruvah*, as he so eloquently pronounces it, on the Instagram page Dylan and I found. Most of Henry's timeline was landscape photography with vague King Arthur references. Dylan settled down a little after we discovered this. The fact that the guy looked a little homeless in the one selfie on the account didn't hurt either. Beanie, sunglasses, dingy white hoodie. Probable weirdo. Definite introvert. The antithesis of Dylan, who doesn't own a shirt without a tiny whale on the breast pocket.

"And Jo," Patrick adds, "he's sort of a wanker. Keep conversation to a minimum and you'll be just fine." His blue eyes power up when he laughs. Lexie and Maddie, my neighbors back home, will be competing for his attention before I even leave the airport. They've been talking about the impending arrival of *the English boy* for a month.

"Wanker. Got it." I chuckle as he hands Mama the phone. But she isn't laughing.

Her hard expression makes her seem older than usual. I have her round face, honey blond hair, and brown eyes, but the similarity ends there. The sprigs of wrinkles beside her lashes have spiderwebbed and spread. The more she worries, the less her face cream works.

"Call me when you get to George's." And without ceremony, she ends the call. Before I can even say I love you.

CHAPTER THREE

: Help! :

THE BRITISH AIRWAYS customer service rep—*Rupert*, his badge says—slides paperwork across the counter to me.

"Fill out this form. Please describe the property in question as accurately as possible."

"Is there a way you can track it?"

Bright lighting above the help desk shines on Rupert's bald head. He jackhammers keystrokes and stares into the computer screen.

"It seems the mix-up occurred in Charlotte. We'll re-route your bags and deliver them once they've arrived. Be sure to include the proper address for where you'll be staying." He gives me a curt smile, and that's that. Rupert moves to assist the lady behind me, but I step in front of her.

"I'm sorry, excuse me." Her eyes widen as she looks me up and down and finds my bare foot.

"So where are my bags now?" I ask Rupert.

His nostrils flare and he sighs. I try to imagine what color his aura is, because no matter how hard I stare, I can't see it. Maybe he doesn't have one. Maybe he's an alien, like the TSA agents in the states, and if you opened up his face you'd find a tiny sadistic alien sitting at a control panel, sending people's bags to all the wrong places.

"Miss Bryant, it appears they are en route to Bangkok."

My mouth drops open. "Thailand?!"

His knuckles pale against his grip on the counter. He probably has these conversations every day. God, who'd *want* this job? Somebody hardcore failed Rupert on career day.

The lady behind me elbows her way back in. "Pardon me, Cinderella, but you aren't the only one with lost bags."

I narrow my eyes and mumble as I slide down to an empty spot at the counter. "Cinderella. Good one." Leaning over, I yank off my other shoe and chuck it in the wastebasket marked *rubbish* next to the wall. Rupert turns his attention to her and they exchange a knowing look. Like *I'm* the drama queen here.

Stiff carpet crunches between all ten of my toes, and a little thrill wiggles loose in my belly. I smile, a few inches closer to the dream. As I fill in my contact information, my phone dings. I set the pen on the counter with a thump and retrieve the text.

I return to the paperwork and fill in the address for George's place, then list the description of my bags and their contents. How specific does *that* need to be? Do I list everything, all the way down to my prescriptions? The tampons, too?

A documentary narrator voice interrupts my thoughts.

"You must be Jojo."

If words were punches, this would be the KO.

My mom calls me Josephine when she isn't yelling (Josie Michelle when she is), and everyone else calls me Jo. Nobody's called me Jojo in a very long time. Hearing it on a stranger's lips slides me off my axis.

A tall, lean guy with messy brown hair steps up to the counter next to me. He wears faded jeans with holes in the knees. Chucks. A t-shirt hoodie peeks out from under his black peacoat. He drops an elbow on the edge of the counter, cool as a vintage cigarette poster. Behind black-framed Warby Parkers, he has the greenest eyes I've ever seen. It's like he's figured out how to use a color saturation filter on his real-life face.

"J-jojo?" I overcompensate for the trembly voice by sticking out my hand for a shake, like we're closing a business deal or something. "Just Jo," I say. "Just call me Jo."

God, I'm so bad at this whole scene. New people. New situations. Awkwardness abounds. If only Pfizer made a pill that could make me say all the right things without thinking, I'd take it with no complaints.

"Just Jo, then." He accepts my handshake politely and pencils in a dimpled smile. Suddenly I'm glad he looked like a weirdo on his Instagram page and that Dylan didn't see *this*. It's like this guy graduated summa cum laude from a boy band.

"And *yeww* must be the *wayn-kuh*." I fake a British accent and grin. Who has two thumbs and on-the-fly wit? This girl, that's who.

But his smile evaporates and he drops my hand.

"Henry, actually." *Ach-chu-ally.*

My joke flails on the ground at our feet. Dying slowly like a Shakespeare character. He doesn't even chuckle. Welp, that settles that. I barely know Patrick, but I'm certain *he* would've laughed.

Instead, Henry looks down and does a double take. His nose *ach-chu-ally* curls, as if there's an odor to accompany the discovery of my toes, neatly pedicured with black polish.

He meets my eyes again. "Did they lose your shoes, too?"

CHAPTER

FOUR

: Baby You're a Rich Man :

I'VE TAKEN QUITE a few retail excursions with unwilling participants in the past.

Mama, for example, is a get-in-and-get-out shopper. Dylan will go with me if it means we get to spend an afternoon on a blanket at Biltmore afterwards. Like most boys, he's motivated by reward. When I take him thrifting, he's always looking over his shoulder—like he's worried his lacrosse teammates from his snooty private school will see him in a secondhand store and assume he's poor. (He isn't; his parents are doctors, for God's sake.) And of course I'm rushed when he does this, which is the most annoying thing. He sometimes makes me feel inadequate. Like he didn't know what he was signing up for when he asked the girl from public school to be his girlfriend. At a lame hospital work party for our parents, no less.

But my current issue is a different situation entirely.

Number one: because I've been to three stores in terminal two, and none have a pair of shoes for less than £200. Number two: because Henry looks more pissed off than anyone I've ever taken shopping with me before.

As I tiptoe through Harrod's, Henry leans against a white column a safe distance away, flexing his jaw and staring at his phone screen. I get the distinct impression that he's only here because someone forced him to be. But I shake off the thought and concentrate on the task at hand. Shoes of every variety are impeccably displayed on gleaming tables. My fingers fumble with the price tags. I can't think of a single place back home that would charge this much for such basic shoes.

A bright orange pair of rubber rain boots called Wellys are the least expensive I find, and they're still £80. I pick up one boot and turn it over in my hands. It smells like a tire shop. The like-new satin knockoff Louboutins I got for junior prom on eBay were only $41. These are ugly rubber rain boots, more than double that. Forget it. I refuse to chisel that much from my budget before even boarding the tube. I only paid $7 for the ballet flats I was wearing before the creeper stole one. Yes, seven dollars! Originally $59, can you believe it? Someday, people will look down into my corpse-stuffed coffin and compliment my outfit. I'll probably use my very last dying neuron to scream IT WAS ON SALE.

My feet make a slapping noise on the pristine white tile as I approach Henry, and something warm and electric sizzles at the base of my skull. It percolates outwards to my fingers and toes—the unmistakable trigger of déjà vu. I glance at the floor. *Marble! From-the-dream marble!* It must show on my face, because when Henry glances up from his phone, he squints.

"Let's just go," I say, ignoring the urge to stare at my feet and grin like I'm full-throttle disturbed. "I have plenty of shoes in my luggage. I'll have to deal till the airport elves can get my things to me."

His eyebrows climb his forehead. "You can't ride the tube without shoes."

"Crap." I cross my arms. I didn't even think about that. "Is it illegal or something?"

He squints again, like my stupidity has a radioactive glow. "Because it's bloody grotty."

I swallow a snicker. Wanker or not, I could listen to him talk all day.

He shoves his phone in his pocket and stands from where he's been leaning. I crane my neck and try not to make it obvious that I'm admiring his station in the cosmos from my position below on earth. Lexie would say he's a taaaaalll drink of water.

A refined voice speaks over my shoulder. "May I assist you with something?"

I pivot to tell the saleslady *no thank you, I'm browsing*, but Henry speaks up first.

"Yes, she'll be needing shoes, as you can see."

I ignore the way he speaks for me and tell her myself, "No, thank you. These are well out of my price range."

She glances down at my bare feet, disapproval darker than her mascara. "Please do let me know if I can help you with anything."

When she saunters away, Henry says, "Nonsense." He glances down at my feet. "What size do you wear? 40 or so? Wide?" He walks over and picks up the Welly boot I put back on the shelf. "I'll buy them myself. The next train leaves in ten minutes."

An incredulous squeak escapes as I follow him. My feet—which by his calculations are dinosaur-like—slap the slick tile as I go. I try to grab the boot, but he does something that makes me fully understand the definition of wanker: he holds it up out of my reach.

Heat engulfs my face. Aren't British people supposed to be polite? This is not polite. I know polite. I am a Southerner.

"Are you serious right now?" I prop my hands on my hips to keep from smacking him. Because manners. People sneak glances at us. The saleslady eyes us from across the store.

"Of course I'm serious." He laughs, but not like *ha*. "You need shoes and you don't have the money for them. I'm your host and will purchase them on your behalf for the sake of time.

This is the third store we've been to. I have things to attend to this evening."

My eyes flit from his face to the boot. He's right. I'm being difficult. But so is he, and I did not ask for his escort service. I jump—actually jump—to grab the boot. God only knows what possesses me. But it doesn't matter because I still can't reach it.

"Your dad is my host. Not you. And I do have the money to buy them," I insist. It isn't a lie. I put two years of saved babysitting money—nearly $2,000—on a prepaid debit card. It has to last the whole five weeks, though, which means I can spend approximately $57 per day, food included. "I just think it's ridiculous to pay that much for a pair of shoes I don't need."

"But it appears you do need them." A mixture of challenge and irritation simmers in his big green irises. Now that I really look at them, they're the color of slime. The Grinch. The Slytherin crest. He's Malfoy, but with better hair and eyes and… well, pretty much better everything, but his actions render him toad-like.

He slowly brings his arm down. I snatch the boot out of his hand, grab the mate, and stomp toward the cash register. Déjà vu ripples through me with each thud.

CHAPTER FIVE

: There's a Place :

MY OVERPRICED BOOTS squeak with newness as I bounce my feet.

Just as I suspected, the transfer from Piccadilly to Jubilee is no more difficult than catching a city bus to Biltmore back home. I'm *even more* irritated with Mama for sending me an unwilling chaperone than I would've been if he hadn't turned out to be such a reject Bond villain.

The train jolts as the brakes are applied. Henry holds on to a pole to keep from falling into my lap in the crowded tube car. The doors open, and people file off and on. He swings around and plops on the emptied seat next to me. A breeze sweeps by and I shiver.

"Are you cold?"

I jump, because it's the first thing he's said to me since he hastily showed me how to use my Oyster card.

"Not at all."

Patrick warned that a tank top was more June-in-North-Carolina weather than June-in-London weather. It was 87 degrees when my plane took off at home. 59 when it landed here. I brought a short-sleeved cardigan, but it's insufficient.

I ignore Henry's smirk and focus on the people nearby—an older man reading a book through thick spectacles, a bedraggled mother with two fidgety offspring, and scores of commuters, attention glued to their phones. I hug my elbows closer.

Henry blows a chest-deflating sigh and scoots toward the edge of his seat. I pretend to pay him no attention whatsoever but watch from the corner of my eye as he shimmies out of his peacoat.

"Here, take it." He dangles his coat right in front of my face. Act of kindness or not, it irritates me something fierce. He's just so pushy, and pushiness is the surefire way to get on my bad side.

"Really. I'm fine." When I flash him a fake smile, a tinge of violet blooms around his head. I blink and it disappears, but the distraction lasts just a split second long enough for him to place the coat on my lap.

"Honestly. This isn't necessary." I try to hand it back to him, but he won't take it. "I'm hot-natured," I plead. "But thanks."

He cocks his head and squints. "Your arms are covered in gooseflesh."

A little boy next to us asks his mother, "Are they fighting, Mum?" She shushes him instead of answering.

"Fine," I say through my teeth, trying to crush the aggravation between my molars. To keep from making a spectacle, I throw the jacket on. The sleeves are so long I have to roll them up at the bottom. It smells a bit like a campfire and, as much as I hate to admit it, is crispy warm.

Shoving my hands in the pockets, my knuckles bump something cool and smooth that feels like rocks. Imagine that: the wanker keeps rocks in his pockets. He probably throws them at elderly people and then offers to help them up afterwards.

I retrieve one from the right pocket. It's the size of a domino, oddly heavy, with engraved letters etched into its rusty brown surface: an N on one end, and an S on the other. Before I can examine further, Henry takes it right out of my hand. His fingertips brush my palm.

"Sorry, I forgot about those." He shoves it into his jeans pocket. "There's one in the other as well." He points to my left side. I take it out and hand it to him.

"Rocks?" I ask, doing an excellent job of withholding the comment about elderly people.

He fiddles with the silver ring on his thumb. "Magnets."

When I realize he isn't going to explain further, I press. "What are they for?"

His eyes move to the tube door. "Just a hobby."

"So, voodoo then?"

He ignores me. At least we've established that Henry has no appreciation for humor.

When we pull into our last stop at Southwark (*Suth-urk*; it sounds nothing like it's spelled), I grab my bag and follow him off the tube.

"It's just a short walk away," he assures me, like he's counting down the seconds to get away from me, too.

We make our way up to the busy street above the station, and London fills the background like someone's lifted a curtain at a play I've been waiting to see all my life. The sky is sterling silver, and everything glistens with dampness. The air smells like food and exhaust fumes and rain.

Three story brownstones flank either side of the wide roadway. Shops and pubs and cafés undulate in every direction. The sidewalks are tidy, with manicured trees and charming wrought iron benches along the street. Like Asheville, but classier. I spin in a circle as I walk, marveling like a muggle.

Why Pop didn't make good on his promise to bring me here himself—before it was too late—I'll never understand. My eyes wander over the windows and doors and business signs, searching, until I find the blocky letters and blackbird silhouette.

BLACKFRIAR'S CROW.

My chest pulls tight as I force my feet closer to the windows. Sadness slips over me, and some irrational urge makes me want to scour the place for Pop. Make certain he isn't inside. People fill the tables in the dining room, eating and talking and drinking, completely unaware of how empty the place is without Pop in it. A bartender towels the counter as he takes orders. I study every face, then the backs of each of the men sitting at the bar. Too old to be him. Too pudgy. Too skinny.

I glance at the flyer pasted on the door: *Open Mic Night, Saturday at 10.*

Sometimes the universe sends messages that seem like they're meant specifically for me. Walrus Gumboot got their start at an open mic night here.

Henry's reflection watches me through the glass, stock still at my back. I realize I'm still wearing his coat. It's enough to make me get myself together. This could get super awkward.

"My pop used to play here." I shrug out of the coat and hand it to him, determined to stay casual as we continue on our way. Of course Pop isn't *still* here. "This is the first—and last—place he ever played." Henry catches up with me.

"Good place." His vowels are suddenly softer. "We're right down this way." He points down a side street. I walk beside him, trying to ignore his pity. I notice every person who passes. I see Pop's face in all of them.

CHAPTER

SIX

: Julia :

MAMA MET GEORGE Pemberton in some Facebook group for people overcoming grief.

George's wife, Julia, died of cancer not long after we lost Pop. Over the past couple of years, George and Mama have become close. When he first came to visit us in the states a year or so ago, I thought maybe they were starting a romance. But then they slept in separate rooms. I could tell they liked and respected each other in a just-friends sort of way. And I was glad she had a friend like him.

Bonus for me: it meant I had a possible place to stay in London.

"We know people there now!" I insisted, over and over. "Maybe they'd let us stay with them!" We don't exactly have a vacation budget, after all. Mama's been an emergency room nurse since before I was born, but Pop's death left us broke in unexpected ways. Did you know it costs nine thousand, three hundred eighty-eight dollars to fly a dead body home from a foreign country? You get a discount if you cremate them first.

Having a free place to stay would've made the trip doable for both of us, but she goes out of her way to avoid things that remind her of Pop. Which by default means we don't talk about

Pop. We don't do things that remind us of Pop, including travel to his favorite places. She wouldn't even budge on *me* coming by myself until a couple of weeks ago, when George made the suggestion. *Let's swap kids for the summer,* George told her. *It'll look good on their university applications.* God bless George for that.

Patrick and I are the same age, just a few months apart. It made sense, so Mom finally agreed. It's too bad Patrick and I can't hang out this summer, though. From the moment he landed in Asheville, he felt like a kindred spirit. Quite different from his brother, the wanker.

When I step through the heavy glass doors of Fox Den Records—George's store—he meets me in the middle of an aisle of vintage vinyl records. He looks older than when I saw him last. A little bedraggled. His salt-and-pepper hair is more salt than pepper. He gives me half-hug-back-pat thingy.

"So sorry I couldn't come meet you myself, love. We had a rescheduled delivery of new inventory and things have been completely mad all afternoon." He steps back and grins. "Here, let me take your bag." He reaches for my carry-on. "Is this all?"

When I fill him in on the luggage, he juts his bottom lip out in sympathy. From the corner of my eye, I notice Henry outside with his back facing the store. When he turns, he has a cigarette dangling from his lips. I physically recoil. *Ew.*

"Come on, I'll show you around." George motions toward the back of the store. "Your mum tells me you're a budding guitarist."

My muscles stiffen to statue proportions. This is just like Mama: saying things that misrepresent me to increase my palatability. I haven't attempted to play since that first psychiatrist convinced me it would help me deal with my grief. Turns out, I suck at it, and since Pop died before he could finish teaching me, it was a pretty demoralizing idea.

"Not really," I say. "It's been a long time."

"Well, maybe it's time for you to pick it up again."

I smile and nod. Zero intentions whatsoever of touching Pop's guitar again.

A few patrons thumb through faded album covers as we make our way to the sales counter. Half the store has used records. The other half has shiny, cellophane-wrapped new ones. Old red phone booths sit in the corners of the room with *Listening Station* written on the glass in chalk marker.

"My office is in that corner, just there," George says as he finishes up my tour of the store. Just inside his office, a huge framed photo of a beautiful woman with dark hair hangs above the desk. I know without asking that it must be Julia because of the eyes. Big, apple-jolly-rancher green eyes, just like Henry's. I turn away.

There's a timeless, eclectic vibe about Fox Den, with its dark shelves and framed album art and festival posters. I scan the list of acts on the one for the 2013 Boomtown festival, and see it listed there, halfway down: Walrus Gumboot. I smile, suddenly feeling at home. I knew I'd be staying above a quaint music store, but my imagination underestimated the level of charm.

The front door opens and a momentary rush of street noise filters in. Henry retreats to the cash register, sinks onto the stool there, and pops a peppermint in his mouth. He opens an old, tattered book to a bookmarked spot.

I stare a hole through the side of his head, but he doesn't notice.

He has *so* many things to *attend to* tonight. Yeah. So busy. He doesn't look up from his book—something called *Ley Lines of Britain*—as we walk past him.

George leads me down a hallway at the back of the store, then up a creaky wooden staircase. There's a little orange bundle curled in the corner of the first landing, and it takes a moment to register that it's alive.

"This is Felix. Namesake for the Fox Den."

I stoop next to him. He opens his sleepy amber eyes, then stretches and yawns. I couldn't be more instantly smitten if you dumped a bag of puppies on my head. Felix stands on dainty paws and his white-tipped tail perks up.

"Patrick told me he was a rescue." I reach a tentative hand toward him so he can sniff it. He does. His little nose is wet. "How old is he?"

"Oh, I guess it's been about five years now," George says.

"He was hit by a car when he was a wee kit. We nursed him back to health, and after that he wouldn't leave us."

"Did you get him at an animal shelter?"

George shakes his head. "No. An old friend of the family found him and brought him to us. Then we lost him to an accident a couple of years ago." He bites his lip, as if deciding what to say next. "That's one of the reasons Felix is so special to us."

Ugh, poor George. Both his wife *and* his friend. I focus on Felix instead of doing that annoying apology thing people do when death is mentioned. Like we are programmed to acknowledge it, lest we be marked. Like silence isn't enough to convey the suckage. When I tell people Pop died, they say *I'm sorry.* I always want to say *Oh, did you kill him?* and walk away. But that would make me a jerk, so I don't.

The little fox presses the top of his head into my hand like an eager cat might.

"We can't have pets at home because my mom is allergic to everything."

My fingers comb the silky fluff behind his ears. I pull my hand back and stand before Felix is ready for me to. He places a paw on top of my foot and cocks his little head with expectation.

"She'll have plenty of snuggles for you later, Felix," George says. "We're busy now." I laugh as he motions around. "The lounge, the kitchen, and my bedroom are here on the second level. Your room is on the third."

We ascend another flight of stairs. The boards moan beneath our feet as we step into a narrow hallway. In one direction, subdued light from a window illuminates the floor. A metal ladder is bolted to the wall in front of it and leads to a ceiling hatch.

"The dark room is up there." He points. I pause, wondering if that's an English term for an attic. In the other direction, two wooden doors with old-fashioned knobs lead to bedrooms.

"You'll be staying in Patrick's room," George says. "I guess he told you that."

I nod as he leads me inside. The bed is made neatly with white linens. There's a dresser with mirror, a desk with an old record player, a bookshelf in the corner stocked with old records, and an acoustic-electric guitar propped on a stand.

I do a double take and I think I see stars.

It's a Gibson Jumbo, with a Sunburst spruce finish and P-90 single-coil pickups. It's just like the one John Lennon played. I twitch at the sight of it. Pop would've drooled over a guitar like that.

"Please do be aware," George says, "that you'll be sharing the loo with Henry. He's promised to be less disgusting."

This snaps me out of my inspection of the guitar. I follow him into the adjoining Jack and Jill bathroom, long and hallway-like, with entrances from both upper bedrooms.

"Just make sure this door is locked when you come in." To demonstrate, he presses the button on the doorknob that leads to Henry's room. I make a mental note to never forget to do that.

George sets my bag on the floor beside the bed and, after offering me food and tea—which I politely refuse—leaves me to rest.

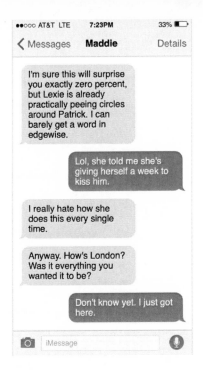

> I'm sure this will surprise you exactly zero percent, but Lexie is already practically peeing circles around Patrick. I can barely get a word in edgewise.

Lol, she told me she's giving herself a week to kiss him.

> I really hate how she does this every single time.

> Anyway. How's London? Was it everything you wanted it to be?

Don't know yet. I just got here.

📷 iMessage   🎙

I put my phone on the charger, then pull out the urn in my bag and set it on Patrick's desk. It's made of dark gray titanium, with a tongue-and-groove locking lid, which destroyed me the first time I saw it. So dull and gray and depressing. So final.

Once I was medicated and able to semi-function again, I started collecting stickers and decorating the urn: A Sgt. Pepper's Lonely Hearts Club sticker. An all-you-need-is-love sticker with a rainbow heart on it. A yellow submarine. A cartoon rendering of The Fab Four. I thought it'd be an appropriate theme for the lead singer of Walrus Gumboot, internationally known Beatles cover band. Almost none of the titanium is visible now, except on the lid.

I run my fingertips over the smooth, curved surface of the stickers.

"Please tell me you're not in there," I whisper. "I know you're trying to tell me something. I'll forgive you if you're really just incognito on this side of the pond."

I push the urn aside and take a deep breath.

The letter I've hidden for three years now whispers to me from my wallet. When I wait a few weeks between readings, it almost feels like talking to him. Now that I'm sitting in the city of his heart, there's no more perfect time to absorb his words once again.

CHAPTER

SEVEN

: Goodbye :

October 9, 2018
Dear Jojo,

I was 17 when I saw this city for the first time. The Salvation Army declared me an adult, gave me a bus voucher and a slap on the back. I'm sure they were quite weary of me ping-ponging through foster homes, only to land on their doorstep again. I used to be much harder to get along with, you see. So off I went to London, with nothing but the clothes on my back and a duffle. Popped into a pub by Tower Bridge and made nice with some uni girls who gave me a covert place to stay for a few weeks. Don't tell your mother, but it was in their dormitory. When their resident chaperone finally discovered me there, it was a catastrophe—I'll tell you that story someday when you're older.

For the first six months, I had the time of my life working odd jobs and couch surfing. It was no way for a proper adult to live, but I had no plans to become a proper adult. I was so in love with the people of this city, and still am: the toothy bartenders and the raven-haired uni girls and the elbow-patched professors and the starry-eyed children. Even the endless rain left the streets looking like polished silver. I think God knows

London rivals heaven, so he makes it rain all the time out of spite.

Just like with any place I've ever been, the restlessness welled up and I had to move on. Like the Beatles, I followed the sun. And that led me to your mother. Ever since leaving, though, I've been lured back. There's something special about it you have to experience to understand. So as I walked in the rain this morning, I made a decision. This is the last time I'll come here alone and let descriptions suffice. Next time I visit, you're coming with me. No more delays. We'll fly out before you start high school. We'll go to Menier Chocolate Factory and gorge ourselves on brownies. We'll dance on the glass floor at the top of Tower Bridge. I'll sneak you into Blackfriar's Crow to watch us play a set. We'll forget our umbrellas on purpose so you can feel the way this rain washes away bad feelings and leaves you with nothing but gratitude. You have my word.

Love,
Pop

PS - I picked up a little something for you today.

CHAPTER EIGHT

: Golden Slumbers :

EVERYTHING IS SMOKY.

Blue and purple lights slice through the haze. There's a vague awareness that I'm floating somewhere outside myself, so I close my eyes and find my center. I zero in on the rough texture of the microphone against my chin to bring me back. As I brush my bottom lip against it, it roars. A deafening kiss. My eyes snap open.

The black stand defocuses beneath my gaze, and a sea of blurred faces spread out before me. Everything is eerily void of sound. I try to blink into focus, but the room is a murky smear. Pop whispers, *Play away.*

My guitar strings brush away the quiet with the melody to *Eleanor Rigby*. I think, for a fleeting moment, there are drums coming from somewhere, too—but no. It's only my pulse hammering the *doot-doot-doot-doot*. I've never performed for a crowd before. But for whatever reason, here I am. I open my mouth to sing the opening lines as the smoke clears.

The grooves of the table, the condensation rolling down the beer glass, the tattooed forearm reaching for it—they all sharpen. Every detail materializes one pixel at a time, until the photo before me is in high definition. Vivid. I know that tattoo. The letters. The delicate curve of the Js, the feminine roundness of the Os. *Jojo*. It's him. There at a table in the front row, staring back at me. Eyes alive and full of *I've-been-here-all-along* mischief, as if we've only been playing hide-and-seek.

Pop.

I knew this day would eventually come. But my fingers stumble and get confused. The song changes. The sad soul of *Eleanor Rigby* morphs into the upbeat jingle of *When I'm Sixty-Four*. The audience rumbles and whispers. I look down at my hands, but they aren't moving. Of course they aren't. I would never choose this silly song. I've only ever used it as a ringtone for...

Dylan.

A jolt sends me back to my body and I open my eyes in the dark. A dream. I was dreaming. I reach for my phone, irrationally angry that Dylan interrupted before I could see more. I manage a groggy hello.

"Finally!" Dylan shrieks. "Thank God. I was starting to get worried. Your mom's been blowing my phone up."

I squint. The clock on my phone says 5:37 a.m., and some quick sleepy math resolves it's after midnight in Asheville.

"Sleeping," I mumble and flop back onto the pillow. "It's early. I was dreaming about Pop—" Tears throb at the base of my throat. It's been a long time since I've had a good cry, since I've even been able to.

"Oh no," he says. "One of *those* dreams? Like the ones before?"

I squeeze the blanket in my fist, wishing I'd never said anything. The one time I tried to tell him about Pop and the dreams, he tiptoed around the implication that I might be a teensy bit crazypants. He said that sometimes, when tragic things happen to us, they warp our perception.

He also thinks my *aura-reading nonsense* (his words) is a byproduct of an overactive imagination, plus a touch of lingering depression. Never mind that I've seen auras for as long as I can remember. Since before. Something I inherited from Pop. That's how I knew they were real; we both saw them. We'd people-watch everywhere we went and take notes.

As frustrating as it is, I can't fault Dylan. Not really. He's the only child of an ER physician and a psychiatrist. He sees everything through the lens of medical practicality. His aura has always been skeptical gray, so it's not like I can expect much else. I do appreciate that he keeps me grounded in the now. Even in the moments I don't want to be here. Arguing with him is stressful, though, so I change the subject. I tell him about my lost luggage instead.

"Were your medications in there?"

I stiffen. "Yes. But I'll have it in a day or two."

"Do you think... not taking them... caused the dream? Because you know, last time..."

I'm silent. He doesn't know I haven't taken them since I packed. Three days ago.

"Tell me about the dream." He switches gears, voice soft like a padded room.

"I don't want to talk about it. None of it made sense, anyway."

I have a rule. I don't divulge details until after they've happened in real life. I'm afraid if I say it out loud, the spell will be broken and they'll never come true.

I yawn into the phone.

"Go back to sleep," he whispers. "I'll call you later."

I don't object. I have a dream to get back to.

But when I finally fall asleep again, I dream that I'm drowning.

CHAPTER

NINE

: From Me to You :

I START MY first full day in London by reading the guilt-trippiest email in the history of the world.

To: Jo {jojobee@att.com}
From: Mom {krisbry@buncombecountyhospital.com}
3:33am EST (8:33am GMT+1)

Josephine,

I was pleased to hear you made it safely to George's. He filled me in, don't you worry. It's clear that you want independence, because you've done nothing but push me away since I agreed to let you take this trip. Hint taken! I can't control you. You have to decide who you'll be in this life. Will you be a woman of integrity? A woman who keeps her word? It's out of my hands now.

We're both going to be busy. I'm putting in extra hours at the hospital, and I'll be showing Patrick around when I'm not working. We won't have much time to talk, so I'm giving you a pass. You don't have to check in with me. You don't have to call me. I'm sure Dylan will keep me in the loop, and George will let me know if something of importance comes up. Have fun. These five weeks are all yours.

-Mama

Sometimes I wonder if my life would be easier if I wasn't an only child. At least then my mother would have fifty percent fewer hours to micromanage me.

Even though I *am* busy all day—George gives me a set of keys, walks me through routines, trains me on the operation of the store, and then invites me to eat dinner with him and Henry when it's all said and done—I can't enjoy it or fully immerse myself in any of it. I'm too distracted by Mama's Jedi mind trick. She put a damper on my very first day here.

So by the next morning, when I've had time to stew on it for a solid twenty-four hours, I decide to call her bluff.

> Are the twins driving you bonkers?

They're twins?

> Fraternal, yeah.

They baked me biscuits.

> You mean cookies?

Yes, sorry. I forgot Americans have such odd names for everything.

> Football is made of pigskin and laces. The sport you play is called soccer. Biscuits are appropriate for any meal and are usually slathered in gravy.

Did I tell you I play football?

> *soccer

> And no. Maddie did.

Oh, did she now? 😊

> Perhaps.

How are things there?

> Okay. Had dinner with your dad and Henry last pm.

Is Henry behaving?

> Define behaving.

behaving: v. the act of not being ones usual dickish self.

> Yeah, I don't think he's stoked about me being here.

📷   iMessage   🎤

CHAPTER

TEN

: Junk :

GOOGLE TELLS ME it takes an airplane twelve hours to get from Bangkok to Heathrow.

But it's been nearly a week, and I still don't have my luggage. George let me borrow some clothes, and I am super weirded out that they belonged to his dead wife. And they're all too tight and too long, which made for some really uncomfortable workdays stooping and bending and sorting albums.

Instead of moping, I'm going to pretend my luggage is gone forever. I'll re-make myself in London. No meds. No helicopter mother. No former wardrobe. No remnants of my previous life. You know what the Beatles did when they got sick of suffocating expectations? They re-birthed themselves and made what Rolling Stone called The Best Album of All Time. I've decided that my time in London will be my very own *Sgt. Pepper's Lonely Hearts Club Band*.

The GPS in my phone narrates directions to a little place called Switcheroo, a thrift store three blocks into the heart of Southwark. The bell dings as I enter and breathe the musk of the secondhand store, hear the low hum of the fluorescent lighting, see the disorganization of the racks. It's a treasure hunt.

Sometimes the life of clothing interests me as much as the clothing itself. Maybe someone wore this elephant tee on a safari in the Serengeti. I put it down and pick up another. Maybe a boundary-pushing explorer wore this beanie to base camp on Mount Everest. Or maybe—and I gasp when I see it—this faded blue Beatles tee, with the album cover of *Help!* on the front, was worn by a fan in the street for the 1969 Apple rooftop concert, the last time the Beatles performed live together.

$76 US dollars will get you two shirts, a dress, a cardigan, pajamas, flip-flops, and a pair of jeans in a UK thrift store. I'm feeling pretty satisfied with myself, so I duck into Joy, a women's clothing store, and buy underwear and socks. They cost almost as much as my Switcheroo loot, but alas. Some things cannot be thrifted.

I meander over to Blackfriar's Crow, killing time before my afternoon shift at Fox Den.

The pub looks different in full daylight. I press my forehead against the glass, straining to see. This time, the chairs are stacked and the lights are out. The place is a shell of what it was the other night. I cup my hands to block the glare on the glass, and they slide through the morning dew gathered there. My Switcheroo bags slide down to my elbows.

At the very back of the room, a small stage and microphone stand are tucked away. It's so dark I can barely make it out, but from here it looks exactly like the stage in my dream.

"Closed till lunchtime, love."

I whirl toward the voice. An older man with a mouthful of tall teeth grins widely at me. The morning brightens around him as my eyes adjust.

"You a singer?" His keys jangle against the glass as he unlocks the door.

"What?" I sway, a little dizzy from the onslaught of sunlight after staring through the dark. "No. Yes. Why?"

"What a strange answer." He laughs. "You look the part."

"Uh. Okay." I shrink back to leave.

"Open mic is Saturday." He calls as he steps in the door. "If you decide you're a singer before then, please do come by."

I'm halfway down the block before it occurs to me that he may have known Pop. I stop and do a dance of indecision. He invited me to *sing*. In a place that looks like the setting from my dream. A swarm of shivers chase each other down my arms.

What if I'm *supposed* to sing there Saturday night? I'd only have three days to learn how to play *Eleanor Rigby* on Patrick's guitar. Pretty much impossible, since I only know how to play one song fluently (*Let It Be*), and it wasn't that song in the dream. I swallow and start walking again, resolve growing with every step.

If Pop insists on laying breadcrumbs right at my feet, I'd be an idiot to ignore them.

CHAPTER

ELEVEN

: It Won't Be Long :

ACCORDING TO MY school guidance counselor, I have a few requirements to fill to get class credit for my five weeks abroad, which will allow me to skip a senior year elective: A hundred hours of community service, which I'll accomplish by volunteering in the record store. Then I have subject-specific tasks to complete, depending on which elective I want to skip.

Of the list, Photography seems like the easiest throwaway class. I'll have to assemble a photo project documenting my time here using each of the various techniques outlined in the syllabus at least once, with thoughtful captions for each. I'll have to do some research to get it right, but it seems a far cry easier than some of the other electives. If I'd chosen Business Law, for example, I'd have to create my own fictional organization set in London and write a business plan for it, then write a long essay explaining how it differs from United States business practices. Hard pass.

It's almost too easy to take pictures. I was going to do that anyway. And by Friday morning of my first week in London, I'm feeling pretty confident the community service portion will be a breeze too. In a week's time, I've learned the ins and outs of Fox Den with no problems.

Well, no problems except Henry.

"Do you plan to play guitar until midnight every night?" he asks, chomping a piece of candy like he has to kill it first. I continue sorting albums by genre, faking indifference better than Ringo.

"Only if it displeases his majesty," I say in my best fake British accent, because I know it irritates him when I do that. We've fallen into this routine where he says something snarky, and then I reply with something equally snarky and/or borderline insulting. He smirks. I smirk. We go back to ignoring each other. I don't know if this is camaraderie or if he actually hates my guts.

My mental inventory of Henry so far: he smokes, but never smells like smoke. He eats peppermint candy like he's trying to piss off his dentist. When we aren't busy with customers, he reads weird scientific-looking books with diagrams of molecules on the front, and I can't tell if it's because he's smart, or if it's because he wants people to think he's smart.

Felix perches at Henry's feet. His tail makes swishy brushstrokes in the air, waiting patiently for a head pat. Henry tosses his book—*The World of Quantum Mechanics*—under the counter and steps over him like he's not even there.

I mentally add *doesn't like animals* to the ledger of treachery.

Felix trots over and does a figure eight through my ankles, looking up at me with a plea. *Pet me.* Unlike Henry, I stoop to pet his soft fur. At least I know Felix's intentions.

"That song isn't really meant for guitar." Henry climbs a step ladder to replace a top shelf rock biography a customer decided against. The graphic on the back of his t-shirt has multicolored intersecting lines with block letters that say *Everyone Wants To Get Ley'd.* I squint, contemplating the spelling, when he turns to me. "Wasn't it originally written on piano?"

Okay, so I don't remember what instrument Sir Paul used when he wrote it. I feel my face crumple like a ball of paper around my reply. "None of the Beatles played an instrument on the final version. It was an orchestra ensemble."

He pauses, one foot dangling midair next to the top step. "Sometimes a song is ruined when you tinker with the arrangement."

"A string octet, to be specific," I add to my earlier thought. But I don't know where to get one of those, and besides—I played it on guitar in the dream. If he can tell what song it is, maybe I don't suck as badly as I thought.

"You're a Beatles fan, then." Henry says this in his sarcastic voice—the one he might as well trademark. Like my knowledge of the string octet is the first definitive piece of evidence that I'm maybe, perhaps, someone who enjoys the greatest band of all time. The *Help!* thrift store t-shirt I'm wearing notwithstanding.

"I mean, isn't everyone?" I give Felix a parting pat and resume alphabetizing the albums I've sorted into genres. "My pop used to say that anyone who claims he isn't a Beatles fan is either a liar or an asshole."

Henry hops off the ladder and crosses his arms. "Interesting." But he says it in a way that makes it sound like he isn't interested at all. "I'm really not much of a fan myself."

I've been telling myself I won't react, no matter what he says. Heat pulses in my cheeks and I narrow my eyes. I asked George if he'd heard of Walrus Gumboot at dinner. He hadn't. Which disappointed me, of course. And also made me wonder how good he could be at his job, since he has a festival poster with their name on it hanging in his store, totally unawares. Henry was sitting right there for the whole conversation. Not participating, but listening. This is an intentional jab. He knows what he's doing.

He smirks and turns away, probably mentally collecting his trophy.

"Oh yeah?" I forget my manners. "Then which one are you? Liar? Or asshole?"

"I'm more of a Stones fan," he says. He glances back at me, purses his lips around a shit-eating grin, and whistles the tune to *Gimme Shelter*.

Asshole then. Clearly.

"Your shirt is obnoxious," I mutter, even though I don't know what it means.

"It's great," he says.

I glare at him, hoping I convey exactly how uninterested I am in his opinion on getting laid. *Ley'd*. Whatever.

"It's referring to ley lines, just so you know." He grins again. "Friend of mine gave it to me as a joke."

I roll my eyes and wander off to the other side of the store so I can google "ley lines" on my phone without being caught.

Maybe working alongside him for a hundred hours will be more of a challenge than originally anticipated.

CHAPTER TWELVE

: Long and Winding Road :

ON FRIDAY EVENING, I get a taste of the strange, angsty dynamic between George and Henry.

"You know the first Friday night is trivia night," George tells Henry with a huff. "I don't know why you'd schedule a session during that time."

As I tidy up some of the front shelves before close, I peek into George's office, where Henry leans against the wall with his arms crossed, pissy stance turned up to eleven.

"I wasn't aware my presence was required," Henry snarks.

"You know I'd like for you to be here," George says, a little more quietly. "I thought we could all have tea afterwards. Your support is important."

"I've already told you my support is heavily dependent on your honesty."

George flexes his jaw, and at that moment, he looks over and sees me standing there, record in hand, eavesdropping.

I quickly put the record down and scurry away like the nosy little rat I am.

"Jo, could you come in here?" George calls.

I squeeze my eyes shut and count to three before I walk back over to the doorway of the office.

"What's up?"

"You're coming to trivia night tonight, yes?"

I stare at him, mouth agape. I certainly hadn't planned on it, even though he brought it up multiple times over the past few days. People from the community (*especially young people!*) come to show off their music knowledge. The winner gets a free album of his or her choice. Everyone eats pizza.

"Actually, no," I say. "I'm sorry."

I hate the way disappointment draws the corners of George's face. He's such a nice guy and I hate disappointing people. It makes it worse that Henry just shot him down. I don't come right out and tell him *Trivia with strangers is not really my speed.* And he doesn't come right out and say *Fine, but I'm going to tell your mother about your antisocial behavior.*

Henry smirks at me as he exits the office and jogs up the stairs. I give him a side eye to slice him in half as he goes.

"Henry isn't coming, if that's why you aren't..." George bites off the end of his sentence. My brows furrow. We play nice when George is around, but he's been holed up in his office the past couple of days. "He won't be there," he says again. "His sessions normally take a few hours and it'll be over by the time he gets back."

"That isn't why. I just... I'm reading a really good book and want to finish it," I lie. Lexie's romance novels are pretty predictable. So far a cowboy has taken off his shirt, built a fence, and sprung a boner. The main female character knows nothing about boners but is interested in learning.

"Well, at least come and get some pizza."

"I'm not hungry right now." *Or ever.* "But I might be later."

George smiles at me. "Brilliant."

Upstairs, I plop down on Patrick's bed and stare at the ceiling. I hate myself for it, but my brain moseys on over to the Forest of Curiosity and digs up what George said about Henry. His *sessions*. What kind of session? My initial thought is therapy, because if anyone could benefit from therapy, it's Henry.

I pull out my phone and check for notifications. No calls. No texts. I scroll through and stare at my mother's contact information. Her email left things in an uncomfortable place, and she's been calling my bluff on calling her bluff.

One of us has to be the adult here. I dial her number. It goes straight to voicemail. I send her a text instead of leaving a message. Several minutes go by as I listen to the sounds coming from downstairs. Chairs moving. Laughter. A faint rhythm on the turntable. My phone dings.

What?! I bolt upright. She's at my favorite hiking spot with my two best friends, my boyfriend, and the *nice* British brother. Without me. Not to be a total juvenile about this or anything—I know the plan has always been to introduce Patrick to my friends, to fully immerse him in the outdoor culture of western North Carolina. That's kind of the entire point of this summer exchange deal. Now that it's happening, though, it chafes.

Meanwhile, I'm here alone in Patrick's empty room, no closer to finding Pop than I was when I left Asheville. And other than the interrupted dream I had my first night here, my most exciting moments have been trading belligerent quips with someone I don't even particularly like.

Screw this. I grab the urn off the desk and put it in my backpack along with my wallet, then shuffle it onto my back and head downstairs. It's Friday night and there's a whole city beyond these doors that might hold clues about Pop.

: : :

I'm five blocks away when I see it.

Through the years, I've read Pop's last letter so many times that I have it memorized. I can close my eyes and see exactly where the pages are creased, where the ink is blotted from stray tears. I remember where the stress marks in his writing are... the way he leaned heavily on the pen when he looped his y's with finality. I see the words so clearly—Menier Chocolate Factory—with the thick ink line on the y.

I stare up at the sign in real time now, pull out my phone, and snap a picture of it.

Caption: wish you were here

I've seen this place on the internet many times, and in my head many more, but it isn't the magic *aha* I was hoping for when I step inside. Though there's a purr of festive energy from the folks seated around the dining tables, a draft blows through the space.

"One?" The *maître d'* asks.

I opt for takeaway, and she points me to the bar, where I order a brownie to go. As I wait, I listen to forks clinking against plates. Ice cubes rattling in glasses. Lively conversation. I wait for him to speak to me. To tell me what to do. But the voice doesn't come. There's life all around, but it doesn't reach me.

This is how it feels before the medication completely wears off—it's like being stranded on an island in plain sight. Close enough to watch the party on the mainland, but far enough away that I can't participate. I wonder sometimes if Pop felt like this. Maybe he wanted off the island.

But why would he have sent me a letter, promising to bring me to London, if he wanted to die? I know what happened was an accident. Mama knows it was an accident. But the insurance company says it wasn't.

A waitress taps me on the shoulder and hands me my order with a smile.

I thank her and leave, walking until I run out of sidewalk. I stop at the Riverfront.

From here, Tower Bridge is a beacon. A million tiny lights illuminate it against the dark sky. The glass-bottomed top level that Pop promised me we'd dance on is closed for the evening, but it glows hopefully in its emptiness. Feet will grace it again tomorrow.

I sit on the concrete ledge next to the water and pull the urn out and set it beside me. I poke at the brownie with a plastic fork. That last letter wasn't the first time he'd mentioned these legendary brownies. I take a bite—velvety rich. No wonder it was one of his favorites. I set the take-out container on the ledge next to the urn.

"You can have the rest," I say.

I remember pulling the letter out of our mailbox cubby in the cul-de-sac and sinking to the ground when I saw the handwriting. I opened it and read it right there. I'd been in robot mode until then, but reading his words fortified my denial. He wouldn't make a promise and then die. He just wouldn't.

His ashes arrived only days later.

I wanted to call the insurance company myself so many times and read them the letter as proof that he didn't take his own life. But it was his last correspondence, the last piece of him I had. I didn't want to share it. So I folded it up, put it in my wallet, and didn't tell a soul about it. Not even Mama.

I might have told her—if she hadn't deleted all traces of him from my email. Back then, she had my password and checked behind me for safety. One day, all of his messages disappeared. She blamed it on the email settings, but I'm not stupid. A couple of weeks before they disappeared, she told me it was *unhealthy* to reread them so much. She still doesn't know about the letter.

"Should I tell her, Pop? Or have I waited too long?"

He doesn't answer, but the light from the bridge dances on the surface of the Thames. The light mist turns into a more formidable rain. Chills scamper up my arms. He's here with me, if only for these tiny moments I acknowledge how much of him I carry in my heart.

Tiny moments are all I can handle, if I intend to keep myself together.

I snap a picture of the drizzly reflection on the water.

Caption: light and dark

Raindrops collect on the surface of the urn, so I pick it up to put it back in my dry backpack. But it's so slick, it slips right out of my hands—tumbling end over end, bouncing off the steep sloping bank beneath my feet, and splashing into the Thames, ten feet below.

I don't think. I just jump.

: I'm a Loser :

WHEN I WAS eight, we took a family vacation to the Outer Banks. Pop and I waded out to where the waves were breaking. My boogie board—a bright yellow one with blue and orange hibiscus flowers—was tethered to my ankle. The waves got bigger and bigger as we got closer to the breaking point. Fear filled every crack in my eight-year-old resolve, but I wanted Pop to think I was brave. *When it crashes*, he said, *start kicking. Kick as hard as you can.* I nodded. *Don't be afraid. The board will keep you afloat.* I nodded again.

But then there was a lull. The waves relaxed for a bit and broke beyond us, rather than behind us. We watched birds and boats and people closer to the shore. We floated over the swells, losing our original position. *Hey Pop,* I asked, peering into the murky water below me. *How come the ocean isn't blue like it looks on TV?*

Before he could answer, I saw the reflection in his eyes: a massive whitecap crashing on the water behind us.

Kic—

The force of it rolled me. My nose, mouth, and ears filled with stinging, burning salt. A smear of drab colors stabbed and scraped at my eyes. I couldn't close them against the pain. I flailed my arms and kicked as hard as I could, just like he said, but the tether attached to my left ankle jerked me around below the surface like a piece of driftwood. I fought hard as my lungs starved for air. Kicking, spinning, clawing. I couldn't find the surface. I spun helplessly in the muck of a decidedly-not-blue ocean until I realized my time was up and there was nothing I could do. A strange sort of calm settled over me and I stopped fighting.

I woke up later, on the shore, mid-cough. Pop was slapping my cheek and shouting at me. I gurgled up salty acid and spit it on the sand. A crowd gathered around us, clapping and cheering. Once I'd shaken off the wooziness, I sat up and looked down at the happy-colored boogie board, still strapped to my ankle. Pop had grabbed it and yanked me out.

But now, there's no boogie board. No Pop.

The river is a thief that steals me from myself.

My limbs disappear as I flail and choke in the freezing water, all heat ripped from my body and sucked out to sea. The urn is gone. I know it's gone, but I can't accept it. I dive down over and over again, struggling against the current as a blurry, burning darkness enters my nose and mouth. As my lungs struggle to expel the water and catch up, a strange sleepiness overcomes me. Everything slows and I see him there, in the deep.

I stop fighting. The ice fills me from toes to head and I sink to him. His red hair fans out in the water, his arms and legs suspended as if he's imitating a seastar. He's so still, so peaceful. But then I meet his eyes, and they're the color of a frozen lake. His expression is harsh, anger carved deeply into the lines of his face. It sends a jolt of dread through me.

He only got angry with me once, when I was eleven. I'd directly disobeyed him and rode my bike across the highway. I didn't see what the big deal was at the time; nothing bad had happened. But he hadn't seen it that way. He'd yelled at me until the vein in his forehead was bulging and I was sobbing into my hands.

He looks like that now.

I wait on him to tell me how I *could* have hurt myself, how this *could* have been really bad. But instead, bubbles rush out of his mouth as he screams a warbled phrase, over and over.

I stare at him hard. Try to concentrate on what he's saying. Finally, it registers.

"It isn't me!"

Something yanks me, hard. I'm rolled, shaken, and then blinded by a bright light. My body sloshes over a blunt edge that digs into my ribs momentarily, and then I plunk into a heap onto a cold, hard surface. A waterfall pours from my mouth. It's endless. I choke and gag and yet still more pours out. My throat feels peppered with broken glass. A gasp rattles my chest and I open my eyes to a shivering blur. A wide, bearded face stares down at me, but it isn't Pop. His hair and beard are gray. His mouth is moving, making the most terrible roaring noise. I shrink away but he grabs me by the shoulders with gloved hands and sets me upright, then throws something soft and thick around me. The world pitches and rolls beneath me as if I'm on a—

I'm on a boat.

I blink. A massive wall of light shines in the sky above me. Ice water drizzles out of both of my ears as the deep voice of the man reverberates against my brain and begins to sound like language. He's wearing a bright yellow rain slicker. It occurs to me that the soft, thick material around me is a towel. With numb hands, I grab it by the edges and pull it tight against me, even though it smells sour, like it was left in the washing machine too long.

"Do ya know where ya are?" he asks. I stare at him dumbly, glance at the light behind and above him that reflects on the shiny material of his slicker. Tower Bridge. That's where the light is coming from. I look back at the man, huddled protectively above me. A jackhammering sensation pulses pain through my jaw. I realize after a moment it's because my teeth are knocking together. "Were ya tryin' to hurt yourself?"

Things click together, slowly. The river. The urn. *Oh my God, the urn!* I try to scramble to my feet but he yells, "Whoa!" as he presses his hands into my shoulders and forces me to sit back down.

"I d-d-d-dropped it!" The shivering only gets worse as icy wind slices me from every angle.

"Ya dropped something? In the river?"

I nod my head, but I don't know if he can tell since I'm shaking so hard. "Y-y-yes! My f-f-f-father..." I can't form the words.

"Oh, dearie," the big man says, "whatever ya dropped, it isn't worth your life! Your father will forgive ya."

· : ·

I don't know how much time passes.

I fight the disoriented feeling for what feels like a long time. After some hot tea, and a whole lot of asserting that I'm fine, I convince my good Samaritan, a fisherman who saw me jump, to take me to the closest access point to where I'd been sitting. By some miracle, we find my backpack still sitting on the ledge, completely unharmed and just slightly wet from the rain.

When the fisherman stops his old truck on the street in front of the Fox Den, I thank him and climb out onto the sidewalk.

"If I see your Beatles jar, I'll be sure to let ya know!"

My shame submerges me more thoroughly than the Thames. I couldn't bear to tell him I dropped my father's ashes in the river. So I told him it was a jar covered in Beatles stickers. With any luck, the locked lid of the urn will hold, and the sealed plastic bag inside will keep the ashes dry. Or it won't, and Pop is clumping like cat litter as we speak.

But better still, maybe Pop was never in there at all.

It isn't me.

I shiver violently as I wave goodbye. Though I'm no longer dripping, thanks to the loaned towel, my clothes are still wet, and the night breeze reminds me of that fact every two seconds. I turn the corner to the back alley and stop in my tracks.

Henry is there, leaning against the brick wall.

George asked me not to use the front door after close. Before I can consider breaking this rule, Henry looks up and sees me. A bulky camera hangs on a strap around his neck. A tendril of smoke spirals the air above his fingers. The closer I get to the door, the more the sickly sweet aroma of Cloves inundates me.

Of course he smokes Cloves.

It's like Buzzfeed writers created him in a lab: the golem of every hipster joke ever told. Smokes Cloves. Wears Warby Parkers. Reads books on quantum mechanics. Is Unimpressed© with everything else, including the Beatles.

His eyes move over me, take note of the towel. He smirks. "Been out for a swim?"

An irritated breath rises in my still-burning lungs. Though he has no idea how terrible my evening has been, his teasing hurts. I give him a side-eye as I shove my key in the lock. "Smoking will kill you."

He takes a drag and blows wispy smoke around his reply. "So will hypothermia."

I glance down at my waterlogged clothes. Touché, Hipster Golem.

"They say kissing a smoker is like licking an ashtray. It's gross." I jiggle the handle, but the door won't budge. I yank the handle and my wrist smarts. Only my Baptist brainwashing keeps me from taking the Lord's name in vain.

Henry flicks his cigarette into the puddle at my feet and it sizzles. He reaches past me and grips the handle, tweaks it just so. The door opens, but when I glance up at him, I'm stunned still. The violet shade I noticed the other day blossoms behind him in the post-rain mist of the alley.

"Been thinking of kissing me, then?" A smile curls his lips, and I hate myself but I look right at them. It takes a moment to remember where my feet are located.

"Nope." I step past him and give the door a little shove.

He drops his grip on the handle. "Good."

"Good," I echo, shaking it off.

Quiet blankets the store. Trivia night has ended and everything settles under the darkness. I follow the dim light illuminating the stairwell. Henry's footsteps thud behind me, so I jog to put space between us.

The moment I'm in the relative solitude of the upstairs bathroom, I lock the door and turn on the shower. I ditch my soaked clothes and stand in the hot stream, washing away the dirt and grime of the Thames. As the heat returns to my body, the reality of what happened sets in, and my shame slowly morphs into regret, and then into self-loathing.

I dropped his urn into the Thames.

But then I remember Pop's words, and I'm able to breathe again. *It isn't me.*

Now that I have time to think about what I did, it frightens me. Pop used to say leap and a net will appear. But I leapt without even considering a net. It never crossed my mind. *You're being impulsive again,* my psychiatrist's gravelly voice says in my head. *You always regret impulsive decisions, so why do you keep making them?*

As I'm towel drying my hair, Henry's voice filters through the door. I catch only snippets.

Got some good shots

Magnetic fields were supercharged

Storms make it easier

Just uploaded them

It's not that I care what Henry is talking about or to whom he is speaking. But I put two and two together and figure out the session George was referring to must have had something to do with that camera around his neck.

I dress in warm, dry pajamas, crawl in bed, and click off the light. But like most things do, my curiosity only becomes unbearably large in the dark. My phone finds its way into my hands and I track down the bookmarked Instagram accounts I don't follow.

Okay, one account I don't follow. Henry's.

I scroll through the recently uploaded pictures. They're all black-and-white photos with heavy contrast. The first one is a shot of the Tower of London, from an on-the-ground perspective, looking up. The night sky frames it with eerie shadows and bursts of light. The caption reads, *Bryn Gwyn: Window to the past. Additional shots in the Places of Power column.*

I scroll through until I come to the ones I've already seen. More landscape photos with references to *Places of Power*. Huh. He must be some sort of a journalist. Not that I care, but I pull up my browser and search Places of Power + Henry Pemberton.

The first result is an interview from an online publication called *New Ages.*

Places of Power is an ongoing column mapping Britain's ley lines, their About Us page reads. Then, beneath the byline: *Henry Pemberton, a ley line cartographer, shares with us his eye-opening theories on the supernatural properties of these sites.*

I snap the light back on and sit up. Then read and re-read it three times. Ley line cartographer? Who is this guy?

Allegedly you can communicate with the other side if you know what you're doing, he tells us. But even a novice can do it on a ley line. Magnetic forcefields occurring at these powerful sites intensify latent abilities. Think of these places like windows between the past and present, the living and the dead.

Magnetic forcefields. Maybe that's what those things in his pockets that first day were about. A Q&A follows some full-color and black-and-white shots, similar to the ones on his Instagram feed.

Q: What began this hobby of sorts for you, Henry?

A: Curiosity, mostly.

Q: Curiosity of...?

A: The notion of supernatural communication. With anyone. Even people we've lost.

Q: Are you attempting to communicate with someone you lost?

A: Yes.

Q: And does it work?

A: (laughs) I'll let you know.

I glance up at the date—two weeks ago. Is he actively trying to communicate with someone now? His mother? And if so, would he teach me how to do it?

I'd probably have to start being nicer to him.

The door lock to the bathroom clicks and the faucet turns on. I remember that I left my wet clothes on the floor and I instantly regret it. As much as Henry irritates me, I don't want him to think I'm a slob. I listen as he brushes his teeth and rummages around. Eventually he turns out the light and returns to his room.

I stand and press my ear to the wall, holding my breath so I can listen. But I'm met with silence. He must be off the phone. I turn the knob to go into the bathroom and clean up my wet clothes, but it's locked.

I exhale and creep down the hall.

His door hangs open a crack. Yellow light spills onto the dark hallway floor. I stop just before I reach the light and peek inside.

Henry's curled up on his bed, with Felix snuggled into a ball against his chest. His head is propped on one hand while the other strokes the length of Felix's back. He speaks softly to him, voice gentle as a heartbeat. My eyes feel like they might roll out of their sockets.

I've never even seen him speak to Felix, let alone pet him. Felix yawns with a squeak.

He looks up and sees me then, as if my gape-mouthed stare is emitting a homing beam. His face changes, but this time, it's the opposite of his usual smirk. It's the look you'd give a squatter after you caught her lurking in your attic. I want to melt between the floorboards.

"You uh—the bathroom door, uh—" I point wildly with my finger. Toward the ceiling, for whatever reason. I guess I'm pointing at all the other planets I'd rather be on.

He nods like my foolishness made sense, but he doesn't say anything as he rolls off the other side of his bed and disappears to unlock the bathroom door.

I can't make my feet move until I hear the click.

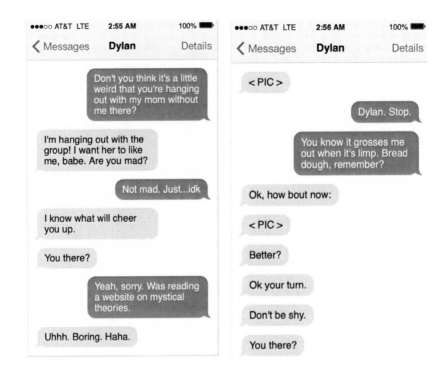

CHAPTER

FOURTEEN

: Child of Nature :

HENRY LOOKS DIFFERENT on Saturday.

A purple halo of light surrounds him. I blink and blink and blink. But the aura stays.

As he rings in customer sales, I sneak peeks at him over the top of the shelves. I can't bring myself to say one snarky thing to him. Usually by now he would've chastised me about my guitar playing or asked me when I expect my luggage, which still isn't here. But he hasn't uttered a peep all day.

When he's quietly working alone, the aura has dark streaks. But when he interacts with customers, recommending Hozier to the older ones and Damien Rice to the younger ones, he's all smiles and thumbs and floppy hair, and the aura brightens to lavender.

I see the auras of every customer in the store. Greens and blues and yellows. They're all there if I concentrate hard enough, but Henry's is vivid. I don't even have to *try* to see his. I've never met anyone else with a purple aura before. Purple auras indicate a highly sensitive, deeply spiritual person. They're prone to depression. Relatable since, according to Pop, my aura is also purple. I wouldn't know; I've never been able to see my own.

Pop's aura was like tie-dye. Never the same color twice.

When the store is empty again, I open another box of albums to shelve and, before I can talk myself out of it, take a swing at casual conversation.

"So. Your dad tells me you're a photographer for a website." Not technically true, since I had to online stalk him to uncover the one clue George did give me. I'm betting on him not questioning my source.

He glances up at me, but his aura doesn't turn lavender when our eyes meet. It darkens.

"I'm a freelancer." He steps away from the register and makes himself busy straightening displays.

I refuel and try again. "So, I looked at the site."

"Hocus pocus, child of nature stuff, but the pay is decent." He doesn't turn around. I narrow my eyes, because I know good and well that purple aura people don't say things like that. Besides, his t-shirt from the other day and his interview responses in *New Ages* contradict him.

"So these ley lines. They're energy lines?" I nudge. "I googled it. They're a possible place of supernatural connection, right?"

Henry leaves his spot and rounds the counter. He reaches into the shelf below the cash register and pulls out a book, worn and frayed on the binding. It's the book he was reading the day I arrived. He hands it to me.

Ley Lines of Britain by Alfred McFadden has a tree in a misty field on the cover. I flip it open. Copyright 1925.

"What is this?" I raise an eyebrow as he returns to his post. The pages smell like a basement. I skim through them, picking up words I stumbled across online. *Geoglyphs. Dowsers. Magnetic fields.* But everything else is watered-down pseudoscience. It doesn't even try to assert itself as fact. A tad different from his quantum-whatever-whatever books.

"Are you trying to communicate with ghosts?" I ask, my voice a little squeaky and unsure. He stacks book after book in the rock biography section like he's building a fortress that will block my attempts to converse. "Because if you are, I want in."

He looks up at me then. Pauses a moment. "My mother…" Henry stops and regroups. "She taught me to be open to every idea, to pursue my curiosity even if the idea appears silly and unfounded. That's all."

The front door opens as more customers enter the store. Henry leaves his station to greet them. For the rest of the day, each time the store empties of customers, he takes a smoke break. I get the feeling he's only doing it to get away from me.

$$\cdot \ \cdot \ \cdot$$

We're closing the store up when he comes in.

"Hello, love, would it be possible to put these flyers…" He squints ever-so-slightly, then his eyes widen. "Hey, I know you! You're the singer! Well, the undecided one."

The man from the pub stands in the doorway and shakes rain off his umbrella with one hand, holding out two neon-pink papers with the other. It's more Open Mic Night flyers like the one I saw the other day.

"Could you perhaps hang these in your window? If you have to ask George, it's fine. He knows me quite well. Trying to drum up a bit of business because the new place down on Scoresby keeps siphoning our patrons and we don't have much in the way of signups tonight."

I turn to get direction from Henry, but he's stepped away. Probably to smoke again.

"Uh, I uh—"

"Nigel O'Neill," the man says. "I'm the proprietor of Blackfriar's Crow."

I take the flyers and smile. "I'm Jo. And I'll certainly ask George about these."

"Lovely." He grins and I try not to stare at his teeth. "Have you decided yet if you're a singer? That is why you were poking around the other day, yes?"

"Well, sort of," I begin, but don't really know how to tell him why I want to play at his pub without betraying weirdo vibes. "My father used to play there, a long time ago."

He raises his bushy eyebrows and chuckles. "Is that right? Back when folks wanted to play there, I guess."

"Nigel!" George's voice echoes through the empty store. Nigel and I both turn. George and Henry file out of the office. He makes a beeline for us as Henry goes to the cash register to pull out the till.

"Well hello, my friend!" Nigel says, as they clasp hands and firmly shake. George looks down at the flyers and asks, "May I?" and then takes them from me.

"I was just asking the young lady here if you could perhaps display these."

"Oh, I think we can handle that. Help me decide the best spot for them." George slaps Nigel's back and leads him to the door.

I open my mouth to say the words. *My father is Nate Bryant. Was. Nate Bryant.* But the moment slips by.

Nigel pauses at the door and looks back at me. He points a finger in my direction. "And I'll see you later, isn't that right?"

This has to be a sign. Has to be.

"Yes." I give him a sincere smile. "I'll see you later."

CHAPTER FIFTEEN

: Doctor Robert :

ABOUT A YEAR after Pop's death, I had the dream that made me desperate for England.

In the two years since, I've dreamed the same one dozens of times, without a single variation. It begins with me sitting on the damp earth in a cool, shady graveyard. It's sunset, and I'm staring at a headstone. Trees reach toward the ground with knobby, arthritic hands. Moss grows over the tombs.

I'm alone but not afraid.

Written on the headstone in front of me:

Eleanor Rigby, beloved wife of Thomas Woods and grand-daughter of the above, died October 10, 1939, aged 44 years, asleep.

There are other names listed above hers, relatives that I could never quite see clearly in the dream. But when I looked up the actual photo of the grave (thank you, famousgraves.com), I was able to fill in the blanks. Though I'd never laid eyes on that headstone until I had the dream, it exists in real life in the church cemetery of St. Peter's in Liverpool—the church where Paul McCartney met John Lennon.

There are a string of coincidences, but here are the most significant: Eleanor Rigby shares a death date with Pop; he also died October 10, exactly seventy-nine years after her. Also in his sleep.

In the dream, as I'm trying to make out the blurry words, Pop steps out from behind the headstone and smiles. Not in my periphery like in the other dreams, but head on. Face-to-face. He's wearing his black button-up shirt, ripped jeans, and boots. His beard is neat, his hair is combed back like a windblown flame, and his eyes glisten with some fantastic secret he can't wait to tell me. He kneels in front of me. *We are finally together,* he says, and then squeezes my shoulders.

Every single time, no matter how hard I try to resist in the dream, I get so frightened by how *real* it feels that I shut my eyes. When I get the guts to open them again, he's gone.

There's something about Eleanor Rigby—the woman or the song—that I'm supposed to know or understand. It leads the way to Pop. Now that I'm in London, things are slowly falling into place. The missing shoe at the airport. The dream about singing the song.

If he isn't in an urn at the bottom of the Thames, maybe he's here. Tonight. And all of these clues were just leading me to this moment.

A toilet flushes behind me and interrupts my epiphany.

With Patrick's guitar slung across my back, I lean in toward one of the tiny, dirty pub mirrors and apply a thick coat of the kohl eyeliner I bought at the drugstore on the way over. It isn't really my style, but neither is singing in front of a crowd of strangers. I'm going for older, bolder me. I finish off the look with bright red lipstick.

Sgt. Pepper's Jo.

A latch clicks and a girl exits the stall. She's tall and dark-skinned, with natural hair and shimmery eye shadow. Her lips are glossed nude. It's effortless beauty, like her makeup came standard with her face. She turns on the faucet and washes her hands.

"Nice shade," she says, eyeing the lipstick tube, and then the guitar. "Are you playing?"

I smile and nod. She's so pretty and put together that it has apparently rendered me mute. I try not to compare myself, but my reflection next to hers is inadequate. I look like I always do: like someone who is pretending.

"See you out there." She exits through the swinging door.

Nobody has to know I'm pretending but me. I straighten my back and wade into the roaring cheer of the bar room. People fill the tables and barstools, but the open mic sign-up sheet fluttering on the end of the bar is empty. My hand shakes as I scrawl my name on the first line.

The last time I did something this unhinged, there was no public humiliation involved. But humiliation just the same. I didn't tell Lexie or Maddie I'd lost my virginity. I only told my psychiatrist, Dr. Robert Aufderheide. I think half the reason I ever trusted him in the first place was because he told me to call him Dr. Robert. (You know, like the song.) At the time, I thought this was a sign from Pop that I could trust the guy.

When I confessed to Dr. Robert that I felt like I was riding a soaring wind—that lights were brighter and smells were stronger and everything that touched my skin felt like electricity so I finally let Dylan undress me—he diagnosed me with mania. He said it was brought on by my new medication. Then he changed my dosage, which made things a lot worse for a while. Go ahead and try to tell your boyfriend that sex was a one-time thing while your brain was on the fritz. Does not stop him from reminding you what's done is done and *hey, remember how good it feels*, and you can't bring yourself to tell him it stopped feeling good the moment you crossed the line. After that, I learned distance and damage control is the way to go. Also: don't tell Dr. Robert everything.

I wonder what Dr. Robert would think if he could see me now, waiting to sing in a bar I'm too young to be in. He'd tell me to practice mindfulness. To reconcile my ideals with reality, or some other bullshit that sounds good but doesn't make any real sense. Good thing I don't care what he thinks anymore.

CHAPTER

SIXTEEN

: You Won't See Me :

"THERE YOU ARE!" Nigel steps up to the bartop. "You've come after all!"

His enthusiasm draws unwanted attention from the old guys perched on their stools. They turn to look at me, and then the Gibson. Do I look older than myself, with the black eyes and red lips? Or is it painfully obvious that I'm seventeen? I always feel so grown until I encounter actual grown people.

I straighten the collar of my white thrift store dress. It has bell-shaped sleeves and stops halfway down my thigh. It's more baptism than bar, now that I think about it. The scrutiny will only feel worse when I'm up on the stage.

Nigel glances at the sign-up sheet, then at me again. "Bryant?" Recognition flickers in his tired eyes, like he's just remembered our unfinished conversation from earlier. "As in Nate Bryant of Walrus Gumboot?"

My heart grows wings and flies away. Nigel pulls me into a hug with no warning.

"My darling girl, of course! I knew you looked familiar! I was so devastated to hear of your father's passing."

I nod into his shoulder. His shirt smells like whiskey and old man cologne. When he releases me, I step back. His eyes glisten. "Nate was a dear friend." He sniffles, composing himself. "Tell me, are the old Walrus Gumboot boys still playing together?"

I shake my head. "Ronnie moved back to New York. We haven't heard from Jim in a long time. Luka plays in a church band now. I guess it wasn't the same without Pop."

"No, no. Surely not."

We stand there for a minute in loaded silence until someone hollers his name from the kitchen door. "Ethan," Nigel says to the bartender with a finger in the air, "this is Jo. Get her whatever she likes this evening. On the house."

Ethan nods as he mixes someone else's drink.

"Oh," I reach for his sleeve. "No, you don't have to—" I'm interrupted by more yells from the kitchen.

"Nonsense!" He looks back at Ethan and nods. "Anything!" He turns to me then, "We'll catch up more in a bit. Duty calls."

I wonder if I should tell the bartender I'm underage, even if it's only by half a year. Legal drinking age here is eighteen. Ethan dries a glass with a towel and steps up to my spot at the bar.

"What'll it be, dear?"

"Uhhh…" I glance up at the menu, shifting back and forth on my feet. Mixing alcohol with meds could land me in the emergency room, but I've been off them for over a week now, and I've just signed up to sing in front of a pub full of people. "I'll have the Jameson."

Ethan gives me a funny look.

"On the rocks," I say. There. That sounds more official.

I exhale and scan the room when he turns to make the drink. My soon-to-be audience is definitely older than me. Like a lot older. Mid-thirties, at least. But then I spot the girl from the bathroom at a table near the stage. Three guys sit next to her. My eyes stop on the third one.

Henry lounges, his peacoat slung over the back of his chair. He's dressed nicer than he does for work: dark jeans and an Oxford, untucked. He smiles as he talks animatedly with his friends. He must feel me staring at him because he looks up. I whirl around, positive he's going to come over before he ever scoots his chair backwards.

A quick estimate: twenty, thirty steps at most, and I could be out the door. Forget about this whole thing. Singing in front of a bar full of strangers is one thing; singing in front of the one person in London who doesn't like me and repeatedly chastises my subpar guitar skills is quite another. Ethan sets my drink in front of me before I can remember how to move my legs. He sticks a skinny straw in the low, curvy glass and grins. "Enjoy."

The smell of it is enough to singe the cells inside my nose.

"Bold choice," Henry says, squeezing in next to me. I shrug but don't look up at him. I study the perfect square ice cubes in my glass instead. He props his elbows on the bar and orders a pint of beer. Beer! Damn, I forgot about beer. I should've ordered that.

"You come here a lot?" I cringe as soon as I say it because ugh, that sounded like a pick-up line from Lexie's cowboy book. I wrap my lips around the straw and try to swallow it back down with a swig of the golden liquid.

Scratch that. Fire. It's actually liquid fire and my throat is on fire and my belly is on fire and the whole building is on fire. Since I'm a girl of southern graces, I flinch only on the inside.

"Not really." Henry's smirk is audible. "But we didn't want to miss your performance. I heard you tell Nigel. You're singing, right?"

"We?" I finally get the nerve to make eye contact. For once, he seems lighter. His eyes are glassy and bright, and his aura isn't dark like it wants to smother me. "Is George here?" I briefly panic that he'll see me drinking and tell my mother.

"No. A few mates and me." Then I notice the barely perceptible slur.

Oh. He isn't happy to see me. He's buzzed.

I glance past him at the table with his empty chair. His friends look away and pretend they weren't watching us. One guy has round glasses and neat, gelled-to-his-scalp black hair. The other is short and stout with bleached curls. The beautiful girl from the bathroom seems out of place there, like she's only settled for their company. But she smiles like she is unaware of it.

Henry picks up his beer and takes a swig. "You ready for this?"

I nod as if my brain isn't screaming protests.

"Let's hope you sound better than you did the other night." He nudges me and grins as he walks away. Effervescent nerves bubble up in my chest. I try to drown it with my drink as I watch him walk back to his table. Nigel's voice on the microphone jars me out of my panic. Or pushes me further into it, I'm not sure.

"Ladies and gentlemen, as you know, it's the season's inaugural open mic night tonight, and we have a few performers lined up to sing for you this evening."

Everyone claps and cheers. I glance over at the sheet. My name is still the only one on it. With one last gulp, I finish my drink.

"Our first guest is a very special one. Some of you may remember a band that used to play here years ago, Walrus Gumboot." A few cheers and whistles sound from the back. I scan the crowd, searching for these holdover fans of Pop's. "Sadly, their founding member went to be with the saints too early in his life, and the band split up." Nigel pauses for dramatic effect. "But tonight, I have here for you the daughter of that founding member. Ladies and gentlemen, Miss Jo Bryant."

My body must've switched to autopilot, because I'm closing in on the stage, but I don't feel like I'm the one working the gears. The current of cheers pushes me forward.

My limbs hang at my sides, useless. Blue and purple track lights shine on me as I step onstage. Suddenly I'm aware of my silly white dress. My neck prickles with sweat. Why did I wear my hair up? I'm too exposed.

The cheers and applause stop as the lights dim. All sound evaporates. I can't see faces in the crowd because of the haze of the lights. Déjà vu clicks me into my place at the microphone stand. I close my eyes, find my center. Though my fingers feel like cold and clammy extensions of my body, they somehow find the frets and the guitar pick.

I wait in vain for his voice to tell me to *Play away*.

A million eternities stretch on, and then the chords bleed warm over the cold silence of the room. My lip touches the microphone. Slowly, I smile around the opening line.

It goes well for one perfect moment.

My fingers stumble and play the wrong chord. Panic rises like the smoke from my dream. That's another difference: there's no smoke in this bar. I push away the nagging feeling and sing through it. My lips stay on task, but my fingers search, search, search for the tempo. I could look up at the crowd, but it doesn't feel right. Not yet.

I finish the first verse, but the guitar is too far off to recover. I slide my right hand down the neck of the guitar, place my left hand over the strings and press until they sting silent against my palm. Then I sing without the music. The lights above me change and shift.

Cheers and whistles filter through the bubble I've created. It sounds better without the guitar. But it also sounds worse, because the déjà vu becomes water in my hands.

I look up, past the haze.

As my pupils constrict and adjust to the captive crowd, I'm drawn to one spot. Condensation slides down a beer glass. A hand reaches for it, but there's no tattoo. There's only a purple aura. I search behind him. Beside him. Around the bar. To the back corners of the room. There's no overlay of images, dream to reality. It's gone.

Nigel told the entire room he was dead; why would he suddenly appear? A stabbing sensation pierces the skin between my shoulder blades. I understand the sensation, but it's like it's happening to somebody else. Somehow I finish the song. Everyone cheers. Henry and his friends, especially.

I take a mental snapshot. *Caption: pity party, table of 4*

They're only applauding because I'm Nate Bryant's daughter. Because of that intro by Nigel. Anyway, it doesn't matter. I wasn't here for them. I was here for Pop.

I step past the microphone to exit the stage. Nigel says something like *Beautiful, darling*, into the microphone and thanks me, but I barely hear him. The path of least resistance to the door is just past Henry's table, but...

An empty chair slides out in front of me, blocking my way and nearly tripping me.

The rubber toe of a green Chuck Taylor props on the chair edge. I follow the line of his leg all the way up the body attached to it, stopping when I get to his face. The corner of his mouth twitches.

"You trying to trip me?" The lump in my throat spreads. Henry's friends watch me carefully, maybe with a tiny bit of suspicion. Henry, though? The look on his face doesn't contain even a hint of malice. He isn't closed off like usual. Open body language, smirky smile, dimples on display. Aura brightest lavender. Sincere.

"Maybe." He shrugs. "Join us?"

CHAPTER

SEVENTEEN

: If I Needed Someone :

EVEN SITTING, I'M dizzy.

"Zara," the girl says, as she reaches across the table and shakes my hand. Very formally. I wonder if Henry told her that's the way I greet people after the airport disaster. "We met in the bathroom."

The guy with the bleached curls lets out a wolf whistle. "Bathroom, eh?"

"That's Mons." Henry slurs a little, pointing at the whistler.

"Calvin Edward Monson the third, as a matter of fact." Mons reaches across the table and yanks my hand to his mouth. He plants a sloppy kiss on my knuckle before I can retract my arm.

"Sanjay." The one in glasses grins and gives me a little salute. "Henry sings your praises."

My praises? I give him a questioning look.

"You're a rotten guitarist, though," Henry adds.

"Don't listen to him," Sanjay says. "Can't bother with him when he's imbibing."

"Or any time, really," I mumble.

They all laugh, even Henry.

"You were right, she's feisty," Mons says to Henry. I shift in my seat, wondering what else he said. Hypothetically. If I cared.

"I've got the next round," Sanjay says as the next guy on stage bumbles about his original song and prepares to sing. "What'll you have?"

It takes me a minute to realize he's talking to me. "Uh…"

"Whiskey, right?" Henry grins. A challenge. Pop would hate the thought of me drinking whiskey in a bar. He told me once that alcohol was for losers and that I would never be a loser. He was drunk at the time.

"On the rocks," I tell Sanjay, feeling at least three years older every time I say that.

Sanjay slides out of his chair and heads toward the bar.

The guy on the stage begins to sing and his voice cracks on every lyric. I cringe. Several people get up and leave. He didn't get a dead dad introduction, so the crowd isn't as nice to him when he finishes. Henry, Zara, and I clap politely. Mons yells, "Thank God!" and a few people around us laugh. He looks directly at me. Like he's making sure I'm paying attention to him. I shift in my seat. Something is off about Mons; where there's a light behind most people's eyes, there's a tunnel behind his.

Sanjay returns with drinks for the table. I take my glass and distract myself with the burn.

"How do you like London so far?" Zara asks. Four pairs of eyes await my answer.

"Oh, it's great." I squirm and glance at the exit. She smiles like she thinks I'll say more. I'm not doing her any favors here, but small talk is utterly painful.

"Are you at university here?" I give Zara my most interested expression. This is a well-known awkward-turtle trick: get other people talking about themselves. It keeps the focus off you. It works a little too well on drunk people. I find out each of their majors. Henry: physics. Sanjay: history. Mons dropped out last year to work in his dad's mechanic shop. Zara tells me she's studying theatre at Saint Catherine's.

"Yeah," Mons cuts in, like he thinks he's the narrator of this conversation. "Our girl is London's next movie star." He tosses an arm around her shoulders. I watch her reaction—calm, subtle, calculating. She shifts her body and shrugs it off. Probably not the first time she's dealt with him. "Here lately, she's also a model."

This doesn't surprise me a bit and I say so.

Zara rolls her eyes. "That's not even a little bit accurate. I needed portfolio portraits, and Henry needed a volunteer to help him perfect his portrait process."

"Henry's great at taking pictures of beautiful women," Mons interrupts again. "Has he asked you to pose for him yet?"

I'm not entirely sure if he's trying to insult me directly or to provoke a fight with Henry, but his tone is instigative. "He won't stop asking," I joke, trying to lighten the mood. "I keep telling him no, though."

Everyone laughs except Henry, but he doesn't correct me. From the corner of my eye, I catch him staring at me. I turn to face him and *whoa*. He looks away, but maybe not as fast as he should have. There's a hint of a stomach flutter. Which, whatever. Doesn't mean anything. I'm probably just hungry; I haven't eaten since lunch. I stir ice cubes with my straw. They rattle and tinker against the sides of my glass. At some point, a third drink materialized beneath my hand and now it's almost gone.

His foot bumps mine under the table and my pulse quickens.

It's not like I'm attracted to him. Please. Not even. He's cute, I mean clearly. But I have a boyfriend. And maybe he has a thing with Zara or something. Mons seems to think so.

I glance up at him again, through my lashes. I don't intend to be flirty, but…

"Why are you looking at me like that?" I narrow my eyes.

He grins as he writes something invisible on the table with the tip of his finger. Then he turns the full force of his gaze on me. "No reason."

It definitely doesn't cause any more flutters. I sit up a little straighter in my chair and drink the remaining liquid in my glass with a slurp. *See? I'm unaffected. And a lady, at that.*

Henry leans in and props his chin in his hand.

"So tell me." He blinks. "How long have you been a raging alcoholic?"

I bite my bottom lip to stop it from trembling. "Only since I met you."

Zara and Sanjay chuckle, and I take a mental victory lap for this round. Henry smiles and holds my gaze for an uncomfortable amount of time. Probably only four or five seconds pass, but it feels like the sun has risen and set again by the time he looks away. His aura is a kaleidoscope of purple now.

"Your aura is purple." It's out of my mouth before I can stop it.

His face scrunches and he laughs. "What?"

"Your aura. Sometimes it's this like, dark indigo up here," I wiggle my fingers around his face, "mostly when you're being an asshole, but right now, it's plum. With a lavender outside edge."

"You read auras?" Zara asks. "Do mine!"

Maybe they'll all have a good time making fun of me about this later, but I don't care right now. I concentrate on the feminine shape of her face, the high pitch of her jaw. Then I let my gaze defocus. Everything's fuzzy, but after a minute, a rich sunflower shade blossoms behind her head. "Yellow," I say.

She stares at me. "My aunt says the same thing. Always yellow."

Maybe she won't think I'm a freak. Or maybe her aunt is a known freak and this inks the certainty.

"What about mine?" Sanjay sits up a little straighter.

"Orange." I noticed his when I first sat down. I don't look at Mons, because his is tar-like. If he asks, I'll lie.

When I'm 64 blares from my lap. I silence the FaceTime call.

Suddenly the room spins. Until this exact moment, I hadn't noticed the effects of three drinks. It's like seeing Dylan's name on the caller ID activates my drunkenness.

"Uh-oh," Mons bellows. "What's wrong?"

I must have made a face because all four of them stare at me like they're waiting for the bad news.

"Nothing." I shrug, and it sets me off-balance. "Just a call I don't want to take right now."

I switch over to the text screen to send him a message instead.

"Pardon me," says a voice over my shoulder. I put my phone on the table and turn around. An older man with a backwards cap and a stubbly gray face smiles down at me. "Are you Nate Bryant's daughter?" He's fuzzy around the edges, but his aura is green. Trustworthy.

"Yes!" I reach out and take his hand awkwardly, hoping he can't tell I'm well on my way to wasted.

"I'm Walter Kingsley," he says, squeezing my hand. "I grew up with your father in Liverpool. We even played music together for a bit."

My throat goes completely dry. I have so many questions for him, but I freeze. It's like I can't remember how to talk. Nigel stops by our table and interrupts.

"I'm so sorry we've not had a moment to chat," he says to me. "Stop back by later this week. After six. We'll all have some tea and discuss your father. Walter, you'll come?"

Walter nods. "I'd love to!"

I nod and thank them, thrilled by the prospect of talking about Pop, and a little grateful I don't have to do it in my current state.

"Walter," Nigel says. "I was able to do that thing you asked me to." He puts his arm around Walter's back and leads him toward the back of the bar.

As they disappear through a door, Walter says, "But what thing?"

I'm discombobulated by this incident, and my hands shake as I reach for my phone, but it isn't there. Across the table, Mons shakes with silent laughter.

"What is it?" Henry and Sanjay both crane their necks to see, but he's clutching something to his chest. I squint. My phone. He has my phone? What's he laughi—

Oh! Oh God.

"No," is the only word I can form. I hold my hand out, hoping he understands I need the phone back, right now.

"Hel-lo?" Henry sings. "What is it?"

Sanjay's gaze pings back and forth between Mons and me.

For one heart-stopping moment, Mons stares at the screen, and I think he might turn it around and show everyone Dylan's last text. The photo. But Zara reaches over and yanks it out of his hand, then gives it to me. I shove it back in my dress pocket as fast as I can.

"I've got you." Zara winks. "Not a word, Mons."

The guys groan, and a blackmail smile unfurls on Mons's face.

I've decided I don't like him. If I felt more capable of stringing sentences together right now, maybe I'd even tell him so.

Ignoring Dylan hasn't discouraged him from sending pictures like that. He's never been good at taking hints. Maybe if I'd just been firm with him, he would've stopped. I make up my mind to delete the whole thread as soon as I'm alone.

Henry finishes off his beer and slides backwards in his chair. "Let's get out of here."

Everyone stands before my brain catches up. I jump up, and the room turns a cartwheel. I reach out and grasp the table edge for balance. This part. Wasn't supposed to happen.

Carefully, I sling the guitar strap around my shoulders and follow them—step slide—to the door. Chairs and tables become moving obstacles. I bump into shoulders and heads with the guitar as I go and *wheee!* Oopsie.

"Sorry," I sputter. "So sorry. Excuse me. Pardon me."

The air is twenty degrees cooler outside, and when the breeze hits my face, it fine-tunes the severity of my situation. Flashes of light orbit my head and I feel like I'm watching one of those awful first-person low-budget films.

"What's the plan, then?" Mons asks, walking backwards down the sidewalk. Zara and Sanjay trail Henry, and I hang way back.

"Dunno." Henry shrugs. "I wanted a break from amateur night."

I open my mouth to point out he wasn't exactly volunteering to get up and sing, but I can't push words past my lips. The lines in the sidewalk wiggle and zigzag like a conveyor belt. Ah, conveyor belts. Now I'm thinking about my lost luggage. And my lost medicine and clothes and all the other important stuff in there. Remake myself, hell. I need my stuff! Rupert is a liar, I tell you that.

"What about that new place on Scoresby?" Zara suggests.

"Their beer selection is shite!" Mons roars.

Beer selection? They're thinking of drinking more? A wave of dizzying heat washes over me. I breathe in through my nose, out through my mouth. The conversation goes on, but their voices taper into oblivion. I look up to make sure they're still there, and the world freefalls. I stagger to a halt next to a trashcan on the street and close my eyes. Warm saliva fills my cheeks. All the liquid in my belly reaches volcanic temperatures, desperate for the chill of the night air.

I barely hear Zara ask, "Hey, is she sick?" from her separate planet in the solar system.

"You all right?" Henry's voice is closer now, but I can't answer. I try to swallow all the lava seeping toward the back of my teeth.

"She looks like she might chunder," Sanjay says.

If that word means what I think it means...

Then, as if Sanjay, with his orange aura, has the power to manifest realities, I lean forward and grab the sticky edges of the trashcan.

And chunder my face off.

CHAPTER

EIGHTEEN

: If You've Got Trouble :

TRASH SMELLY HOT throat palms sweating gurgling empty stomach head pounding humiliation eyes watering muscles clenching life over.

Hushed voices confer behind me. An obnoxious cackle—I think from Mons—thunders through. I'd crawl right into the garbage if I had the wherewithal to make my muscles cooperate.

"I'll stay," Henry says. "Go ahead without me."

Oh God, no. Breathing through my mouth doesn't prevent me from smelling the contents below me. I pretend there aren't people walking by snickering and gaping. If only Pop could see me now, amirite?

"Here," Henry says, and hands me a wet napkin. I don't know from whence he acquired this miraculous object of relief, and I don't care. It could be soaked in chloroform at this point and I'd happily bury my face in it.

The cool cloth wipes away the sweat and ickiness on my face and lips, smearing red lipstick everywhere. I realize it a moment too late and whimper. Henry hands me a peppermint. I dizzily unwrap it and pop it in my mouth.

"Feel better?"

I grunt. He stands, hands in his pockets, casual as ever. Not a care in the world about the passersby. His glassy eyes twinkle behind square frames and he smiles. Just like the smile he gave me in the pub.

Oh. I get it now. He's amused. This is fun for him.

My anger flares hot and sudden on the back of my neck. Come Monday, he'll be reminding me how I embarrassed myself with a guitar and then yakked in a trashcan. And I'll have no defense, because look at me. I'm a complete mess.

The universe decides things aren't bad enough, so it starts to rain. Cold, stinging drops sizzle against my flushed skin.

"Go find your friends," I say. "I don't need an escort."

But he just stands there. Doesn't say a word. I pack up my shame and start walking, but before I make it very far, the sky opens up. Again. Of course.

Something tugs at my back, and I have to step backwards to keep from falling over. Henry pulls me under an awning as I whirl around, and he lifts the guitar by the strap over my shoulder.

"At least let me carry the guitar," he says. "I'll wrap it in my coat so it doesn't get ruined."

"Since when do you care?" I stumble.

He narrows his eyes. "I don't. But Patrick might."

He has a point. I hand it over and then zigzag into the downpour. It's so infuriating the way I know where I want my feet to go but they won't cooperate.

By the time I make it to the back door of the Fox Den, I'm drenched to the bone. Freezing water rolls down my forehead, into my ears, down the front of my dress, which is suctioned to me like a second skin.

I press my key into the lock and turn, but the handle doesn't budge. I fiddle with it, becoming more water-logged by the second.

"Getting drenched is becoming a habit for you." Henry steps past me, balancing the wrapped guitar on his back. He holds an umbrella, dry as can be beneath it.

"Nice umbrella," I mutter.

"I borrowed it. You could've walked with me." The grin in his voice pisses me off more. "Allow me." He takes the key from my hand and my reflexes are too delayed to stop him. I cross my arms over my chest. He deftly fits the key in the lock, lifts and jiggles the handle and opens the door, then raises his finger to his lips. "Shh."

When we step into the dim hallway, the door closes behind us and mutes the roar of the rainfall. I'm acutely aware of the chill on my skin, the quiet drip of water off the hem of my dress, the amber glow of the hallway and all the colors of the famous albums lining the walls. Henry closes the umbrella and sets it down. Before we get to the stairwell, he drapes his coat over my shoulders and clamps a hand around mine. I startle at the sensation of sudden warmth.

He narrows his eyes. "Go slowly. And be quiet."

It hadn't occurred to me until now that I should worry about George catching me sneaking in drunk out of my mind. If he told Mama, I'd probably be on a plane home tomorrow.

We tiptoe up the steps, and I'm so dizzy I'm glad he's holding on to me. The drip of water from my dress hits the wood. *Thud. Thud. Thud.* His eyes stay on me as we go. It's dark in the stairwell, but his aura is different now. The lightest I've ever seen it. Henry likes me better drunk. Clearly. I giggle aloud.

He shoots me a warning glare and I button my lip.

When we finally make it to the third level, he drops my hand. I stare at him for a moment, wanting to say something, but he turns and goes to his room before I can.

I head to the bathroom for a towel. In the mirror, horror awaits. The black eye makeup has drizzled down the sides of my face like charcoal lines in the snow. Red lipstick is smeared across my cheek. The colors pool on the collar of my dress. I look like Harley Quinn on a drunken bender inside a gas station car wash.

When I remove the coat and hang it on the towel rack, it's even worse. No wonder he covered me up. White dress plus lots of water is a really bad combination. I don't stop to analyze whether it was because he was helping me preserve modesty or because he was repulsed by me.

I strip down and towel off my hair and ruined face. Maybe if I scrub hard enough, I can remove all the humiliation of to-night along with the water and clown makeup. I brush my teeth to get rid of the puke-and-peppermint taste, then stumble into Patrick's room.

There's an ever-present spinny feeling, and it makes simple things difficult. Like putting on a clean t-shirt and pajama pants from my thrift store pile, and brushing the tangles out of my wet hair. I fall on the bed. Closing my eyes makes the spinning worse. I clench my fists, despising being so out of control.

"You're a liar, Pop. There's nothing magical here."

I lie awake in the dark for a long time until the sickening turmoil begins to subside.

I'm nearly asleep when cabinets squeak in the bathroom. Doors open and close. I pretend it's a stranger in there, because it's easier than thinking about who it actually is and endlessly analyzing his behavior. He's not some puzzle to be solved. Even though maybe, if he was someone else and I was someone else and we hadn't gotten off to such a weird start, I'd like to be his friend.

The light strip under the bathroom door disappears and I listen to his quiet footsteps. Into his bedroom. Out into the hall. For one nauseating moment, I think he's coming to my door. But then there's a loud creaking. Footsteps fade and then get louder again—a thudding on the ceiling above me. The attic?

Above, Henry's voice is faint, but he's talking to someone. I can't make out the words—just the baritone warmth of his voice. I creep to the door and crack it, ever-so-slightly and peek out.

A pool of light spills onto the hardwood across the hall. Above it, the trap door is open. Henry's voice sifts down. I tip-toe toward the ladder and listen.

"...had to be hard for her, knowing her dad played there."

I stop dead in my tracks and hold my breath. There's a liquid sloshing sound.

"Right, right. I tried to tell him that. Nobody ever listens to me."

Except me, right now. I'm listening to him. And tried to tell who what?

"Right, then. Talk to you tomorrow."

I attempt a sneak-away but step on a squeaky board that announces my location.

"Hello?" he calls, somewhere out of sight. Then a moment later, he peers down at me.

"Sorry," I bumble. "I heard someone talking and—"

He reaches down through the opening in the ceiling. "Come up here. I've got something for you."

CHAPTER

NINETEEN

: Something :

HE TAKES MY hand and helps me up the ladder.

It occurs to me for the first time how big his hands are compared to mine. My head swims as I get my bearings. Old brick walls surround us and slant upward. The pitch of the roof in the middle of the room is just tall enough for Henry to stand without ducking or stooping. On either side of the room, long tables line the workspace. On one side, there's a sink and several plastic trays. On the other, there's equipment of some kind, which I assume is for developing film. Rows of pictures hang from clothespins on wires above it. The ceiling has alternating white bulbs and red bulbs that illuminate the windowless space.

It hits me then that George meant this was literally a dark-room.

In the corner opposite the workspace, there's a counter with a microwave and an electric tea kettle, and a table and two chairs. Henry pulls out one of the chairs for me.

"This is my studio." He pulls two mugs from a shelf above the kettle and sets them on the table, then sets a box of tea beside them. I sink into the chair.

"Hangover prophylactic," he says, and places a bag in each mug.

I read the label on the box. "Mugwort?"

He half smiles. "Drink this and take two aspirin, and you'll wake up good as new." He pours the steaming water from the kettle into our mugs. The aroma is rich and peppery, almost hypnotic.

While it steeps, he takes a jar of honey and a spoon from one of the shelves and sets it on the table. His hands move non-stop. Sliding the kettle over. Turning the mugs. Turning the ring on his thumb. Wiping his hands on the back of his pants. I survey the room and pretend not to wonder why he's so fidgety.

"Look," he says, sliding into the chair opposite me. "I owe you an apology. I should've done a better job looking out for you."

I stare at him. "What? Nobody asked you to look out for me, Henry."

"Actually," he twists his hands together, "my dad did."

My spine stiffens. "George asked you to go to the Crow tonight?"

He nods.

Oh God. It comes to me one detail at a time. "I'm guessing you had different plans with your friends before he asked?"

He gives me a half-shrug, half-nod.

Here I'd been thinking that he came because he wanted to be there. Not to mention his friends changed their plans! All to witness my series of incredibly stupid decisions. Then Henry ditched them. And not because he cared that I got back safely, but because he felt responsible for me. Glancing down at the tea mugs, I feel sick all over again.

Even this hangover tea is his way of keeping his word.

I stand up. "Look, you don't have to do this. I didn't realize. I'm sorry I ruined your night."

"Wait." He reaches out and takes my hand for the third time tonight. "Sit down. I promise you'll feel better."

"I'm not gonna tell your dad, okay? Don't worry about it. This is pretty much a regular thing for me. At home, I mean. Partying."

The corner of his mouth turns up.

"Super regular thing." I dig the hole a little deeper, fully committing to the lie.

He bites down on the inside of his cheek like he's trying not to laugh. "Sit down, Jo."

I think it's the first time he's ever used my name. My legs wobble as I sink onto the chair. He lets go of my hand and pushes my mug toward me.

The liquid is warm and a little bitter. I add honey and stir, spoon clinking against the cup. We sip quietly for a few moments, and he peeks over the rim of his mug at me. The closeness becomes a little too much, so I stand and pace the room with my tea, studying the pictures hanging on the lines. Unlike the landscape photos on his Instagram page, these photos are of people. Nobody I recognize, until I get to the end of the line.

Two photos of Zara stare back at me. Some of his photos look like commissioned portraits, but these look like *art*. She's draped in a blanket, bare shoulders and legs sticking out, lying on a hardwood floor. It occurs to me that she's probably naked under the blanket, based on the placement of the fabric. A strange pang turns over in my gut when I imagine myself as Henry and look at her through his eyes.

"Are these the pictures Mons was talking about tonight?" I glance at him.

He nods. "Yeah. He's a little jealous."

"I kind of picked up on that."

"I'm sorry about him, too, by the way," he says. "We call him Mons Pubis. I'm sure you can guess why."

"Because he's a dick?"

Henry chuckles. "Nothing gets by you."

I glance over at him. "Why do you hang out with him, then?"

"Old habits die hard and all that."

We both go quiet for a moment.

"So how does all of this work?" I point to the red bulbs on the ceiling.

He reaches up to a light panel on the wall and flips off the light, putting us in momentary darkness. Then flips another switch and bathes the room in a hazy red glow. He joins me in the workspace and feeds some film into the viewfinder, then turns on the big bulky machine that looks like an oversized microscope.

"Go ahead, take a look."

I peek down through the lens at the negative. It's one of the photos of Zara, but in this one she's wearing a dress.

"The red light," he explains, "won't expose the film the way the white light will."

I look up at him. Our proximity suddenly occurs to me. I could move one inch forward and touch any part of him.

Jesus. Not that I would! I take a step back, bumping into the table behind me.

"I see the tea is sobering you right up." He smirks and places the negative back in its sleeve. "A warning, by the way. Mugwort produces extremely lucid dreams for some people."

"Oh, great." I look down and swirl the sepia liquid around in my mug, watching the steam rise from the surface like a spell. "More of those."

"More of what?"

I meet his eyes. "Lucid dreams."

Henry leans back on the table and tilts his head to the side. His eyebrows knot together above his nose. He doesn't ask me to elaborate, but the shadows in his expression do.

Maybe it's because I can't possibly embarrass myself any more than I already have, or it's the comfort of the relative darkness, but something about him makes me want to open up my head and pour my negative reel of thoughts directly into his viewfinder. Let him pick through them and develop them at will. "My pop has been communicating with me through dreams."

He doesn't laugh. "How?"

I shrug. "I keep getting these premonitions. Of things I'm supposed to do and places I'm supposed to be. I'm going to find him. It just hasn't worked yet."

Henry says nothing. Just stares at me like a museum exhibit.

"Forget it. I sound unhinged."

He shakes his head. "I have dreams like that sometimes. My mom died, too, you know. And we lost a close friend a few years ago. Sometimes I talk to both of them in my dreams. It always seems incredibly real until I wake up. Never premonitions, though."

But it isn't real. That's what he's implying. We sip from our mugs for a while, not talking. The peppery aroma dazes me. It's like being suspended in that moment just before you sneeze.

"I only sang tonight because I dreamed it."

He looks up at me.

"In the dream, Pop was in the audience. I thought maybe if I could recreate the dream exactly, it'd make it real and he'd be there."

He watches me carefully. The fact that he's not freaking out only encourages me. I tell him about the gumballs. And the shoes at the airport. And all the other times I had dreams about mundane things that later came true, with Pop waiting quietly in the periphery. The only thing that didn't come true was Pop.

He doesn't say anything as he goes back to the table, switches the red lights for the white ones.

"I came here to find him." I squint as my eyes adjust, wondering if the mugwort has some sort of truth serum property.

"Find him where?" Henry asks. "I don't mean to pry, but... I saw the urn."

My stomach falls through my feet at the mention of the urn. I think about it, lying on the river bottom, or washed out to sea. I wonder what he'd think of me if he knew I lost it.

"Thing is," I stare at the floor, "I can't be sure it's him in the urn. I never saw his body."

Henry opens his mouth to say something but stops short. He returns to his place at the table and I follow him.

"There's this one dream," I say. "I keep having it over and over. He always shows up at this one place, and even after what happened tonight, I have to go there. To make sure."

"Where?"

I hesitate. "It's in Liverpool, where he grew up."

"But where, specifically?"

I shake my head. "I can't tell you. I don't talk about the dreams until after they've happened in real life. Kind of a superstitious thing."

He nods as if this makes perfect sense. I twirl my tea and make a tiny typhoon, knowing good and well this conversation is not normal. That *I'm* not normal.

"You asked me about ley lines." He meets my eyes. "There's a theory that you can communicate on ley lines. Telepathically." It's casual, non-committal, the way he says it. He doesn't know I read the interview in *New Ages*, and there's no way I'm confessing to it.

"I'm a physics major," he continues. "So this whole ley lines thing—at first, it felt like an identity crisis. But the more I studied theory, the more it made sense. We're all made of energy, and energy can be neither created nor destroyed. What comprises a soul? Where does it go?"

I take a breath. "I don't know."

"It's not just science that aligns with it. In maths, there are coincidence points. Two lines occupying the same space, like an overlay. If you apply the properties of ley lines to any number of physics or even mathematical theories, things become... possible."

I sit up straighter, not quite following. "The possibility of?"

"Deliberate, conscious communication."

Something squeezes inside my chest.

"So what does science say about premonitions?"

"Well, they're mostly regarded as pseudoscience because they violate the principle of causality, which says an effect cannot occur before its cause."

I look down at the table.

"But some physicists," he continues, "believe that time is fundamental. That disordered causality may exist."

I look back up at him. "So science can both confirm and deny something, depending on the scientist doing the analyzing?"

He slides his glasses up on top of his head. I've never seen him take them off before, and my face flushes like he's ripped off his shirt. I blink the embarrassing thought away and pull myself together.

"Our perception of reality is a lot like uncorrected nearsightedness. For instance—" he leans over the table, close to my face, and lowers his voice "—when I look at you now, up close like this, I notice the precise details. The texture of your hair, the shape of your face, the freckles on your nose, even the little flecks of gold in your irises."

His peppermint-scented breath vibrates across my lips and heat crawls down my neck. I don't breathe. I *am* those little gold flecks right now: small and hidden but discovered. Terrified because I'm being seen.

He moves to his original spot and all the air in the room shifts with him. "But further away, I can't see any of that. It's a blur. Our reality is shaped by what we can see. What we can capture with a lens." He gestures absently to his workspace. "And we can't see everything." He slides his glasses back onto his face. "Physics works like my glasses. It's a tool that corrects the nearsightedness of our perceived reality. Imperfectly, nonetheless. It's still blurry if I look to either side instead of directly through the lenses."

"Tool?" The word comes out in a whoosh. "Like the magnets?"

"Well, I meant the principles of physics. But since you brought it up, we can apply one to the magnets, too. The magnets help me find ley lines. They work like dowsers. But there's something called the Observer Effect. It's a principle that says by simply observing something, you change the nature of it."

Kind of like he just did to me a minute ago, one impulsive moment away from my face.

"That sounds... complicated." I swallow.

"Okay, think of it like this. When you check the pressure in an automobile tire, you can't use the gauge without air escaping. The change is small, but present. So when I use magnets to locate a ley line, it may alter the nature of them. The location or the quality or the movement. The Observer Effect explains inconsistencies in mapping them, to a point."

"I see." I don't see. I'm still a little wasted.

"I'm saying the answers are all out there for the taking. But we're far from grasping them all, separately or together."

He smiles and launches into theoretical physics—a passionate stream of concepts I might struggle to follow even if I was fully sober. He talks about inclined planes, string theory, multiverses, quantum entanglement. I'm listening, but more than anything, I'm watching the way his eyes light up as he talks about synchronicity and combined energies and ionic bonds. He gestures in front of him like he's painting a picture in the air. He's a constant ripple of movement and thought and energy.

One thing is for sure: Henry isn't *pretending* to be smart.

He blows out a tired breath at the end. "I said all of this to say that I've been trying to make contact, too, but it hasn't worked yet."

Though the rest seems like alien language, I understand this part. And also the disappointment in his face when he says it. He and I at least have this in common.

"How do the magnets help you find the lines?" I empty the rest of my tea, lick the last of the honey off my lips, and set the mug down, feeling sleepy and warm.

"It's hard to explain but…" He pauses and locks eyes with me. The air between us crackles, like a chemical reaction is taking place. "I could show you sometime."

I take a mental snapshot.

Caption: wowzer

I glance at his lips. Just a peek, long enough to observe the pillowy quality of them. What would physics say about that? Were his lips that plump before I looked at them? Or was it the effect of my gaze that made them that way?

When I meet his eyes again, I know he saw me look. The bottom of my empty mug suddenly becomes the most interesting thing in the observable world. If there were leaves there to read, they'd say *Hey, remember Dylan?*

Dylan would be crushed if he knew I was sitting here in this intimate space, telling some other guy all the things I can't tell him. Some other guy, who takes my word for it when I tell him irrational things instead of asking about my meds. And I keep thinking things about this other guy that I should not be thinking. Because he is only babysitting me as a favor to his dad, and ultimately, my mom.

Alcohol makes me stupid.

"I'm really sleepy. I think I should go to bed."

Henry nods. I stand and head to the ladder. When I glance over my shoulder, his eyes are waiting for me.

"Thank you for the tea," I say. "And the babysitting."

He smiles at me as I leave.

CHAPTER TWENTY

: I'm Only Sleeping :

SUNLIGHT SHINES ALL around us as my mouth maps a shady trail over his skin.

Behind his ear, down the tender side of his neck, over the point of his throat. I part my lips and taste the sticky sweetness in the divot where his collarbones meet. A shudder settles over me as I inhale the peppery, intoxicating scent. He's a dreamy nightcap in the middle of the day. Warmth beats down on my exposed back. My knees chafe from friction with the crisscross embroidery of the picnic blanket. The thread makes little x-shaped indentions on my shins.

Dylan's chest rises and falls beneath me, leaner than I remember. It's only been a little more than a week since I've seen him, but I've somehow forgotten his details. My hair fans over him, trickling over the ridges of his stomach—defined muscles I never bothered to notice or appreciate before. He shivers as my mouth dips further and further south.

It's different this time.

Long fingers grip the tops of my arms and pull me back up. Even with my eyes closed, my face finds his in an instant. Like an ionic bond, we fit. I smile against his lips.

My fingers draw invisible lines on his collarbones, over the puckered ridge of a scar on the left side of his chest—another detail I've somehow forgotten. I linger there, tracing it, trying to remember what it looks like. I can't process all five senses at once. His hands are everywhere.

My bare thighs slide over the protrusions of his hipbones—skin on slippery, damp skin. Though I know what comes next, for the first time, the curious anticipation of it makes my legs tremble.

I sit up, lashes fluttering against the glittering daylight. Body bared and back arched. I'm not a girl, but a physics lesson: the inevitability of an inclined plane. Our energy is combined at a single meeting point. We are perpendicular lines occupying the same shimmering vibration. Synchronicity in human form.

I balance, fingers stumbling again over the raised scar. I'm drunk on sensation and my eyes can only process color. First the white of the scar, then the flesh surrounding it. The green of our hillside. The endless blue of the sky. The gray stone tower jutting up against the horizon.

His aura bleeds into my vision. It's not the usual slate, but deepest plum—the exact shade of an African violet. I know a moment before I look at his face that it's Henry beneath me.

The shock of it changes none of the euphoria I feel.

I trace a thumb over his fleshy bottom lip, breaking its seal with the dramatic cupid's bow of the top one. My fingertips read the braille of stubble on his jaw. It says *don't stop*. His hair is a mess on the ground, and I don't know how I managed to miss the difference, how something didn't give this away immediately. Of course everything feels different: because it is.

He is an atlas of perfect destinations. I'm lost in the deep green forests in his eyes as I sail the ocean currents on his hips. Something hazy and inaccessible taunts me from the deepest recesses of my mind. Something about magnets and maps and a mission—the thing we came here to do. Except we ended up doing this instead.

I look down at Henry, and the angles of his jaw clench sharper. The furrow of his brow, deeper. He knows we've gone off course. I close my eyes again, trying to hold on. Begging the powers that be for another minute. Thirty seconds, even. But it's too late, because my brain has identified this for exactly what it is. The moment you realize a dream is just a dream, a cruel breaker trips and it's gone.

I fling back into my body with a high-voltage jolt. In Patrick's room. Middle of the night. Curtains blowing. My throat is ragged; I'm panting like I've run a race. My hair and t-shirt stick to my skin. I throw the blanket in the floor and peel off my pajama pants. The cool night breeze from the window brushes over my damp knees. I'm a live wire left behind by a storm.

Only a Jack and Jill bathroom separates my room from his. I dart upright. I could walk in there right now, crawl into his bed, whisper this secret to him.

But...

Reality returns to me in degrees. Henry and I are barely even friends. We only just had our first real conversation last night. My heart pounds and I quake with disappointment. That was the way it's *supposed* to feel. I don't know how I know; I just know. The shame I couldn't feel in the dream submerges me now. *Why* has it never been like that with Dylan?

Maybe not taking my medication is messing up my perception of things.

Tears well and I cover my face with my hands. My throat aches. I need water.

My feet glide over the smooth floor planks, across the rug at the foot of the bed, over the threshold and onto the cool tile of the bathroom. I paw around in the dark for the light switch. I find the wall, closer than I thought it was, but it gives way and...

"Sorry," says a startled voice, moments before the light flips on.

Not a wall.

Henry and I freeze, face-to-face in the narrow bathroom. There's bare skin everywhere. My legs. His chest and arms. We're immobilized by the exposure, by our eyes adjusting to the light.

His hair sticks to his face the way mine sticks to me. He shimmers with sweat-sheen. He crosses his long arms in front of him, following the v-shaped lines that dip down into his boxers, which I am not looking at. At all.

We stand frozen. Maybe only seconds have passed. I can't tell.

I feel his eyes all over me, but I avoid them, diverting my gaze to his collarbone. My stomach plummets when I see it there: *the déjà vu.*

A small, puckered scar glistens white on the left side of his chest. I've never touched it, but my index finger twitches with memory. I know what it feels like, even though I've never seen Henry with his shirt off until this exact moment.

A drizzle of perspiration rolls between my ribs, down my stomach, into my bellybutton. It shoves me in motion. I dash from the bathroom and shut the door behind me.

"Sorry," he says again, from the other side of the door. "Was getting a drink of water."

Instead of replying, I hold the knob in the vise grip of my sweaty palm, praying he won't turn it. We're both silent. I wait there until the strip of light under the door disappears and I hear him go back to his room.

He never even turned on the faucet.

CHAPTER

TWENTY-ONE

: Rain :

I LIE IN bed until noon on Sunday, listening to a downpour that rivals the hurricane remnants that swept through Asheville last summer.

The streets flooded and Dylan and I took his dad's kayak down main street. The muscles in my neck wince at the memory. It's a good memory I don't really deserve.

I squirm under the blankets—my own personal shame fortress. I've had to pee now for approximately three millennia, but I refuse to go in the bathroom. Or even leave this room, for that matter, until Henry goes downstairs. Because I am super mature.

The store is closed on Sundays so that George can attend church. Henry apparently doesn't, however, because his voice filters down the hallway. Talking on the phone, laughing, and moving around in his room. There is no clear prediction for when I'll be able to pee. I hope I can outlast him.

I don't even let myself think about the fact that he and I are here alo—see? Won't even complete the thought.

The bathroom door opens and I pull the blanket over my head. I give it a minute before I peek out. When the push button lock clicks, I breathe again. Faucets squeak as he runs the shower. He's totally naked on the other side of the door. But it's not like I'm picturing it with perfect recall or anything.

My phone buzzes on the desk, so I sit up and glance at the caller ID. Dylan. Again. I reject the call and throw myself backwards on the pillow. I know it's ridiculous, but I feel so guilty. And he will sense the guilt the moment he talks to me. I made it worse by not answering his calls last night. I scroll through all my missed texts.

I reply to Maddie first.

You should see his brother.

I think it instead of typing it, then shove my phone under a pillow and groan. I can't do this. I have to work with this guy for weeks. I can't go getting a crush because we finally talked to each other like human beings. Or because of a stupid dream. A dream with the same eerie qualities to the ones that have come true. *Disordered causality?* Nope. Not gonna think about it.

It makes no sense that I feel betrayed, but I do. Mama is hosting co-ed sleepovers for my friends? This is not something she would normally do. It's not like it's a youth group lock-in at church or anything.

My phone starts ringing again. Dylan.

I turn it off and toss it aside. Now there will be no doubt that I'm avoiding him.

I close my eyes and listen to Henry's movements as he leaves the bathroom, opens and closes drawers in his bedroom, and then disappears down the stairs. I take the opportunity to make a mad dash to the bathroom.

It's locked from my side.

I press my forehead against the cool frame of the door.

Drawing a deep breath, I tiptoe to the hallway and poke my head out. When I'm sure the coast is clear, I dash to his room and push the door open. My heart pounds in my throat. I glance behind me before I slip inside.

His walls are covered end-to-end with astronomy posters. Constellations. One that's solid black with the definition of quantum entanglement on it. In case you're wondering: *a physical phenomenon that occurs when pairs or groups of particles are generated or interact in ways such that the quantum state of each particle cannot be described independently of the others, even when the particles are separated by a large distance.*

I think I fell asleep before I finished reading it.

The room is a wreck. His bed is unmade, dark blue sheets twisted around the foot of the bed. Above it on the wall are pictures of his family and friends. His dad and Patrick. Mons and Zara and Sanjay. Then there are squares where the paint on the wall is a little brighter, like photos used to hang there, but have been taken down. I wonder how many old girlfriends he has. Maybe he even has a current one.

Footsteps on the stairs jar me out of my nosy investigation. I fly into the bathroom and lock the door. A moment later, the door handle jiggles.

"Jo? You in there?"

I have to pee so incredibly bad, but I don't want to do it with him standing outside the door.

"Yeah," I call.

Silence descends. I can't tell if he's still standing there, but I keep holding it, listening to the *drip, drip, drip* of the rain outside. My eyeballs start to float.

"You feel okay?" His voice is muffled through the door.

"Yep, great." *Please. Go.*

A pause.

"I'm headed out to meet Zara," he says.

I stare at the tile backsplash over the sink, legs shaking. Why is he telling me this? And worse, why does it make me jealous?

"Have fun!" What else can I say? His shadow under the door disappears, returns, hesitates.

"The deli on Brixton, if you want to come over." His shadow vanishes before I can answer.

I should go, I think. This is good. A step forward. But then I remember we only hung out last night because of George's request. Maybe he told him to invite me to this, too.

So I stay in my room all day instead.

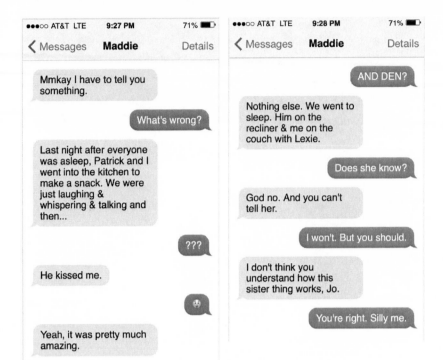

Left screen:

Mmkay I have to tell you something.

What's wrong?

Last night after everyone was asleep, Patrick and I went into the kitchen to make a snack. We were just laughing & whispering & talking and then...

???

He kissed me.

Yeah, it was pretty much amazing.

Right screen:

AND DEN?

Nothing else. We went to sleep. Him on the recliner & me on the couch with Lexie.

Does she know?

God no. And you can't tell her.

I won't. But you should.

I don't think you understand how this sister thing works, Jo.

You're right. Silly me.

CHAPTER
TWENTY-TWO

: Act Naturally :

I HAVE ONE goal when Monday rolls around: Be cool.

I tossed and turned all night, afraid to dream. Each time I'd feel myself falling asleep, I'd startle awake again.

When I get downstairs, Henry's reclining on a counter stool with a book in his hands, green Chuck Taylors propped next to the cash register. My ears burn at the sight of him. At least he's wearing clothes now.

"Good morning," he says, glancing at his watch and then up at me.

"Morning." I don't bother to point out that it's nearly lunchtime. Instead, I make myself busy straightening shelves and do my best to avoid talking.

The awkwardness hangs between us like a smoke screen all afternoon. The store is so dead that I check to make sure the Open sign is lit up. Twice. He doesn't bring up Saturday night or his ignored lunch invitation, and I pretend to be very interested in running new inventory reports. By mid-afternoon, George wanders out of his office with a big cardboard box.

"Favor to ask." He drops the box between us on the floor. It's full of wooden shapes that look like puzzle pieces.

"I need this display put together for the front window. We're out of shelf space and a shipment for the Boomtown Festival is arriving tomorrow."

Henry and I nod silently.

"Work together." He says this like he assumes that's the last thing we'd want to do. Henry lifts the box and takes it to the front corner of the store and I follow. He drops it on the rug by the window and sinks to his knees.

We organize the pieces on the rug, according to the directions sheet.

"This one goes over there." He hands me a wooden piece that matches others in a pile I've made. I take it and set it down. He glances up at me a couple of times and I pretend not to notice. How can I not notice, though? His emerald green University of Bristol tee brings out the color of his eyes so much that his face may as well be a Venus flytrap for idiot girls.

I click the base together while he reads the directions.

"Were you hungover yesterday?" he asks, voice low.

I glance up at George's office door. He chews on a pen and stares at his computer screen. Far enough away that he can't hear us. Or isn't trying to.

"I didn't feel great, but I wasn't sick."

He nods. "The tea always helps me." I can practically smell the peppery herbal aroma when he mentions it. Which rings a bell: I could smell the tea in the dream.

Do Not Think About That.

"Yeah, I'm sure it helped." I swallow. "Thanks for that."

"Sure." He corrects my wobbly display base, adding a piece to stabilize it. He starts building the next level and I hand him the pieces in order. "So how were the dreams?"

I drop the display piece in my hands. Then quickly pick it up. The blush crawls the length of my body. Even my toes are blushing.

"What dreams?" Becoolbecoolbecool.

He full-on stares at me. I swallow. Swallow again. *Why is there so much spit in my mouth?*

"The lucid ones." He narrows his eyes like I'm a moron. "The ones we discussed."

"Oh." I shrug it off like this is Definitely No Big Deal and I'm not at all worried that *he freaking knows or something.* "I didn't dream anything at all. Or can't remember if I did."

It doesn't sound remotely true. I re-sort the display pieces and pretend I didn't just say that in my Liar Liar Pants On Fire voice.

"That's interesting," he finally says. "Mugwort always makes me dream."

"Not me. I was out like a light." My voice squeaks on the last word.

Henry chuckles. "You all right?"

"Yep." I don't look up. It's not like he can read minds. Right? I hope to God that isn't a quantum physics thing. Or a ley line thing. Or a Henry thing.

His eyes are still on me, and I make the mistake of meeting them. Mischief swirls like a whirlpool there. My stomach drops when he says, "I had crazy dreams after. Woke up in a sweat."

"Yikes," I say, and grab the directions. I stare at a blank spot in the middle of the page, pretending to study meticulously.

"I mean it wasn't unpleasant." The *way* he says it... "I got up to wash my face, and that's when I kind of barged in on you by mistake. Sorry about that." He pauses. "You seemed a little off-kilter yourself."

"Who, me? No. Maybe sleepy." I stare harder at the page, wishing there was a volume button for my pulse. I swear it's shaking the whole building now. I don't know how he knows about The Dream, but it feels like he has read the script and seen the movie.

"You, uh, figuring those directions out?"

I nod and squint, bringing my eyes up to the words. They're upside down.

Henry reaches over and takes the page out of my hands, flips it around, and hands it back to me. "Might be easier to read it this way." His dimples wink.

Inside my head, I'm summoning the meteors. Crush me right here where I sit, please.

"I probably need glasses," I mutter.

We fumble with the display for a few more awkward minutes until my phone rings in my back pocket. *When I'm 64* blares through the store. I could silence it and ignore, but I'm so desperate to get out of this embarrassment quicksand that I press the answer button.

Dylan's face lights up on-screen. There are pillow lines on his face.

I glance at the clock on my phone. "Did you just wake up?"

"I didn't sleep much, but yeah. I was worried about you."

I can see his aura again. It's the color of a storm cloud.

Henry continues working on the display but keeps glancing up at me. I stand and walk to the opposite aisle and crouch down behind a collection of Ramones albums. Appropriate, because I wanna be sedated.

"There's no reason to be worried about me. I'm fine."

"I've been calling you for two days." His eyes well up and he frowns.

I swallow a lump of guilt. Dylan cares about me. It may not be in the way I need him to care about me, but he does care.

"I know. I'm sorry. Our schedules are opposite right now. And I've been going to bed early. Why don't we set up a specific time to talk every day?" I say it with a lot more conviction than I feel, and then punctuate it with a smile.

"You seem strange. Are you taking your meds?"

"Of course I am."

"So your luggage finally made it?"

Oops.

"Yep," I fib. "Saturday, actually."

Dylan seems to relax a little. "Well, that's good. Might take a little while to feel like yourself again."

My teeth clench. I used to love it when he said things like this. It was comforting that he didn't think I was wounded in some way because I had to take medication. But now? He makes me feel like I'm a wild thing to be controlled. Like I'm not me if I'm not taking meds. And I feel more like me right now than I have in a long time.

"Look, I've gotta go, I'm working." It sounds like a brush-off. It is a brush-off. My nose burns like I need to cry, and if I talk to him for much longer, I'm probably going to.

"Okay. What time do you want to talk?" He sits up on the edge of his bed and runs a hand across his face, covertly wiping his eyes. "Tell me when to call you and I will."

"I'll text you," I say. "We'll figure out the time then. Talk to you later."

I hang up. Leaning against a box of unsorted records, I take a deep breath and close my eyes, then wait a full thirty-second count before I re-join Henry on the rug. He's got the display half assembled. He works diligently, snapping wooden pieces together and securing them with screws. I drop to my knees and stare at the remaining pieces.

"That your boyfriend?" He works without looking at me.

"Yeah."

"He seems a little…" Henry glances over. "Annoying."

Like I need people pointing out obvious things to me right now. I sigh.

"We've been dating for a year. This is the first time we've been apart."

Henry raises an eyebrow. "Ah. That explains all the crotch selfies."

My mouth falls open like a broken door. He chuckles.

"Oh, come on. Did Mons seem like a guy who'd keep secrets?"

"I don't know what you're talking about." I clamp my teeth together and yank a corner piece out of his hand and position it where it goes.

"Look at you, all flustered." He laughs, teeth on full display. "It's charming. Really."

"I'm not flustered." I say this even as I try to extinguish the flames on my cheeks.

"Some unsolicited advice," he says, quieter now. "Don't let him pressure you."

I shove him before my brain approves it. He looks surprised at first, but then grins.

"My God," I grumble. "Did Mons read the whole conversation?"

"It shocked me, too. I didn't even know Mons could read."

We both laugh. The tension in the air dissipates a little.

"Look," he adds, "stand your ground. If your dad were here, he'd probably say something like that."

The mention of Pop is an unexpected jab. He has no right to assume what Pop would or wouldn't say when he didn't even know him. "Oh, are you my dad now? Or anybody's dad, for that matter?"

He blinks at me. "Well, no. But—"

"Thank you for the advice," I say, narrowing my eyes. "But I've already heard the abstinence speech from church ladies and my mother and all her co-workers."

I have no intention of telling Henry about Dylan and me, or the fact that it's too late now to take his decent advice.

"You're awfully knotty today. More so than usual."

I ignore him.

He soldiers on, though. "I'd think you'd be in a great mood, since your luggage finally arrived."

I cut my eyes at him. He chews on his cheek, suppressing a grin.

"What are you studying at Bristol again?" I ask, unruffled. "Espionage?"

He gives me a sheepish grin and a shrug. "You're the one who lurks outside doors."

"Looks marvelous!" George blessedly interrupts, walking over with an armload of albums. "Henry, could you set it there, by the front window?" Henry does as he asks.

"When are you leaving for Bristol?" George asks him.

"Tonight. Hopefully back by the weekend."

"Make sure your dorm transfer is squared away," George says. "You've a little under a month before classes begin."

I stack albums on the newly built shelf, trying to ignore the submerging sensation that coincides with the news that Henry's leaving.

"I will. And don't forget Zara is coming by tomorrow to pick up prints."

"I won't forget," George says to him, then elbows me as he bends down to help me stack inventory. "What are your plans for next weekend?"

My brows furrow. "Next weekend?"

"We're closed up for inventory on solstice weekend. I have a hired crew coming in for fiscal year counts. Your mum said you'd be doing some exploring then. Visiting schools, yes?"

I mentally scroll a calendar and recall my plans.

"Oh. Yes, I'm taking a day trip to Liverpool. Touring Hope University."

"Ah, Liverpool. Beatles tour while you're there?"

I nod. "I have this photo project to do for school, so I'm going to practice taking pictures there."

"Perhaps Henry can give you some pointers. He's a photographer, you know."

Henry gives me an indecipherable look. "Where in Liverpool?"

"Well," I start. "Penny Lane is a given. And Strawberry Field."

"Of course." George smiles. For the first time, I notice his aura. It's yellow at the center, but with a big band of murky brown around it. Troubled.

I fiddle with my hands. "I'll definitely see Eleanor Rigby's grave at St. Peter's, too."

"Oh, that's a good one," George says. "I've never been. But I've heard it's quite spooky."

I swallow the lump in my throat and it plunks into my belly like a stone. George stands from where he was kneeling and brushes off the front of his pants. "You know, they say Paul and John wrote that song without ever knowing the grave existed. Right there in the graveyard of the church where they met."

"Conspiracy," Henry says. "They planned it all. Media manipulation."

George rolls his eyes. "He's such a negative Ned, isn't he?"

"My pop died the same day as her. October 10th. 79 years later."

He's quiet a moment as he straightens a shelf. "Oh."

I shrug. "Coincidence, probably."

Sympathy registers on George's face. Henry stares at the floor. I guess I'm a Negative Ned, too. Because I've gone and made it awkward.

I did it.

What?

Kissed him.

Omg. Where?

On the mouth!

No shit. I mean WHERE as in setting.

Don't be mad.

LEXIE

In your room. But don't worry, nothing else happened.

Dare I even ask why you were in my room?

We went to grab some of your vinyls.

Idk what to say.

About the vinyls? We put them back.

ABOUT THE KISSING

He was really sweet, but I don't think he was into it. Maybe I scared him.

So... on to the next romantic hero?

What? You think I'd give up so easily?

CHAPTER
TWENTY-THREE

: I've Got a Feeling :

THE SUMMER BEFORE I started sixth grade, Mom and Pop moved us into a two-bedroom townhouse close to downtown Asheville.

It was closer to the hospital for Mom than our cabin in Mills River, and since Pop was gone so often with the band, he agreed to anything that made life easier for her. They didn't ask me my opinion about the move. I had to change schools—which was completely traumatic at the time. After a failed runaway attempt—that time when I rode my bike across the highway—I decided I'd confine myself to the back porch and stay mad at them until I could move out. Seemed like a completely reasonable plan at the time.

One day, a Frisbee sailed over the fence into our small yard. Two girls showed up at the gate moments later to retrieve it. Instead of thanking me for handing it for them, the one with darkest hair openly studied me.

"Are you the new neighbor?"

I nodded.

"Come over and play." It wasn't a question. She just opened the gate for me, and I went.

Lexie and Maddie and me were like that from then on. There was never a question.

As I scroll social media, looking at all the pictures Lexie uploaded to Instagram, emptiness crawls into all my corners.

There are hiking selfies from the parkway of Maddie and Lexie and Patrick and Mama. Then there's another of all of them, plus Dylan, minus Mama, in front of the French Broad River Rafting Center. Still more with Lexie and Maddie and Patrick at the ice cream shop, wet-haired and all smiles after their rafting trip. Patrick fits in like he belongs. Maybe it's just like that with Lexie and Maddie, no matter who you are. It's impossible not to love them both.

I can't shake the feeling that I'm letting them both down now. By being so far away, by keeping their respective secrets, by not yelling at them both to focus on something besides whatever guy they're fighting over this time.

A quick knock on the door rouses me from my pity party. I sit up and smooth my hair behind my ear, and Henry steps through the cracked doorway. My nerves ricochet.

"Hey, I'm heading out," he says, eyes darting around, "but in case I don't see you before you leave for Liverpool, I thought maybe you'd like to borrow this." He drops a spiral-bound book on Patrick's desk. I pick it up to get a better look. The front cover is a glossy map of England. It's like one of the fancy travel guides you get in visitor centers.

"An atlas?" I turn it over in my hands. It's a little heavier than I expected.

"Sort of," he says, running a hand through his hair and leaving it sticking up in ten different directions, which definitely doesn't do things to me. "It's an atlas, yes, but of ley lines. Throughout Britain."

I flip it open. There are large scale maps, and behind those, smaller breakdowns of each area covered. There are additional annotated notes on every page in compact, precise handwriting, and marker-drawn lines plotted between points like a graph.

"Wow," I say, gently turning the worn pages. "Thank you."

"No problem."

We stand there for a moment, not talking. At least not out loud. There are indecipherable conversations going on between our eyes.

Henry grabs the doorknob and takes a few steps backwards. "All right, then. See you later."

"See ya," I mumble, and look back down at the atlas. Henry is the only person in the world who knows the real reason I'm going to Liverpool.

And instead of trying to talk me out of it, he's trying to help me.

· · ·

Seagulls squawk overhead, and I take a deep breath and inhale the salty breeze.

The rain is inevitable, certain, looming at any moment, but I move forward—away from any possible shelter. My footfalls thud gently over sodden boards. Between the cracks, thirty feet below, the sea is a dark, choppy mirror of the sky. Other people pass me on the pier, but I don't see their faces. I only see one man, to my left, near the iron railing. He's old and hunched over, gray hair sparse in the front and long in the back, and his brown trench coat is tattered at the edges. He stoops down and unbuckles a music case, then pulls out a violin. I stop to watch him, glancing up at the sky, anticipating the drops I know are coming.

He pulls a bow over the strings. The melody is familiar. Cheerful.

Here Comes the Sun.

It's such an antithesis of the sky that I laugh. I hear my own laughter, the way it stirs the air far away. It doesn't feel real. I'm light as helium, floating, a balloon on a string. Somewhere behind me, a muffled voice says, "Ta-da!"

I laugh again, and the string that tethers me snips. It sounds like a text message coming through—a familiar click.

That's what wakes me up.

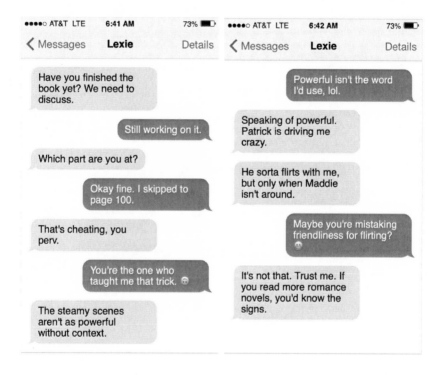

CHAPTER

TWENTY-FOUR

: Searchin' :

WITHOUT HENRY, THINGS are busier.

Maybe he works more than I've noticed. Once the shipment is unloaded and the customers have filed out, George leans on the counter and sighs.

"So. Have you visited any of the universities in London yet?"

There's something about the way he says it, the overly casual way he looks at me as he scrutinizes one of the ignored action items on my London itinerary. It isn't a George question. It's a Kristina question.

"Did my mother put you up to asking?"

He creases his eyebrows and makes an offended tsk. He starts to say something—a denial maybe—but then thinks better of it and changes direction.

"Your mother adores you, Jo."

I grit my teeth. Rather than talking to me, she prefers to have her friend watch me and report back. I'm certain that's why George had Henry follow me to the Crow, now that I think about it.

"Adoration in the form of spying is always my favorite."

George sighs. "She isn't spying on you. She's checking in."

"With you. Not me."

"It's hard for her not to talk to you."

"Which was her idea."

"She's giving you space."

"Is she, though?"

George sets down the stack of albums he's collected from the listening center. "I don't tell her *everything*."

Record screech. This feels like a trap to get me to admit something. Definitely not falling for it.

"I haven't done anything I wouldn't tell her about."

George quirks a brow. "Nothing?"

"Nope."

"Not even drink so much you get sick on the street?"

I stare at him, wondering why Henry would've told him about that. Especially after all the sneaking around and tiptoeing and apologizing that night. I let the anger simmer for a minute before I say anything.

"Okay. Maybe not that."

"Nigel told me, by the way," George says, as if he's read my mind. "Henry tells me nothing."

Oh.

"Nigel knew my dad," I say.

George turns the depth of his gaze on me now, a sincere look in his eyes. "I absolutely hate that you lost your father. It's miserably unfair."

I take a deep breath. George knows all about unfair, too, I remind myself.

"But go easy on your mum, okay? She worries about you. We all worry, as parents. I worry about Henry. But I can't talk to him about it or he gets defensive. And he stays angry with me." He dumps the records into their respective shelf space and returns to the register. He punches a few buttons to zero it out.

"I never noticed," I say.

His face stretches out with surprise. "Oh, you never got the perpetually angry vibe from him?"

Okay, to be fair, yes. But I'm feeling strangely defensive on his behalf. I glance sideways at George but just shrug. His aura's still muddy brown. Maybe he's too wrapped up in his own struggles to understand Henry's.

As I'm making my way to the front of the store to lock up, a flash of yellow zips by the front of the plate-glass windows and opens the front door. I'm just about to tell the person we're closing up when I realize it's Zara.

"Made it!" She looks past me, a little out of breath. "Sorry I'm so late! My evening class ran over."

"Come in," George says. "I have them for you." He digs beneath the register for the photos Henry left for her.

"You look better than last time I saw you," Zara whispers to me conspiratorially. "You doing okay?"

I nod, suddenly nervous. Like I need to impress her in some way.

"Hey, you don't happen to know what days Saint Catherine's does tours for prospective students, do you?"

"Oh. I have no idea. Why? You thinking about Saint Catherine's?" She wears a proud smirk as she says it.

George rounds the counter with a sealed envelope marked DO NOT BEND. "Good luck with this," he tells Zara. She takes it and thanks him.

"Thinking about it," I answer her question.

"If you want to come over tomorrow around ten, I could show you around myself. I'll be on campus and should have a break then."

I look at George. "What do you say?" I ask him. "Would it be all right if I come in a little later tomorrow so I can tour Saint Catherine's in the morning?"

George narrows his eyes at me, not at all fooled by my performance. "Of course. I think it's a splendid idea."

"Here." Zara hands me her phone. "Put your number in."

I do.

"Text me later for details."

I lock the door behind her when she leaves with her pictures. Before I go upstairs, I turn to George.

"Make sure you tell Mama I'm taking a private guided tour of a liberal arts university tomorrow. With a current student." I give him a little wink.

. . .

In my room later, I study the atlas Henry left for me.

I flip to the Liverpool page and read his notes again.

Two main lines, perpendicular: Glastonbury Tor to Aberdeen, 2nd longitude W, and Tibradden (passage tomb) to Ohlsdorf (cemetery), 53rd parallel N.

The note strikes me as familiar for some reason. I remember something about Glastonbury on his Instagram page, so I pull it up. A few moments of scrolling brings it front and center.

I almost choke when I see the picture of Glastonbury Tor: the rolling green hillside with the perfect angle of sunlight. A tall stone tower in the background. It's only missing a picnic blanket and two very specific people. Flashes from my dream come back to me.

This explains why I had such a perfect visual of the place stored away in my brain: I'd seen this picture before. His caption beneath it says, *"yet some men say in parts of England that King Arthur is not dead..."* —Thomas Malory.

I scroll his photos. Every single landscape picture correlates to places plotted in the atlas. Based on the dates—they go back two years—Henry has been visiting ley lines for quite some time.

The map is color coded, and there are notes for each that list the endpoints. I try to make sense of them but can't see exactly where they are at the street level. Frustrated, I pull up the browser on my phone and type *ley lines Liverpool*.

The very first result is a link for a site called Magical Mystical Locator. The home page has an interactive map of the entire United Kingdom. I zoom in on Liverpool. Two ley lines intersect just south and inland from Liverpool, perpendicular. They appear to match Henry's hand-plotted lines. The longitudinal line connects Glastonbury Tor with standing stones in Aberdeen, Scotland. The latitudinal ley connects a place called Tibradden in Dublin with Ohlsdorf Cemetery in Hamburg, Germany. I skim for more information and conclude that all of these places have rich history and are shrouded in myth of the dead— or undead, as the case may be.

I know from my amateur research that a place where two ley lines intersect is called a vortex. What that means, exactly, I don't know. But the internet's explanation goes something like *Magic! Fantasma! Much Amaze!*

I zoom in as far as I can. The intersection occurs in a green space just beyond Church Road in Woolton.

I pull up another browser window and put Church Road into Google maps. Zoom in. In. In. In. And *oh my God*, I suck all the air out of the room. It's the road St. Peter's church is on.

My fingers fly furiously over the screen. I compare the two maps and zoom in to street level, to the exact location of the intersect. The screen fills with a street view outside a graveyard, a large red-brick clock tower in the background. I stare gape-mouthed, no sound but my roaring pulse.

The vortex is in the graveyard where Eleanor Rigby's grave is located.

∙ ∙ ∙

That night, I dream of a bright green piece of paper.

It's folded four times, lines creased like it's been left in a pocket too long. Maybe even put through the wash. As I'm unfolding it, one rectangle at a time, Pop's voice whispers in my ear: *It's a good idea.* But before I get the paper completely open to see what's on the inside, my alarm wakes me up.

CHAPTER

TWENTY-FIVE

: Tomorrow Never Knows :

I RIDE THE train to Saint Catherine's and meet Zara in the main student courtyard.

She stands from her spot next to a fountain when I pass through the lumbering main gates.

"You made it!" Her eyes twinkle with the sort of kindness you'd expect from someone who offers to spend her morning break giving a tour to a girl she barely knows. Every time I look at her, I think about the photo that was hanging in the darkroom and I get a sour feeling in my stomach. Which is ridiculous and makes me one hundred and twelve percent more punchable.

"Thank you for doing this," I tell her. "My mother's nagging me via George about doing all the things I came here to do. Like visit universities."

"I think you'll be glad you did this." She adjusts her bag over her shoulder and motions for me to follow her, then smirks as she says, "Creativity abounds here, even in the summer session."

I look around for the first time and consider what that actually means. Students lounge on the grass, deep in their books. Others gather around tables and discuss politics or art or upcoming tests. I pick up bits and pieces of their conversations as we pass.

I raise my phone and take a panoramic photo. *Caption: the real world*

Zara takes me through the sliding glass doors in a state-of-the-art building. It smells a little like a library inside. She motions to doors as we pass. Science wing. Arts wing. She explains the different campuses and what each specializes in.

I snap pictures the whole time as I take it all in.

"Do you know what your major will be yet?"

I shake my head, a little sheepish.

She places a reassuring hand on my arm. "You'll figure it out. It took a bit for me to decide on theatre."

"Everyone I know seems to already have a life plan in place." Dylan's going to Duke to play lacrosse and be a doctor like his parents. Lexie wants to go to SCAD in Savannah and design clothes. Maddie is going to whichever school offers her a soccer scholarship. "I've failed miserably at coming up with a plan of my own."

We stop at the end of the hallway.

"You can't fail at something you haven't even done yet." She smiles. "If so, I'm failing at breakfast right now. You hungry?"

My stomach has been a mess since I boarded the train. But I nod anyway.

"Come on. I'll show you where the café is."

We walk through more identical hallways until we get to an area that looks like a food court. As we take our trays and place items from a buffet style setup, she tells me her experience with Saint Catherine's.

"First year took some adjustment. I was really busy. Barely had time for anything, including friends. I missed Henry and Mons and Sanjay, of course, because we'd been together for so many years that I wasn't sure how to function without them."

I nod. "I texted with my friends back home every day when I first got here. Now it's super sporadic."

She shrugs. "It happens. Sometimes it's good to peel ourselves from our comfort zone, though. It forces us to grow. Discover who we are as individuals. Even though sometimes that means growing apart from the people you care about."

We sit down at a table in the courtyard. It's a rare sunny day in London, but I'm wearing my rain boots. I prop them on the chair across from me.

As we eat our breakfast, a guy approaches us with an armful of papers. He hands me one. It's bright green. *Free community workshop sponsored by the Photography department.*

I read over the details, considering.

"I wonder if Henry would be interested in this," I say. Zara leans in and reads over my shoulder.

"Probably not. This is more entry level."

"Oh. Yeah, he's definitely not entry level."

"Have you seen his work?" she asks.

I shake my head. Lying like a guilty lying liar.

She leans down and reaches into her bag and pulls out the envelope she picked up from the Den last night. Carefully, she slides the photos out on the table.

"He shot these for my acting portfolio. I'm trying to get some side gigs while I'm in school. Build my resume a little."

I shuffle carefully through the photos, stopping when I get to the picture of her on the floor. I widen my eyes and pretend to see it for the very first time.

"Wow. This one is…" I look up at her. "Intimate."

She casts her eyes downward at the photo, maybe a little shy.

Fighting the sour stomach feeling all over again, I point to the contrast in the picture.

"He's good."

She nods. "I don't know why he wants to waste his life being a boring ass scientist."

We both laugh.

She tucks the photos back into the envelope and into her bag again.

"So are you two... like...?" I bite off the end of the sentence, wishing my mouth ever bothered to ask me for permission before saying things.

Zara shakes her head. "No, not anymore."

Ah, so there's history. I try to gauge the way she feels about it.

"Henry is the best friend anyone could ask for. He's fiercely loyal. He'll take a secret to his grave and keep it for the next three lifetimes after that if you ask him to. He's of course funny and smart and not difficult to look at, by any means. But..." She pauses and picks at her fingernail. "I love Henry, but not like *that*. Going there was a mistake. He's terribly messy. We're better as friends."

I choke down the obnoxious relief gathering in the back of my throat and look over the workshop flyer again.

"Funny, I'm actually doing a photography project for school. This workshop covers some of the techniques required for the pictures I have to take."

"You should do it."

I glance at the dates again. "I won't be here long enough. I go back home before this starts."

She shrugs. "Can you extend your time in London? It might give you a feel for campus life here."

I concentrate on the flyer as I consider. "I'd have to buy a real camera."

"I'm sure Henry would let you borrow one."

I start to shrug it off, but as I fold the bright green piece of paper, one, two, three, four times, a little prickle of déjà vu dances along the edge of my consciousness. I lift my hips and tuck it into the back pocket of my jeans, along with the idea.

CHAPTER

TWENTY-SIX

: Got to Get You Into My Life :

THE REST OF the week passes in a blur.

I barely have time to process all the competing ideas at war in my head: the photography workshop, the vortex at Eleanor Rigby's grave, the excitement about spending my Saturday in Liverpool. I drop in on Nigel to see if he and Walter can chat, but Ethan tells me he's out, and that he'll be sure to relay the message that I stopped by. I leave my number for him. George and I work side by side diligently, and he seems satisfied by my visit to Saint Catherine's. I guess Mama gave him the stamp of approval.

On Friday evening, as I have my regularly scheduled FaceTime call with Dylan, I notice that his aura has become progressively darker.

"What if you love it there?" Dylan leans back in his chair and crosses his arms. He's talking about Hope University in Liverpool, where I'm supposed to visit tomorrow, though I never bothered to make an appointment. I didn't even tell him about Saint Catherine's.

"We'll deal with it when the time comes. Don't worry, okay?"

"You know, Duke is a pretty amazing school." He gives me a half-hearted smile.

Dylan is a shoo-in at Duke, both for his lacrosse accolades and the fact that his father gives them big fat alumni checks every year. A few months ago, I made the mistake of saying I might apply there. I thought it was pretty noncommittal at the time, but he brings it up each time this conversation arises. There's no way in hell I could afford to go to Duke without the same level of scholarship I'd need to go somewhere overseas, and the fact that this completely eludes him annoys me.

"It sure is." My face feels like it may crack from smiling. "Nothing is set in stone yet."

Every night, we talk via FaceTime at 9 p.m. my time, 4 p.m. his. Around the ten-minute mark, my gaze starts drifting towards the clock.

"I get why you want to at least look at the place," he says. "But think about how much easier the transition would be if you go somewhere in North Carolina. In-state tuition, easier to see your mom on the weekends, easier to see me…"

He lets that hang there, but I don't take the bait. A frown has replaced my carefully composed expression at some point, and I watch as his smile fades, too. The distance between us is vast. More than geography.

I have to hope that once this trip is behind me, once I've done what I came to do, Dylan and I will be okay. If the meds were the problem all along, then maybe we will be fine since I've stopped taking them. Maybe a college in North Carolina will be perfect. But right now, I'm more interested in filling in blanks from my past than penciling in an outline of the future.

"We don't have to think about it yet." I try to muster some enthusiasm. "We have senior year ahead. The best year of our lives, right?"

Dylan nods, unconvincingly, and in the middle of it, the screen lags. I wait a few seconds, but it doesn't refresh. After a full minute of staring at his paralyzed expression, an unflattering technology glitch, I hang up and text that I'll call him tomorrow.

Packing is tricky because I'm not sure how long my investigation will take. Maybe it'll be a day trip, or maybe I'll stay overnight. Depends on what I find there.

This ley line intersection feels like the key to something important.

My late-night research has led me to a couple of promising theories: First of all, a vortex means double the power. If there's any place I might have a chance of finding Pop, it's in a vortex. And it can't be coincidence that one happens to exist in the same place I've been dreaming about finding him for years.

Henry couldn't have known how significant this atlas was when he gave it to me.

I need to know how his ley line theory is connected to the dreams about Pop, though. There has to be a simpler explanation than a dizzying crash course in quantum physics. I want to be prepared, with whatever equipment is necessary, but I can't find a single thing about the magnets online. I could buy some, but I don't know what they do to locate the ley lines.

I'm going to have to ask Henry.

I search the texts in my phone until I find where he texted me at the airport. I save his number to my phone.

●●●●○ AT&T LTE   9:33 PM   44% ▪️

‹ Messages   **Henry**   Details

> So that Ley line atlas you gave me? Interesting stuff in Liverpool...

> It's Jo, btw

Jo who?

> ??

😊 And I lent you the atlas. Didn't give it to you.

> Rude.

So what about Liverpool?

I wait a few extra minutes before I respond.

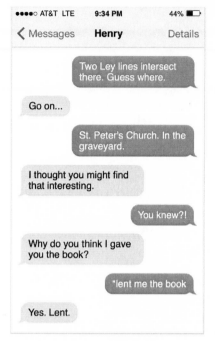

I imagine him sitting wherever he is, in some dorm or whatever, or at the pubs near Bristol, smirking down at his phone the way I'm smirking down at mine.

The type bubble pops up and disappears. Pops up and disappears. Then finally...

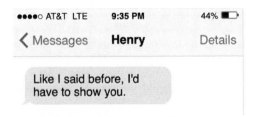

I set my phone down. He can't very well show me right now, and I'm leaving in the morning. I get up and finish packing. Some extra clothes. My phone charger. Brush. Toothbrush. When I'm finished, I drop the bag next to the bed and crawl under the covers.

As I'm lying awake, mind racing, footsteps get louder on the stairs outside my door. Then down the hall. Henry's door opens and shuts. I sit up and pull the covers up around my neck. *Is that...?* He said he'd be back this weekend. It's Friday night, so technically it's the weekend.

My phone dings.

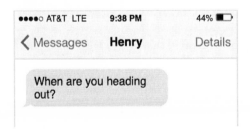

I hold my breath, listening as he moves around in his room. Shuffling things. Opening and closing drawers. I wipe my sweaty palms on the blanket and reply.

The notification dings on his phone in the other room. He doesn't respond. All is quiet. I lean back, in utter stillness, waiting. Then footsteps again. Coming toward my door. I'm torn between rolling off the bed and crawling under it, or making a mad dash to the bathroom to lock myself in. But I have no idea why.

A gentle knock. "Jo?"

I sit up and smooth the blanket over my lap. Clear my throat. "Yeah?"

Henry opens the door and peeks in. His hair is messy and his eyes are tired. He looks like he's just solved some week-long math problem.

"What time does your train leave?"

It's weird to resume a text conversation in person. "Nine a.m."

He stares at my packed bag at the foot of the bed.

"And how long will you be gone?"

I shrug, heart in hysterics. Maybe he had a weird case of missing me this week, too.

"I was gonna play it by ear."

He nods.

"You, uh…" He scratches his head and drops his hand. "You want some company?"

CHAPTER

TWENTY-SEVEN

: Day Tripper :

WHEN I WAKE up, I have three missed calls from unknown numbers.

There's no voicemail. I check my messages—a goodnight text from Dylan. Nothing else.

I'm surprised to find Henry waiting for me at the bottom of the stairs. Some part of me believed he'd sleep in and pretend we never had that conversation last night. Not that you could exactly call it a conversation, per se. He said *you want some company?* And I said *sure.* And shrugged. Oh, the dichotomy between inside me and outside me. Other than discussing what time we'd need to leave, we said our goodnights and I drifted off with one eye open.

He stands from the bottom stair, dark jeans and white button-up neatly pressed, and shuffles into a backpack. His hair is a little unruly, like he rolled out of bed without combing it. It works for him.

"Ready?"

"Totally," I squeak. *Totally?* God save the queen. Who am I, even?

We don't talk on the walk to the tube station, but I'm thankful that he doesn't try to fill all the silence with small talk. I keep a polite distance but close enough that I can smell his bath soap—something herbal, with a hint of eucalyptus. (It sits on the shower ledge in a little black bottle. Not that I've ever un-screwed the cap and sniffed it. Definitely not something I would do.)

The tube takes us to Euston station, where we purchase tickets for the London Midland Train, which will take us the three hours to Liverpool. As we're standing on the platform, waiting to board, my phone rings. Another unknown number. I answer it this time.

The British voice on the other end of the phone has a vague-ly familiar croon. "Josephine Bryant?"

"Yes?"

"This is Rupert with British Airways."

Ah, Rupert. Here it comes. Your luggage has been lost in a freak plane disappearance over Southeast Asia. Your luggage is in the Australian outback. Your luggage was stolen by rogue penguins in Antarctica. It's been two weeks. Nothing would surprise me at this point.

"Your luggage has arrived." He says this so proudly, I im-agine him growing a tail just so he can wag it.

"Uh…"

"We'll have it out to you within the hour."

I pull the phone away to glance at the time. "I'm actually boarding a train to Liverpool at the moment."

"Oh," Rupert huffs, like this is a massive inconvenience to him. "Shall we re-route it there?"

"No!" Who knows where it'd end up then. "Please deliver it to the address listed. George Pemberton can accept it on my be-half."

"Let me just write that down. That's George P-e-m-b-e-r-t-o-n?"

"Yes."

"Right then. So sorry for the mix up."

I thank him and hang up. Henry stares at me as I send George a text to let him know.

"Luggage is finally on its way. Of course."

Henry gives me a puzzled smile but doesn't say anything.

We board the train and take our cushy seats next to a picture window with a table in front. It's much different from the crowded discomfort of the tube. I take the window seat and Henry takes the aisle. Nervous energy swims around in my belly. Maybe I'm just hungry. I happily accept a ginger ale and some crackers from the trolley service as the train begins to move.

"I have a question," Henry says, at precisely the moment I bite into a cracker.

"Mmm?" I chew fast.

"Why did you fib to your boyfriend about your luggage arriving last week?"

I chase the cracker with some ginger ale to buy some time. "None ya," I finally say.

"Too bad." He smirks and pushes his glasses up his nose. "My relationship advice is quality."

"I like to keep some things private. But thanks for asking." I give him my best RBF.

"You know, Jo," he says, tracing the end of his armrest with an index finger, "sometimes it's good to talk things out. Instead of taking the whole load on yourself."

I give him a funny look. "Thanks? I guess. But I'll choose what I do or don't tell Dylan."

"I wasn't talking about him. The guy's a duffer. I was talking about... well, anyone. Me, even."

Something flips in my stomach. Why does he think we're in a place for me to talk to him about my relationship? Maybe Zara told him about our conversation at breakfast the other day. I scoot closer to the window.

"You're being weird," I finally say. "Did your dad send you to babysit me again?"

"I'm being serious." Definite sincerity detected in his voice, lavender aura to match. "And I'm here because I want to be."

"Besides," I say, ignoring that last thing he said and the way it made my heart beat a little faster. "I don't know what duffer means, but Dylan's a great guy. Just sometimes I don't feel like telling him everything."

Like, you know, the entire reason for this trip. Which Henry knows about. But whatever.

He flexes his jaw. "I'd want to keep things to myself, too, if someone oscillated between lecturing me about medication and sending me boner pics."

I jerk my head to look at him, take a mental snapshot of his narrowed eyes.

Caption: judging you

"I don't love that you unapologetically bring up sensitive information your dickhead friend invaded my privacy to get."

"Fair point."

"Where I come from, we at least attempt to be polite," I snip.

Henry rolls his eyes. "I'd rather be direct than polite."

"Good for you." I cross my arms.

He turns toward me in his seat. "Is this how we're going to spend the day?"

"You're the one who wanted to come along," I say. "I didn't ask you to."

"I know what it's like to go on these excursions alone. I thought you might need a friend."

I'm more surprised by this admission than anything.

I narrow my eyes. "So we're friends now?"

"Apparently not. Tackling everything solo is working quite well for you so far." He leans on his opposite armrest and gives me a wounded look. For the smallest moment, I want to hug him. But I also kind of want to thump him between the eyes. I do neither and look out the window instead. The city fades into a series of industrial buildings. Everything becomes a green and silver blur.

"I've been where you are," he says quietly. I turn and look at him. There's no hint of snark. "What do you say we call a truce for this trip?" He sticks his hand out to me like he wants to shake, the same way I did when we first met. "Outside of London, we're friends."

My eyes pan down to his hand—smooth skin, long fingers, short nails—and then back up to his face. A tentative smile waits for me there. This feels like a do-over, however temporary it may be.

I reach out and take his hand. It swallows mine up in warmth. "Deal."

CHAPTER

TWENTY-EIGHT

: Here Comes the Sun :

WE STEP OUT of the Lime Street station under a blanket of imposing clouds. The air feels pregnant with a storm that's weeks overdue. Looming buildings in shades of brown and gray climb skyward with their ancient spires. There's a stillness about the city that demands reverence.

I pull up the bus schedule on my phone.

"We have half an hour before the next bus to Woolton."

"Come on." Henry walks ahead of me. "That gives us time to see something before the rain."

I hoist my bag on my shoulder and give the sky a concerned glance.

"Not to worry," Henry grins over his shoulder. "I brought an umbrella." He pats his backpack. "Perhaps you'd even share it with me this time."

My phone dings in my hand.

"Just a sec."

●●●●○ AT&T LTE   12:11 PM   94% ▬▷

‹ Messages   **Dylan**   Details

Did you make it to Liverpool okay?

Yeah, we just got here a few minutes ago.

Who's we?

Shit.

Henry huffs and walks back to where I'm standing. "I promise you'll like it."

I shove the phone in my back pocket. I came here to do something, and I'm going to do it. Henry hails a cab and we climb in. It smells like old cheese inside the enclosed space. The cab driver throws a meaty arm up on the back of his seat and turns to face us.

"Where'll it be, kids?"

Henry instructs him to Pier Head. When the cabbie turns back to the wheel, we shrink down in our seats. Henry pulls the collar of his shirt over his nose and rolls his eyes back in his head. I stifle a laugh and pinch the end of my nose. He pretends to gag and fall over dead.

"Don't mind the aroma, it's just me lunch!"

I glance up and meet the cabbie's eyes in the rearview. Oops. He's seen the whole exchange. Henry and I exchange a *busted!* snicker and stare out opposite windows.

Once the cab door is shut behind us at our destination, we both take a minute to gulp the fresh air. Well, fresh-er air. Here, it smells like fishy saltwater—that ocean smell that is exactly the same on every coast I've visited. I follow Henry out toward the waterfront. Seagulls swarm overhead and squawk. When we get to a grouping of statues, he turns and holds his arms out. "Ta-da!"

My heart stutters.

Not because it's a statue of the Beatles—because, yes, that's extremely cool—but because of that *Ta-da.* I think back to the dream from a few nights ago. The sensory memories. Someone behind me saying ta-da. Was it Henry's voice in the dream? Yes, now that I think of it.

"Earth to Jo, are you okay?" Henry snaps his fingers in the air.

"Yeah, sorry." I look up at the bronze statues of Paul, John, George, and Ringo. "I'm a little starstruck is all."

I turn my camera on front-facing and attempt to take a selfie. I can't quite get them all in it with me.

"Let me," Henry says. I hand him my phone and he steps back, examining me in the viewfinder. I'm suddenly self-conscious. Are my jeans too tight? Is my shirt too clingy? Is this how Zara felt on that floor under the blanket?

I smile and attempt to project all the confidence I don't feel. When he snaps the picture, I turn and throw my arms around the statues and pretend to kiss them all. "I love you Paul, I love you John, I love you George, I love you Ringo."

Henry returns my phone and lets go of a sigh. "What must it be like, to know pretty girls visit your hometown to gush over a rock in your likeness?" He glances from the statue to me like he wants to backspace what he just said. He turns to walk along the waterfront again.

I could let it slide, but nah. "Pretty girls?" I ask as I catch up.

"Purely hypothetical." He grins but doesn't look at me.

"Are you flirting with me, Henry the wanker?" I shove him with my elbow.

The embarrassment seems to fade, lines in his face going smooth, eyes sparkling with challenge when he looks down at me. He leans in and lowers his voice. "If I was flirting with you, you'd know it."

Well, okay then. You'd think this was page 100 material from the way my cheeks flush. I focus on the choppy water below, and it isn't lost on me that my stomach feels equally turbulent. To my left, an old man stoops down next to the railing and unbuckles a music case. My body slows to a stop, like a pause button has been pressed.

His coat is tattered and brown. His gray hair sparse. He pulls out a violin. Props it on his shoulder. Positions his bow.

Henry slows down and looks back at me, and then at the man. "You coming?"

As the first note sings across the strings, the gentle purr of déjà vu dances around the goosebumps on my arms.

Here Comes the Sun.

"Right behind you."

CHAPTER

TWENTY-NINE

: Penny Lane :

THE DOUBLE DECKER bus drops us at the cross street of Smithdown Road and Penny Lane.

The original bus station sits derelict next to the new one. Under the rounded roof is a bank of darkened windows. Graffiti covers the outside walls. *Rory loves Daphne*, in bright red, with a crown over his name. Rory must think a lot of himself.

Across the street, a restaurant sign claims to have Liverpool's best fish and chips. Caddy-corner sits a brick building which houses a coffee shop and a furniture store. In the busy roundabout in front, engines of passing cars roar through.

Everything feels like déjà vu now. The buildings. The shops. Even the people. It's all familiar—not from a dream, but the song. The dark clouds still threaten, but they no longer feel ominous. I'm like an extra in Magical Mystery Tour, the movie. Everything is a fulfilled promise, and I'm light on my feet. It's as if my heart has lived here all along, waiting for the day I would find it. I stop at the street sign and stoop down next to the brick barrier to snap a picture.

Caption: the promised land

"We're on one of the lesser ley lines now," Henry says. He turns his phone screen to face me. It's a map like the one in the borrowed atlas in my backpack.

"I find it interesting that so many Beatles landmarks sit on ley lines," I say. "Don't you think that's weird?"

"It makes perfect sense, actually. The inspiration thrums here." He stretches his arms above his head like he's summoning the force. He drops his arms and looks down at me. "Don't you feel it?"

Loaded question.

He pulls the magnets out of his pockets and sets them on the ledge of the brick barrier. I step closer. "What are you doing?"

"Just testing them." He sets them down, positive ends facing one another. Nothing happens. He adjusts them a little, presses them ever-so-closer together. Still nothing. He tries the negative ends instead.

"Shouldn't you flip them over? Positive and negative facing each other?"

"That's how magnets usually work," he says. "But on a ley line, the opposite happens."

My expression must betray my skepticism.

"You'll see."

Henry tinkers with them for another minute before snatching them up and dropping them in his pocket, a little gruff.

"Onward then."

I want to apologize for his frustration. Like my doubting jinxed it or something.

"But they've worked like that before?"

He nods as we walk. We pass a law office, a wine bar, and a thrift store. I put on the brakes and peek through the windows at the tightly packed clothing racks and the overflowing shelves of trinkets and blankets and art. The place is delightfully stuffed full of junk.

"Just for a second?" I grin at him over my shoulder. He's got that hesitant look in his eye, like he's having shopping flashbacks from Heathrow. "I promise not to spend hours," I add sweetly.

Though I didn't ask him to, he follows me into the store. I push through crowded aisles and look at the hats, sunglasses, and sweaters shoved everywhere, all willy-nilly. Henry picks up a pair of rose-lensed sunglasses, replaces his glasses with them and squints his eyes at me. He pokes his lips out and says, "Life is what happens to you when you're busy making other plans." It's an excruciatingly poor John Lennon impression, but no matter; it makes me snort.

Henry's silly side is my new favorite thing.

When I look past him, I see it.

My throat goes dry. The crisscross patterned picnic blanket hangs off the edge of a shelf. I scoot past Henry and pick it up, the texture of the pattern pressing my fingertips. I can almost feel the indentations of the threads marking my knees.

"What is it?" Henry asks over my shoulder.

I jump. "Oh! Just. This blanket. I've seen it before."

"Oh yeah? Where?" He reaches down and traces his fingers over the seams.

"In a…" I clear my throat and set it down. "In a dream I had once."

"You aren't going to buy it?" he asks as I walk away. "It's only eleven pounds."

I shake my head, blushing from head to toe. There's no way I'd buy that blanket. That would be like trying to will it to come true. "Nope, I don't want to carry it around."

He catches up to me on the other side of the store.

"Which dream? One you told me about?" The question is innocent enough, but it makes me feel like I'm covering some high crime. Behind him, a restroom sign dangles from the ceiling.

"No. I'm going to run to the restroom, okay? Be right back." I don't wait for him to answer, just push past him and go.

When I'm safe again, inside the cool, dark fortress of the toilet stall, I pull out my phone. I have more missed texts from Dylan.

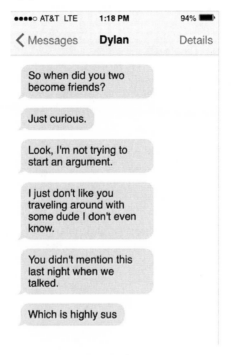

So when did you two become friends?

Just curious.

Look, I'm not trying to start an argument.

I just don't like you traveling around with some dude I don't even know.

You didn't mention this last night when we talked.

Which is highly sus

I take a deep breath before typing my reply.

*You have nothing to worr_*

But then I backspace it all. Now is not the time to have this conversation with him. I mute the thread and put my phone back in my pocket.

Henry's waiting for me outside the store. He's wearing the rose-colored Lennon sunglasses. I laugh and shake my head.

"What? You don't like it?" He pokes his lips out again. "All we're saying is give peace a chance."

I shove him. "If I didn't know better, I'd think you were making fun of John Lennon."

"Never." He smiles at me, and I wish we'd called this truce weeks ago.

We pass a series of soccer fields (*football*, he insists) as the street turns more residential. Shops and restaurants are fewer and farther between.

"You hungry?"

"I could eat."

Henry nods to a large white building ahead. It sits at the end of the shopping district and looks like a cross between a Victorian bed and breakfast and a haunted house. When we get closer, I read the green and gold sign—The Dovey.

"Wait. Is this the same as Barny's?"

He grins. "Yep."

"The Quarrymen played here!" The geek out consumes me as I imagine young John and Paul crossing this very threshold.

"Freddie Mercury once lived here, too." He takes off the rose-colored specs as we step into the dark interior, and he puts his glasses back on. The floors and tables are a warm, rich wood and it has an old world feel—like the building is a history book, rather than something out of one. The food smells fantastic, and my stomach rumbles as the hostess seats us at a cozy corner table. We set our bags down and order drinks. He gets a pint; I stick with water.

"Last time I visited Liverpool with Patrick and my mum and John," Henry says. "And we came here and sat at that table over there, by the window." His aura shifts and changes, darkens and lightens, like the memory gives him conflicted feelings.

"Who's John?"

"Family friend," he says. "The one who passed a few years back."

I feel bad that all this time, I've never even asked him about his mother, or the friend that he lost. He never seemed like he wanted to talk to me, though, especially not about this.

"We all loved him. He was really this sort of cut-up guy, and he kept making the waitress laugh. When she brought us our drinks, she dumped an entire pint of beer on Patrick by mistake." He chuckles a little. "You should've seen his face."

"You know," I say. "This is the first time I've ever really heard you talk about Patrick. Do you two not get along?"

A telling look flashes over his face for a split second before he smooths it away and shrugs. "Brothers fight." He doesn't elaborate further. The waitress brings us our drinks and takes our order. Cheeseburger for me. Shepherd's pie for him. My phone dings, and I tense up as I check it. But Dylan's thread is still muted. It's Lexie this time.

I glance up. Henry stares down at his own phone, so I tilt my camera viewfinder up, stealth-mode, and press the shutter button.

A bright flash snaps over his face.

Caption: FUUUUUCK

Henry looks up at me, eyebrows furrowing as a smirk crawls across his mouth. Every cell in my body begs for death as I stare down at my traitor iPhone. Henry must've turned on auto flash when he took the picture for me at Pier Head.

"What's wrong with this thing?" I mumble. And I shake the phone. Because, you know, I'm extremely competent at mitigating embarrassing situations.

Henry chuckles. "What does shaking it accomplish, exactly?"

"Huh? Oh. I don't know." I pretend to be very enthralled in my screen's contents. My whole head is a ball of flames. I did, at least, get the picture. I send it to Lexie immediately and then delete it from my camera roll.

"You taking my picture on the sly, Beatlemania?"

"What? *Pfft.* No." I turn my phone around to face him, camera roll populating the screen. See? Proof.

"You deleted it." He grins. At that moment, Lexie replies: DAYUM.

I shove my phone in my bag. "Okay, fine. I took your picture, okay? My friend Lexie asked me what you look like. She's a little boy crazy." I roll my eyes like I'm sooo above her.

"What'd you tell her? That I'm a handsome, strapping lad?" He sits up straight and adjusts his collar. "Six feet, two inches of sculptured man?"

I laugh a little and it sounds like a gurgle. "No. I was taking a picture so she could decide for herself."

"You really are quite charming when you blush. Have I told you that before?" He leans in a little and cups the sides of his beer glass with both hands.

Actually, yes. He has.

"Shut up. I'm not blushing. I'm having an allergic reaction to your conceit."

His smile only widens. The temperature in the restaurant rises and my skin goes fizzy, like the top layer of a Coke.

We're friends now. This is no big deal.

CHAPTER THIRTY

: Strawberry Fields Forever :

AFTER GORGING OURSELVES at The Dovey (food tasted good for the first time in forever!), browsing all the shops in the area, and taking a narrated tour of the city, the evening bus dumps us in the misting rain on Menlove Road.

Someone has scrawled the word "head" at the end of the street name in spray paint.

At least there are people in the world less mature than me. Bright side to everything.

We stand at the sign, chewing on peppermints from Henry's stash. He reaches into his bag to get the umbrella, and something catches my eye as he starts to zip it back up.

"Wait, what's that in your bag?" I reach down and yank the zipper like that isn't super rude. Maybe he's starting to rub off on me. He doesn't stop me, though. His Union Jack umbrella opens with a little click above our heads, but I barely notice it when I see the hidden thing in his bag.

"I bought the blanket." He shrugs, looking a little caught. He re-zips the backpack and shuffles it over his shoulder. *The blanket* from the thrift store. The one from *The Dream I Don't Think About At All.*

I squeak more than ask, "Why?"

"Why?" He laughs. "Because it was only eleven pounds. And obviously it means something to you."

The rain gets a little harder, forcing me under the umbrella, and by default, closer to him. A quick inhale confirms that yes: he still smells good. I take a mental snapshot.

Caption: this is not going to end well

"Why do you care if it means something to me?" I look straight ahead at the sidewalk in front of us.

"Maybe I don't." He nudges me with his elbow. "Maybe I like the blanket."

I button my lip. My eyes well and I blink furiously to dry them out.

He stops. "Hey, are you okay?"

Nope. "Yeah, of course."

"What's the significance? Of the blanket?"

There it is. The point-blank question again, and I have no bathroom to duck into.

"I'd really rather not talk about it."

He looks at me funny but mercifully leaves it alone. We keep walking. I watch my feet move along the sidewalk, creating shadows in the puddles as they go. I try to think about anything else. I'm glad I bought the rain boots, glad I decided to wear them. But I'm worried about the rain. There was no rain in the cemetery dream. Cars pass and we step to the inside of the sidewalk so the tire splash can't reach us.

"Did you know John Lennon promised his son, Sean, that he'd bring him here someday? But then he died before he could. Yoko had to bring him."

Henry glances down at me, expression grim. "No. I didn't." It's like he knows I'm talking about me as much as I'm talking about Sean Lennon. But I don't know how he could know.

When we turn the corner, the red gates stand out against the bleak background. The wall surrounding it is covered in faded graffiti. It hits me all at once that Pop used to live here. He lived at Strawberry Field when the Salvation Army owned it. He came from the place that inspired the song. Maybe that's why John was his favorite Beatle. (Paul > John, if you ask me. We used to argue about it.)

My throat burns, but I resist the threatening tears as we approach the gate.

"Pretty anticlimactic, really," Henry says. "It's been closed down for awhile, but they've plans to turn it into a community center soon."

I run my fingers along the cool, wet metal. Just beyond it, overgrown weeds and shrubs have swallowed the courtyard. It's a suburban jungle.

"This gate is a replica. The original is in the museum downtown. They replaced it a couple of years before I came here the first time."

I drop my hand.

"Sorry to be a buzzkill," he says. "Liverpool's a little underwhelming compared to the songs about it."

Negative Ned strikes again. I clamp my teeth down for a moment before I turn to him.

"I think you're missing the point. This is the town where they grew up. The place they met their best friends and wrote their first songs and fell in love for the first time. It's where their fates began. *That* is the magic of it all."

His eyebrows lift. "Yeah, I guess I could see—"

"They captured the mundane in a way that made it seem special to the rest of the world. Some people may see a plain red gate that's been replaced, or a suburban lane with a few little shops and think, *this is it*? But it's magical in the song because they let us see it through their eyes. Through the context of what it meant to them. What it meant to my pop, even." Tears well up again. My emotions wriggle a little further from my weakening grasp. *What is wrong with me?*

"So, your pop grew up here?"

I nod. "Someone dropped him off on the doorstep of this place when he was two years old. He never even knew his parents. He used to joke that he was a changeling."

Henry peers past the gate like he's trying to imagine it himself.

"I think that's why he related to the Beatles. John Lennon was going to garden parties here twenty years before Pop arrived. He grew up in their literal shadow. As a cover band, sure, but he walked the same lanes. He understood their roots. I think that's what made Walrus Gumboot such a great cover band."

Henry doesn't say anything. I search the names written on the concrete columns in multicolored paints and markers, pens and pencils. I know better than to think I'll see his actual signature on a wall that's been scribbled over many times in the years since he died. But I look anyway.

"There's a piece of him still here," I say. And I know it's true.

Henry passes me the umbrella handle and then reaches to get something out of his bag. He comes up with a Sharpie and hands it to me.

I stare up at him. "We're gonna vandalize the wall?"

He bobs his head side to side, faking indecision, then grins. "Nothing to get hung about."

Dimpled Henry quoting the Beatles is my *new* new favorite thing.

He takes the umbrella from me and I pop the top of the marker and look for an empty space. I stoop down close to the sidewalk and write *I miss you, Pop. Love, Jojo*

Henry squats and ducks under the umbrella beside me. I swallow my sadness and pass him the marker.

"I wanted to write something profound, but it looks like someone's beaten me to the punch." He gestures to a phrase a foot or so away from my message. It says *Percy is a tosser.* A chuckle sneaks around my tears.

I know what he's doing and I'm grateful. He taps the end of the marker against his bottom lip for a few moments before leaning toward the wall with it.

Next to where I signed, in bold all-caps handwriting, he writes: *This place is bloody magical. -Jojo (and Henry)*

I laugh for real this time. "I don't think that was exactly what I said."

"No?" He looks over at me and grins. "I paraphrased. Hence the *and Henry*."

He crouches under the umbrella with me, even though the rain has slowed to a sputter. We stare down at the signatures.

"Why did you call me Jojo the first day you met me?" He hasn't since, until now.

His eyes meet mine. It feels like we're in our own little private bubble, beneath the red and blue fabric of the umbrella and all the silver wires that hold it together. There's a sort of purple mist around us. Maybe it's the colors of the umbrella bleeding together, or maybe his aura is swimming around us both now.

"I dunno." I watch the way his lips move when he talks, the delicate way they come together and pull apart, then rest when he pauses. "You just look like a Jojo."

I stare at his mouth too long. I don't know if I moved closer or if he did. His breath tickles my mouth before I glance up at his eyes, hazy and unfocused. There was no dream to foreshadow this, nothing to warn me. I scramble backward, out from under the umbrella, and stand up.

"Let's take a selfie!" I blurt, and dig in my pockets for my phone before I remember I put it in my bag. As I unzip pouches and search, he stands up.

"We can use mine." He clears his throat and pulls his phone out. "I can text it to you."

He steps close to me again and holds the camera up at an angle. The red gate fills the background. Our arms press together. We both smile, pretending what almost just happened didn't almost just happen.

CHAPTER

THIRTY-ONE

: Eleanor Rigby :

WE MAKE THE mile-long walk to St. Peter's as the clouds finally give way to the evening sun.

An occasional passing car whooshes through the remaining rain puddles. When we turn onto Church Road, I point to a red brick building next to the church.

"That's it right there. The place where John met Paul."

We both stop and stare. Me, in reverence; him, far away in his own thoughts.

I wonder if he feels the impact of the history and the mythology of the Beatles the way I do. Seeing this place, knowing what began in this very location, sends sentimental chills racing over my skin.

"I know you aren't really a fan, but what if John and Paul had never met, and the Beatles never existed? Like in that movie where lightning sends the guy to a parallel universe where the Beatles were never a thing?" His featherweight gaze lands on me, and I continue. "If there had been no Quarrymen, there would've been no Beatles. It's hard to imagine a past, or even a future, where the Beatles never existed. At least for me. That's why I love them so much. They changed everything."

He considers this for a few moments. Quiet. Reflective.

"Scientists can't rule out the possibility of a multiverse. But we can only live in one at a time, as far as we know. I don't think it's reasonable to consider the absence of things that've already happened—here, in this one. Everything happens for a reason, right? You can't undo it once it's done, so there's no use even trying to imagine an alternative present unless you have the ability to travel to one."

I know he's talking about the Beatles, but when I apply that to the reason we're standing right here, right now… it's uncomfortable. Damp air and unwelcome logic hang thick around us.

He says quietly, "You all right?"

It's stunning, the way he picks up on my emotions, for someone who barely knows me.

I nod. "It's just that I came here for an alternative present." We start walking again. "But the best case scenario is a conversation with a ghost."

I don't tell him how much I'm hoping Pop is still alive. That he will somehow warp from some parallel universe and come back to me. Or that I will leave this present and go to one where he's still alive.

I would give up everything to have Pop back.

We walk until we reach the graveyard gate. A roof rises above the brick pedestals separating it from the sidewalk, and it's outlined in black. Two white flowers are etched into the point below the pitch. The sun has made its debut, only to begin a descent toward the horizon.

"I need to find the tombstone before sunset."

"Why sunset?" Henry asks.

"It was sunset in the dream."

"Ah."

I finally meet his eyes. They're sea-glass green in the warm evening light.

"I have to go alone."

He bites his bottom lip and nods. "So it was just you, then. In the dream."

"Well, yeah. Me and Pop."

He dips a hand into his pocket, then reaches out and places the magnets in my hand. He closes it inside my palm—long, sturdy fingers wrapping around mine. I stare down at our joined hands, feeling a sense of connection with him. He knows what I'm feeling right now because he lost someone he cared about, too. Two someones. When he lets go, he takes a step back and hops up onto the brick wall.

"I'll wait here."

Before I step inside the gate, he calls out. "Jo?"

I glance over my shoulder. His feet dangle and swing and he smiles down at me. A sad smile, backlit by a melancholy indigo. "Good luck."

I clutch the magnets tighter in my hand and go inside.

The déjà vu sets in before I find the precise location. Twisting, ancient oaks dot the landscape, and rows of crooked headstones pile in beneath them, huddled together like an anxious crowd.

I wander the path until I somehow know to look up. My eyes fall directly onto the words. The trembling starts at my chin and shimmies all the way down my body. My ability to separate the dream from reality dissolves like a sugar cube in hot tea. I'm in the thick of it. I'm part of it and it's part of me. I pull out my phone and snap a picture, capturing the way the diminishing daylight frames the moment. *Caption: this is it*

Greenish-gray moss webs the headstone. In the distance, there are car horns and voices; but here with me, there's only the whisper of stray sticks skittering across the ground. I read the inscription again, paying special attention to her name in the sea of names on her tomb.

Eleanor Rigby, beloved wife of Thomas Woods and granddaughter of the above, died October 10, 1939, aged 44 years, asleep.

I glance down at the ground. She's here. Below my feet. The evidence of her existence could be unearthed with a few shovelfuls of soft, damp dirt. Pop, though? He has no headstone with a listing of ancestors. No birth date besides the estimate he was given by the Salvation Army.

Panic taps me on the shoulder. When we're past the part I've already seen in the dream, what will happen? What will I say to him? *Hi, are you dead?* Because there's no physical evidence of him left. No bones to unearth. Even if he was in that urn, the urn is gone now.

There are also no facts to support what I'm about to do. It's not what a mentally healthy person would do, and I'm at least self-aware enough to know this. No matter, though. I slowly exhale and center myself, conjure a sense of calm. A sense of assuredness.

When he steps out, I'll tell him that I love him. That I forgive him for choosing his band and his addictions over Mama and me. I'll tell him that, even if the insurance company was right, I forgive him. And that I'm going to be okay. Even if I'm not sure how true that last part is.

I set the magnets down in front of me, on the edge of the stone barrier of the grave. The southern ends cut a flip and they meet in the middle. It happens so quickly that I jump. Henry was right. The magnets *really do* work backwards here. And if that is possible, surely many other things must be.

I close my eyes and concentrate on the sensation of fading sunlight on my closed lids, just like in the dream. The warmth slowly passes over them, centimeter by centimeter, like a golden fleece being drawn away. When the light touches my lashes, I open my eyes. No matter what happens, I'll keep them open. I won't blink him away again.

I wait.

The sun keeps sinking.

And wait.

Time staggers, uncertain.

And wait.

The graveyard is empty, except for me. Just as it looked in the dream. I've dreamed it over and over. It's so exact that it feels like I'm like walking around inside my own dream at this very moment. The only thing missing is Pop.

Any moment.

I stand up, look around. Turn in a circle.

Maybe I didn't do it right. Maybe standing messed the whole thing up. Maybe the sunset has to be almost complete. Clinging to hope, I sink to the chilly, wet earth and try again.

I close my eyes and wait. But only the approaching darkness joins me. The sun sinks below the trees until there's no light on my face.

"We're finally together," I say aloud. "That's your line, Pop. You're late." I open my eyes and smile, tears streaming down my cheeks. The warmth is foreign to me. I've forgotten what it feels like to cry. "I'm still waiting on you. It won't be a big deal if you just come out now. The dreams are different than real life sometimes. I know this." Only a gentle breeze and a sleepy bird call responds.

It's a shitty ending to an otherwise perfect day.

I know the truth, deep in my bones. A harsh, angry stream flows down my cheeks and neck now. One that has been dammed up for months. Maybe even years. I cry and cry and cry, until I'm a girl-shaped river. Until my face is raw and tender.

I cry for Pop. I cry for Walrus Gumboot. I cry for my mother. But most of all, I cry for me. That I came all this way, that I've separated myself from people I care about, only to pursue the impossibility of a conversation it's too late to have. Because he's gone. He's been gone for three years, and I'm only now accepting it.

A little while later, I'm not sure how much later, footsteps crunch gravel behind me. I draw a shaky breath and stuff my face inside the collar of my t-shirt, smearing the wetness with soggy fabric. I sense him without seeing him, smell the pepper-mint. He stops at my side and sinks to the ground.

We sit for a long time in silence.

When my chest stops heaving and we're both still, he whispers, "Did he show?"

The hope in his voice is so sincere that it feels vulgar to say the truth aloud. I shake my head and crumple into myself, pressing my lips together. He hands me a handkerchief. In my emotional hysteria, I laugh at this. Maybe all English boys carry handkerchiefs in their pockets. But I somehow doubt it. He's an old man of a boy.

He leans in close, shoulder touching mine. "I didn't mean to upset you again."

I shake my head, trying to form the words without my voice cracking. "It's not you."

He doesn't rush me to talk. The horizon melts into shades of purple, like an extension of his aura. I feel safe because of it. The moon peeks out, waxing full, before I'm able to say a word.

"When he died, a lot of questions never got answered." I glance over at him and he looks away. "He died here. Well, in London. In a hotel. I don't know if you knew."

When he doesn't say anything, I continue. "You know, we never even had a funeral for him. He had no family but us, so Mama and I spent weeks crying on the couch, while friends and neighbors brought us casseroles."

I feel guilty saying all of this. I know Mama did the best she could do with the resources available to her at the time. Henry stares at me, patient. So I keep talking.

"It was going to be really expensive to fly his body home. So we had him cremated before the embassy made arrangements. Even that wiped out my mom's savings completely. Then his life insurance company denied the claim, because the medical examiner thought—" My voice cracks on the end. I take a few deep breaths to compose myself. "The tox screen showed really high levels of opiates and alcohol. He had a history of depression, and a previous suicide attempt. So the medical examiner used that information to rule it an intentional overdose."

"Jo…" I hate the sympathy I hear in Henry's voice. The pity.

"He wouldn't do that," I say through my teeth. "Not again. When he did try, he ended up in the emergency room in Asheville. They were in town for a show. My mother is the nurse who took care of him. He used to say that she was his angel, that she pulled him back from the brink of death. They fell in love and got married and had me. He was happy, Henry! He hadn't done drugs in a long time. He'd been clean! He promised us and I believed him, because he was the most honest person I ever knew. I still believe him. He just made a mistake."

Crickets begin their faraway chirping, like sad mood music in a movie. The streetlights buzz on, but the graveyard darkens. Henry's eyes glisten as if he may cry, too.

"He wouldn't have done it." My heart thuds the next words before I say them. "And I have proof."

I don't know what makes me decide, at this moment, to share a secret I've kept for three years, but I dig my wallet out of my bag, and then the letter out of my wallet. I hand it to him. The Adams apple in his throat moves up and down as he takes it from me, carefully unfolding it. I watch him as he reads by the light of the moon.

When he meets my gaze, he hands it back to me. "Wow."

"That arrived a few days before his ashes did," I tell him as I put the letter away. "I never told anyone about it. Not even Mama."

Henry picks up his long arm from where it's propped, holding him upright, and he wraps it around my back.

"It sucks so much, Jo. I know it sucks so much." He squeezes my arm and pulls me closer to him. I drop my head onto his shoulder and forget all the uncertainty and awkwardness between us. I forget that we almost kissed earlier. I forget that our friendship—if that's what we'll still call it when we're back in London—has been a little unconventional. Instead, I focus on his warmth. The current of sadness that connects us.

After a few minutes, he whispers, "We should go soon."

He's right, but leaving feels like giving up. Accepting Pop is gone means I'll never get any real closure. But sleeping in a graveyard on the cold, damp ground won't exactly solve anything, either.

I nod and grudgingly pull away. He stands and reaches for my hand. My stiff legs shake as he pulls me to my feet. He doesn't let go, even as we walk out. Our fingers lace together, steady and solid. It feels like I could dangle from the end of his arm and never touch the ground. It's the first time I've felt like somebody's got me in a very long time.

If my heart didn't hurt so much, the feeling would probably make me swoon.

"Do you want to tell me about the Eleanor dream?" he asks, as we turn onto the halogen-lit sidewalk, toward the bus stop.

I hesitate. Maybe it's time. It didn't come true. Keeping it to myself wasn't some magic trick to making sure it happened. I don't even know where I came up with such silly superstitious nonsense, now that I think of it. So as we walk, I tell him. All of it.

The whole thing.

CHAPTER
THIRTY-TWO
: Ticket to Ride :

"SORRY LOVEY," THE rosy-cheeked ticket lady says to Henry. "The last train to London left over an hour ago. Next one is bright and early at 7:05."

Guilt ripples through me. If not for all my graveyard sobbing, we would've made it back to Lime Street in time. Now we're stranded. Henry glances over at me.

"I'm sorry."

"There's nothing to be sorry for. We'll make another plan." If he's irritated, it doesn't show.

"There's a bed-and-breakfast at the north exit," Rosy Cheeks says. "And if you can't wait till morning, there's a bus station two blocks north. A few night bus routes could have you back in London before you'd board the train here."

We both thank her and step aside. Henry looks down at me.

"I don't know about you," he says, twisting his hands together, "but I'm pretty knackered. We could get a room for the night." His eyes widen and he quickly adds, "Surely the B and B has one with two beds."

My ears go hot. The thought of spending the night in a hotel room with Henry, even one with two beds, sets off alarm bells.

It's one thing to sleep in a room down the hall from him. It's quite another to sleep in the same room.

"Couldn't we stay here until morning?" My voice gives me away too much.

Henry bites the inside of his cheek and points to the hours printed on the doors. "They close up at midnight."

My palms start to sweat. "Oh."

"Let's go check out the bus schedule," he says.

: : :

At the bus station, we purchase tickets to Birmingham, which is a three-hour ride. The ticket attendant informs us that once there, we'll change buses and ride another three to London. We missed the last non-stop, doubling our trip time back. Figures.

Only a dozen or so stray travelers sit on the benches near the doors. Closer to the back of the room, a homeless man slumps down in a chair, half asleep with a newspaper open on his lap. The edge of his brown coat is tattered and...

It hits me when I see the black case at his feet.

It's the man from Pier Head—the one who was playing *Here Comes the Sun* this morning. My heart leaps. I don't know why he's here or what it means, but my emotions are all over the place. I want to laugh and cry. Irrationally, I want to hug the man and thank him for being real.

"Check it out," Henry says, stirring me from my reverie. He points to the right side of the sterile white station, where a larger-than-life painting of Paul McCartney in thermodynamic colors hangs. It warms the entire wall.

"He's my favorite, if I had to pick." I wipe my eyes. "I've always felt connected to him."

"Why's that?" Henry asks as I tilt my phone up and snap a picture of the painting. "Send that to me," he adds, pointing at the picture I took.

"His mother died when he was fourteen, same age as when I lost Pop. And she communicated with him through dreams."

Henry's jaw drops. "No way."

"Way. That's where *Let It Be* came from. She whispered it to him in a dream. When he woke up, he wrote the song in one sitting. People always think that song is some religious ode to the Virgin Mary, but it's not. His mother's name was Mary. Mother Mary was his mom."

"I never knew that," Henry says, pulling up the photo I texted him.

"Well, you're not a fan. So." I sniffle, teasing.

He flashes me a weary grin and then studies the picture I sent him. "You have an eye for capturing light," he says.

"Thanks," I mumble.

I'm still processing the compliment when a commotion on the other side of the station distracts us. A hefty bus station employee nudges *Here Come the Sun* man with a broom, so hard that it knocks the newspaper off his lap. "If you're not buying a ticket, you've got to move on."

The man jumps to his feet, suddenly awake. "Don't touch me!" His voice echoes through the station. A hush falls over the waiting passengers.

"Bloody hell," Henry mumbles under his breath and stands.

I want to jump up and defend the man, to tell Henry about the dream, but there's no time and I can't find my voice.

"I said," the station employee reiterates, wielding the broomstick like a weapon, "If you don't have a ticket, You. Must. Leave."

"He's got a ticket," Henry says, stepping between them. "I'm getting it for him now." He motions for the man to follow. After a moment of laser-staring at the employee with the broom, the homeless man grabs his violin case and limps behind Henry, mumbling obscenities under his breath. Everyone in the station watches in silence.

"What's your name?" Henry asks him as they approach the ticket counter. Their voices carry through the quiet.

"Duncan."

"And where are you headed, Mister Duncan?" He points to the music case. "Someplace that appreciates good music, perhaps?" Henry's smile betrays none of the heaviness of our evening. He's lively. Charming. Kind.

"I've not been headed anywhere in years."

"Well, it's your lucky night, because you can go to Leeds, Sheffield, or Birmingham."

The man thinks about it for a moment. "Leeds."

Henry nods and buys the ticket, pats the man on the back, and sends him back to his spot.

My heart is a puddle of goo by the time Henry resumes his spot beside me.

Pop used to say that you can tell a lot about a person's character by the way they treat people with nothing to offer them. I can't help it; I give him heart eyes.

"What?" He says this like he hasn't done something extraordinary. Something most people wouldn't.

"You're very kind."

He shakes his head, mouth quirking up on one side. "No. Just altering the trajectory of a gravitational wave."

"I don't know what that means," I say. He glances down at my lips, then back up to my eyes.

"Me either, really."

I'm mentally cataloging all the shades of green starbursting from his pupils when the loudspeaker crackles to life.

"421 line to Birmingham now boarding."

"That's us." Henry stands. I follow behind him, a little dizzy from the staring contest.

CHAPTER THIRTY-THREE

: Hard Day's Night :

WE SIT NEAR the back, away from the other passengers.

Henry offers me the window seat. I drop my bag and watch out the window as I listen to the announcements and safety warnings. The *Here Comes the Sun* man steps outside the bus station and lights a cigarette. It hits me then. I turn to Henry.

"I haven't seen you smoke today."

He squirms around in his seat, getting comfortable, but doesn't look at me. "I'm trying to quit. Bad for your health, you know."

I smile.

As the bus moves out onto the highway, the lighting dims. Beams from the streetlamps and moonlight pour in. Some passengers reach up and click the dome lights above their heads. I leave mine off, pressing my face against the cool window. Trees and road signs zoom past as I settle into the melancholy of leaving.

"I'm pretty sure that was a sign." Henry says.

"What was?"

"The man at the station." He searches through the contacts in his phone. "He chose Leeds. My mother is buried there. She was from there."

I stare at him, not quite knowing what to say.

"I haven't visited her grave since her funeral."

"Why not?"

He looks out the window for a minute, takes a deep breath.

"I haven't been able to forgive her."

I swallow, hard. "For dying?"

"For a lot of things." He looks over at me. "But yeah, mostly for dying."

"I know how you feel."

He nods. "I know you do."

"What about your dad? Is he still having a pretty hard time with it?"

"Dad and I aren't on the best terms either." He shrugs, and for the tiniest irritating moment, I think maybe he's going to blow me off and not tell me, even after everything I've told him today. "When Mum died, I was angry at him. For being so harsh to her while she was sick."

I struggle to picture George doing such a thing.

"He was harsh to her?"

Henry looks up at me. I see the pain there, the reluctance to say whatever is bothering him.

"She stepped out on him. Patrick and I have different fathers, but she never told any of us that. She kept it buttoned up until my dad confronted her with some of Patrick's medical paperwork. A sports physical for football, of all things. B negative blood type. Both dad and mum are O positive. Two Os can't make a B."

I'm so stunned I don't know what to say.

"Then my father remembered John was B negative."

"Wait," I say, "the friend of your family's who died?"

Henry nods. "There was a huge blow up. Patrick and I heard him accuse her. And as preposterous as it sounded, a few things made instant sense to both of us. First being that Patrick looked nothing like Mum or Dad, but exactly like John."

Henry's tall, Patrick's not. Henry's got brown hair and green eyes, Patrick's got red hair and blue eyes. The difference hadn't really made me think anything of it, because Lexie and Maddie are *twins* and they look nothing alike.

"I was so angry at all of them. At her for doing it. At my father for always being away teaching classes, for making her feel so lonely she turned to someone else. At John for doing such a despicable thing to my family. And at Patrick, for being the reason I knew I had to accept it."

His fist clenches on the armrest. Thinking back to what George said about Henry's perpetual anger, it makes sense now. I reach over and loosen his fingers. Something washes over his face. Surprise, maybe, at the gesture. He relaxes his hand but pulls it away.

I clear my throat. "Did your dad confront John?"

Henry stares down at his lap. "John was already dead. That's how my father knew the blood type. He'd been the one to identify his body after the accident. He'd seen all his medical files."

"God."

"Yeah."

"So they were close?"

Henry nods. "John was Mum's friend originally, but she introduced him to my father early on in their relationship. John was in a bind with his living situation and my father helped him. Anyway, she couldn't pull herself together to go see him. You know, after. He was like family. Like an uncle to Patrick and me."

Uncle, not father. Patrick must've been so hurt and confused. I couldn't imagine what it would've been like to find out someone you'd known and cared about wasn't who you thought they were. Especially after it was too late.

"How did Patrick take it?"

"Like Patrick takes everything. Badly." There's a sharpness to his words, and it makes me feel even worse for Patrick.

"Really? He always seems so positive about everything."

Henry cuts his eyes sideways at me. "That's because he overcompensates."

"He really doesn't seem to me like—"

Henry reclines his seat backwards and gets comfortable. He turns his attention away from me and to his phone. The conversation seems over without my permission. Why am I defending Patrick?

"I don't know him like you do," I concede, and press my own recline button. But nothing happens. The button sticks, and I press again. This time, I really dig my shoulder in. Still nothing. Won't budge. Doors, seats, empty graveyards: nothing ever works for me. Everything is such a struggle, all the time.

Henry looks up from his phone as I angrily dig my shoulder in. "Won't go?"

He sits up and presses the button on my armrest until it gives. "Lean back now." I try, but it may as well be a concrete wall. He places his hand on the back of my seat and presses the button again.

I fly backwards at Mach 3 and my head bounces off the seat when I meet resistance.

"Bloody hell!" His eyes bug out. His curse echoes through the bus. There's a commotion among the other passengers, some rustling and talking. He leans down and whispers. "Was that loud?" It's his sheepish tone that does me in. Laughter crashes over me and I can't stop.

"Bloody hell," he says again, quieter this time. "You must have a head injury. How many fingers am I holding up?" He holds up two, then four, then five, then one. Never for more than a second or two. This only makes me laugh harder. He chuckles along and leans back in his seat. Once I finally settle down, he says, "Seriously, are you all right?"

I look over at him and nod. Reclining side by side in our seats like this, face-to-face, feels intimate. Not bed-and-breakfast-room intimate, but enough that my nerves fray. I look away and watch out the window as we move away from the lights of town.

Keystrokes click quietly next to me as he types something into his phone. I wait as long as I can stand it before I sneak a peek. *You'd be furious if you knew what I almost did today.* I try not to make it obvious that I'm reading, but he glances over at just the right moment and catches me.

"I hear Bristol has an excellent espionage program," he says.

"Sorry," I mumble. Busted.

He tucks his phone away. It's dark in the bus, I feel his smile on my skin.

"I still text my mother," he says, and my heart breaks a little more for him. "Sometimes it helps."

I wonder what he *almost did* today that would upset her. Sleep in a bed and breakfast with a girl? I don't know anything about his mother or what would have upset her, and I wish I did.

"What was she like?"

He shrugs. "Fucked up. Selfish. But she was ours."

I relate to that a little too well. I shiver inside my shirt.

"Are you cold?" He sits up and flips on his dome light overhead before rummaging in his bag. Then he pulls out a blanket—no, *the* blanket. "Here."

I shove frantic arms back in my shirtsleeves and push the blanket away before he can spread it over us. "No, I'm okay. I'm not cold. Really."

He gives me the same exasperated look he gave me that first day in the tube. "Really? Are we still doing this?"

It doesn't have to be a thing if I don't *make it a thing.*

"Fine. Okay. I'm cold." I pull the blanket up.

"I promise not to get handsy." He flips the dome light off and his joke hangs there in the dark. I force a laugh, but inside I'm not laughing at all. I'm wondering what it'd be like if he did. I close my eyes and let the forbidden dream replay like a movie reel in my brain. I promise myself when we get back to London, I'll never think of this again.

Henry's breaths rise and fall next to me. I risk a peek at him. A patch of moonlight rests on his face, and he stares back at me, green eyes piercing the dark. He looks like a still frame from a comic book: the whole world is black and white, except for his eyes. He looks at me like he knows me. Really knows me. Like we've shared something nobody knows about but us.

"Can I ask you something?" I breathe it more than say it.

He gives me a drowsy nod.

"That night. After the Crow and the tea in the darkroom. You said you dreamed something intense. What was it?"

He looks down, hiding under the shadow of his lashes. Opens his mouth and closes it. Opens and closes it again. His eyes search my face, resting finally on my lips. It isn't a quick glance this time.

"I probably shouldn't say."

My voice comes out raspy. *"Probably* shouldn't?"

He grins and squeezes his eyes shut, as if debating. When he opens them again, he says, "I definitely shouldn't."

It could've been about anything. But my pulse is making some pretty grand assumptions. We lie just like that, facing each other in the dark. Streetlights illuminate our faces every few seconds. He bites his bottom lip and traces the stitched edge of the blanket with his index finger. My eyes follow it.

"Can I ask you a question now?"

I want to say no, but I nod.

"Did you dream about this blanket before or after you got to London?"

I inhale, exhale. "After."

He nods. "I thought so."

Trying to fill in the blanks is dizzying. "What are you saying?"

His pupils dilate. "What do you know about quantum entanglement?"

Well, that took a hard left. I try to remember the definition on the poster in his room. Can't think straight enough to remember the words.

"Less than I know about playing guitar."

He chuckles. "It's a theory that says when some particles become entangled, they remain connected even after they're separated. Einstein called it spooky action at a distance."

"I'm sure it will surprise you that I'm still confused."

He turns so he's lying on his side in the seat. He props his head up. "The theory is based on very small particles, at the atomic level. But remember what I said about how we only see a very limited part of our universe?"

"The physics-as-our-glasses comparison, yes."

"Right. Communication is an even more finite science, but a lot of scientists think quantum entanglement can very well explain that, too. Think of how a flock of birds instantaneously change direction and rhythm. Have you ever noticed that?"

I nod. "Sure."

"How are they communicating that? I know people don't do that, but some people are able to communicate better nonverbally than others. Is telepathy just thought particles that become entangled when people spend a regular amount of time together? Or rather, *become entangled?*"

I glance down at the blanket. "So you're saying you picked up on some nonverbal cue about the…?"

"No," Henry says, a little squirmy. He rolls back on his back and stares up at the ceiling of the bus. "I'm saying I bought the blanket because I've dreamed about it also."

The statement itself is innocent. But all the words unspoken, the ones in between, hiding in the curve of his lips—those are the ones that whisper flames into my ears.

"So perhaps we've dreamed the same thing." The corners of his mouth turn upward, just slightly. "At some point."

I turn my head and zoom in on a fingerprint on the window. Ringo is playing the drum solo from Abbey Road in my chest.

When I get the courage to look over at him again, his eyes are closed.

After a few still, quiet minutes, I whisper "Was the blanket in the dream you shouldn't tell me about?"

His eyes stay closed. I can't tell if he's sleeping or playing possum, but I feel dodged-a-bullet relief when he doesn't answer.

Maybe it's better if I never know.

CHAPTER

THIRTY-FOUR

: Tell Me What You See :

"PICK A CARD. Any card." Henry's dimples wink as he grins.

He leans on the front counter of the Fox Den, fanning a set of jet-black cards with gold filigree musical notes on them. Henry and me. Me and Henry. I can't get the thought out of my head. It's hard to reconcile falling asleep on the bus and waking up here with him, back at the store. My memory is a puzzle with missing pieces.

"Am I supposed to ask the question aloud?"

He shakes his head. "No. Just concentrate on it. Focus with your mind. Then pick the card you feel drawn to for the answer."

I close my eyes and take a deep breath. Our trip flashes in a series of reverse-motion still shots in my mind. He's asleep beside me on the bus. Then he's holding me in the graveyard as I cry. He's leaning toward me under an umbrella at Strawberry Field. He's grinning across the table from me on Penny Lane. Then staring at me through a camera lens at Pier Head. I ask the silent question: *What's the outcome of this thing between Henry and me?* My hand reaches for the cards until they stop on one. I peek through my lids and pull it away from the deck. It's warm in my hand, shiny gold border contrasting the ink-black of the card.

"Flip it over on the counter," Henry says. I don't look at him, in case those thought particles he was talking about have somehow transmitted to him what I've asked. I flip the card over. In the same shiny gold filigree, two figures—a man and a woman—face one another. Behind them, swirls dominate the sky like they're suspended in the cosmos. An angel reigns over their heads. At the bottom of the card: THE LOVERS.

CHAPTER

THIRTY-FIVE

: Good Day Sunshine :

"ICE CREAM AND dabbing!"

Somewhere, through thick darkness, an English voice shouts this over and over. *Ice cream and dabbing!* It makes no sense with the context of the tarot card. The voice grows progressively louder. More insistent. Then Henry's voice joins the bizarro chorus.

"Where did you say?"

I open my eyes as I process it: just a dream. No tarot cards. We're still on the bus. Hazy morning daylight swirls inside the bus with a heady mix of diesel fumes. I try to imagine what *this* dream was supposed to mean. Ice cream and dabbing?

Henry rubs his eyes and yawns. There's a lingering feeling that we've missed something important, that something is not quite right, but I can't put my finger on it. The bus driver props a thick arm on the seat back in front of us and says it again. But this time, it's clearer.

"High Street and Abbey. Last stop, ladies and gentlemen. Wakey wakey."

Out the bus windows, a drowsy English town awaits. There are old brick buildings and Tudor houses, but the thing that catches my eye is the mural on the side of a building. It's a painting, in psychedelic colors, of a hand holding a sword.

Henry stretches his back and looks out the window, surprise dawning over his face. "Is that...?" He leans over me to get a better look. A smile creeps over his sleep-wrinkled face, and then he throws his head back and laughs.

My grasp of the geography here is imperfect, so I can't see where we are on the map in my not-quite-awake brain. Arriving at the last stop on the bus line means we slept through the stop at Birmingham. That much I've put together.

"How far are we from London?"

"About three hours," he answers.

I pull out my phone to check the time and our location, but it's completely dead. Great. I scratch my head. It's itchy from getting my hair wet in the rain last night. I throw it all up in a messy bun with the tie around my wrist. Henry keeps chuckling as he folds the blanket and stuffs it in his backpack.

"Tell me again how this is funny?" (I'm super not a morning person.)

He glances sideways at me. "It's serendipitous."

"What is?"

"Come on, you'll see."

∴

Once we've located the bus station bathrooms, we go separate directions.

The ladies' room door swings shut behind me and I set my backpack on the sink. I splash water on my face and brush my teeth. It would've been so much nicer to wake up in a bed and breakfast this morning. To take a real shower. But then I remember the weird chemistry with Henry and the tarot card dream, so I backspace that thought in my head.

Once I brush my hair and redo the messy bun, I pull my change of clothes out of the pack and step inside a stall. I quickly change into the dress I brought: the one I wore the night at the Crow. The mascara came out in the wash and now it's good as new. I shove my dirty clothes and rain boots inside the pack and pull out the flip-flops I brought. The nail polish on my toes is badly chipped now, but whatever. It feels good to have my feet out of those boots.

Henry's waiting for me outside the bathroom, fresh-faced, with two coffees in his hand. He gives me a once-over and hands me a cup. "Feel better?"

I nod. "Much. Thanks."

"Let's go." He heads toward the exit. I follow a few strides behind, looking for signs, trying to get my bearings.

"We're not going to find another bus?"

He glances back over his shoulder. "Not yet." He motions for me to follow him as he pushes the glass door open. We step out into the foggy morning air. There's a sense of otherness hanging in the breeze. We veer off the sidewalk and climb a hill. The flip-flops don't have the same grip as the boots, and my knees go unsteady. Dew dampens the bottoms of my feet and I slide. I squeeze my toes together to keep the shoes on.

"Where are we going?"

He smiles over his shoulder at me. That smile. "The first ley line I ever discovered, the first time the magnets worked for me away from home, it was here."

I try not to let myself hope. Not after last night. "They react as strongly as they did at the graveyard?"

He nods. "Stronger." He reaches into his pocket and pulls out his phone. His pace slows as he scrolls the screen and I catch up to his side.

"How do you still have a charge? My phone's dead."

"External battery. Here." He puts his phone in my hand.

"Remember how I said I still text my mother? This is the first one I ever sent her. After."

I scan the screen. It's dated two years ago.

Remember that time we talked about King Arthur? The way they destroyed his bones and left no trace of him? People can't be erased, you said. His soul is still there on Avalon. Like magic.

Science tells us matter can't be created or destroyed. If souls are matter, then they can't be either. So where do they go? Let's find out. Meet me there. On Avalon.

He studies me, a shy look I've never seen before, then puts his phone back in his pocket.

"I always come here thinking she'll be waiting. Much like people come here to unearth King Arthur, summon his spirit, or what have you."

The land flattens and we step through a wooden gate. A winding path of stepping-stones climbs upward. With the way the fog hangs, hazy and dream-like as it obscures visibility, it feels like we're ascending into the clouds. My skin tingles as we walk through the mist.

"This is kind of trippy."

He laughs a little and looks down at me. "You feel it, right?"

The way he looks—hope glistening behind dark-rimmed eyes, messy hair surrounded by a halo of lavender in the subdued morning sunlight—knocks the breath out of me. I feel something all right. As we scale the hilltop, the remnants of fog burn off and clear.

On the horizon, a tall tower stands against the clouds. The hillside rolls in shades of green. It's déjà vu. The scariest one yet.

"What's wrong?"

I shake my head and try to stay calm. "Nothing. Just. This place feels familiar."

He nods. "You've seen Glastonbury Tor before?"

"In dreams?"

"Yes, of course," he says, like he already knows.

The sun rises higher in the east, painting the surface of everything in pearly gold. We take the path all the way up. I get dizzier with each foot of altitude, terrified of what I'll find when we get to the top. We stop at the base of the tower: a lumbering stack of ancient bricks. They climb the morning sky like a wild, mortar-laced vine.

Henry sinks to a squat and sets the magnets on the ground, far apart from one another. I watch as one wiggles, then the other. In the space of a snap, they fly together—negative end on negative end.

Henry looks up at me, smiling with his whole face. "See?"

He moves them further apart. It happens again. "This only happens on ley lines. And it only happens this strongly at one other place."

"Where?" I watch in awe as he moves them further and further apart still, even as the magnets continue to interact and find each other. Sinking to the cool concrete, I pull the atlas out of my pack and study the lines.

He presses his lips together for a moment. "Did you notice the leys in London?"

I glance up at him and shake my head. "I really haven't looked at the maps outside Liverpool yet." But he has to be asking for a reason, so I flip over to the London map. There are several cross sections around the River Thames.

He leans over, shoulder touching mine, and points to a spot. "There."

It takes a minute to settle in. "The Fox Den is on a ley line?"

He nods. "Mum bought the property for that reason. She believed it'd draw people there. That it'd mean inevitable success. She was right about the first part; wrong about the second. It used to be called Ley Line Records. My dad changed the name after she passed."

"Why?"

"Ley lines are excellent communication conduits. Business models, not so much. Especially for a record store in the age of digital music. It's the only other place the magnets react this strongly, though. At least for me."

We're quiet for a while, sharing oxygen and studying the atlas.

"Wait. Why didn't you tell me this before? Couldn't you have shown me what the magnets do that night in the darkroom?"

He grins. "Yes. But I worried you'd think I was some sort of head case."

My eyes narrow. "Really? You watched me puke in a trashcan that night. On a very public sidewalk."

"It was a dainty puke. Not like a full-on man puke, if it makes you feel better."

I smile. "It does. Somewhat."

More silence.

"Okay fine. Then why couldn't you have shown me the other night? In Patrick's room? After I texted you about it, I mean."

"Because," he offers me a sheepish grin, "that was my excuse to tag along on this trip."

For the first time, his aura sizzles red around the edges. It makes my stomach do somersaults. His eyes are so sincere. So intense. His lips part, ever so slightly, and they look like they were designed with kissing in mind. I stand before I can entertain the thought any longer.

"I should tell you," he continues. "I was conducting an experiment that night. With the mugwort tea." He rubs the side of his face and looks away. "It's great for hangovers, of course, but I wanted to see if lucid dreaming on a ley line created a conduit of communication. A sort of telepathic link. I wanted to see if I could send you a message."

My heart leaps in my chest. Oh my God. *The dream.* Sweat erupts on my palms. I wipe them on the back of my dress. He watches me carefully and I do my best not to react.

After a long moment, he says, "But I don't think it worked."

My heart is hammering now, ninety miles a minute. I decide to be bold. "How do you know? What was the message?"

He smiles and it's inexplicably sad. "That I want to help you find your father."

A sinking feeling settles over me, and I can't tell if I'm grateful or disappointed.

CHAPTER

THIRTY-SIX

: Fool on the Hill :

WE SPEND THE morning wandering around the tower and testing the magnets at different spots, keeping our distance from the crowds of tourists.

He outlines the theoretic principle that could explain why the magnets behave differently in certain places: the Faraday effect. I feel dense trying to wrap my head around it, even though he breaks it down in the simplest possible terms.

The view below us is spectacular. Various shades of green spread out like a patchwork quilt over the countryside. When we finally find a place to rest, it feels like we're sitting on top of the world.

"You want me to lay the blanket out?"

"No!" I protest. With an exclamation point.

He looks at me funny. "Okay."

I change the subject. "I wish my phone battery wasn't dead so I could take pictures."

Henry lifts his hips and pulls his phone from his back pocket. He presses the camera icon and puts it in selfie mode. I squint into the glare on the screen as he scoots closer to me, until his shoulder touches mine. He lifts the phone at an angle and snaps a picture.

"I'll text some to you," he says, standing and stretching his long legs. He pulls a tiny lens attachment out of his bag and puts it on the viewfinder of his phone.

"The lighting is perfect today," I say as he snaps panoramic pictures of the hillside and the town below.

"Mmm," he agrees.

I sit up on my knees and tuck my feet beneath me, lacing my fingers through the little white flowers that spring up through the short blades of grass. The ground is sunbaked now, all of the morning dew sipped away. When I glance up, he's got the lens pointed at me. He smiles, and I catch it like something contagious. A soaring feeling churns inside my chest, a familiar and terrifying one.

"So you've tried to contact your mother here?"

After tucking his phone away, Henry sits down again and leans back on his hands.

"Tried. Yes. I came over on a whim a couple of winters ago."

"What happened?"

"Well, it was snowing, and there were warning signs posted because things were slippery. I ignored them. Scaled the hill on my own. There wasn't a soul around." He tilts his head back like he's remembering, then he looks over at me. "I was sitting right here on the fresh powder. Talking to both of them." He shifts his weight to one arm—the one closest to me—and points at the sky, drawing an invisible circle with his finger. "Then something shifted up there. It was probably just a reflection in the snow flurries. But the more it flickered, the more convinced I became that it meant something. I stood up and reached for it." He drops his hand. "For a moment, it looked like I could climb right into the shimmery disc. But it was out of reach. And the harder I concentrated on touching it, the smaller it got. Until it eventually disappeared altogether."

I imagine him, standing alone in the snow, reaching for something that may not have even been there. I would've done the same thing.

"I had something extraordinary at the tip of my fingers. Possible proof of... *something*. But I left empty-handed. There was no conversation, no proof, no earth-shattering discovery. Just more questions."

"You're describing everything I've felt over the past few weeks. All the excitement and hope that just led to heartbreaking disappointment." He nods. I'm suddenly convinced that nobody on earth has ever experienced this kind of pain except us. The connection between us feels stronger by the minute, and I don't know what to do with my feelings. My pulse hammers in my chest, my knees, my scalp.

"That's not even the worst part." I watch his lips as he talks. "There was a fresh layer of snow by the time I left. I couldn't remember where the path was because my footprints were covered, so I made a best guess. I guessed wrong. My foot slipped and I tumbled all the way down." I gasp, peering down the hill into town, and become instantly woozy at the thought of a fall like that. He motions below. "I finally stopped tumbling when I got to that patch of trees just there. I lay there for a while, on my stomach, certain I was badly injured. But nothing was broken except my glasses. That wouldn't have been too bad, except when I stood up, a piece of one of the shattered lenses was sticking straight out of my chest." He puts his hand on his chest, above his left pec. "Impaled me."

"That's where you got the scar." It's out of my mouth before I can stop it.

His eyes widen. "How did you..."

I fight as hard as I can against temptation and lie backwards against the grassy hill, breaking eye contact. "How did you get help?"

He's quiet for a while. I feel him staring at me, but I just lie there and burn.

"I hobbled into town, bloody and bruised. An old lady gave me a lift to the health centre, where they removed the shard, sewed me up, and gave me painkillers. My dad freaked out completely when I got home. He assumed I'd been in some pub brawl since it was nearly three in the morning by then."

"You don't really strike me as a pub brawler." I glance over at him. He smiles.

"I did punch Mons once. Or twice."

"He probably deserved it."

We both laugh, and it's a relief.

Birds chitter in the distance, and the breeze blows grass around us in a way that makes each blade look like lit candles in the sunbeams. If there's any place on earth that could lead to another dimension, a multiverse, a series of parallel universes, I'd have trouble believing that it's anywhere but here. That giddy feeling rises up inside me again, electricity on my skin, exploding colors all around.

"If you could say anything to them now, what would it be?"

It takes him a moment to respond. "I'd tell them I'm buried under the questions they left behind, and I wish things had been different." He pauses. "What would you say to your dad?"

I blow out a shaky breath. "Pretty much the same thing."

The clouds above us shift and change. I concentrate on their movement, on the sound of his breathing. The energy between us, all around us, is palpable.

"I haven't been the same since he died. Mentally, I mean. I've been on and off medications, in and out of therapy. Nothing makes it better."

It feels good to say this aloud to someone.

"It was the same for me. For a long time."

His admission makes me feel more accepted than I've felt maybe ever. We're quiet for a few moments. I concentrate on my breathing, calming little by little.

"How'd you know about my scar?"

The adrenalin roars to life again. "Your what?"

He shifts onto his side, facing me, and props his head in his hand. "C'mon, Jo. You heard me."

A low hum emanates from the top of my head and trickles down until it's in the tips of my fingers, my toes, my lips. I feel as though I could stand and leap onto the wind. Effortlessly fly the distance back to London.

"I noticed it," I say, in a voice that's meant to be chill, but is decidedly not. "That night in the bathroom." I turn on my side and mirror his position. So close that I can feel every molecule in my body buzzing.

"Really? We were only in there for like five seconds before you practically barreled through the wall to escape."

"I did not."

"You did!" He laughs. "You ran off like you'd never seen a half-naked man before."

I narrow my eyes. "I've seen plenty of half-naked men." The blood drains from my face when I realize what I've said. "I mean, not like that, but—"

He cracks up laughing and I shove him. As he goes backwards, he grabs my arm and pulls me with him. We roll a few times down the slope of the hill, laughing and squealing, until he digs his heels in and we come to a stop. I don't know if I control the moment or if the moment controls me, but I sit up and swing a leg over his hips. My knees dig into the grass, and my hands splay over his chest. A steady staccato thumps under my fingers. Neither of us moves. The memory of the dream sizzles around the edge of reality. Things begin to shift. Henry's Adam's apple slides up and down.

Before I can blink, we're two magnets flipping end over end to meet at our mouths.

His fingers press little dots of pressure into my hips, through the fabric of my dress. His hair is soft in my hands, just like I knew it would be. I'm terrified by how good it feels. Whatever I did before—that wasn't kissing. *This* is kissing. It's like the dream, but better because it's real. And I want more of it. I want all of it. I want every sensation from the dream, and I know I won't be satisfied until I have it all. I slide my hands under his shirt, searching for the scar.

But then suddenly, his grip on me loosens. He grabs my wrists and pulls them out of his shirt.

"Jo," he breathes against my lips, rolling me over onto my back. He pulls away and looks down at me. "We... we really shouldn't."

It takes me a moment, but I slide out from under him and sit up. He studies me, eyes hazy and cautious. I'm so horrified that he stopped me, I can't speak or breathe.

"It's just that," he starts again, fidgeting with his hands. He won't look at me. "You and me, we're... I can't... You're just..."

The rejection stings. It more than stings. It guts me. I've told him things that I've never told anyone. I've let him in. Worn my crazy for him like a technicolor dream-coat. And he doesn't even have to finish his sentence for me to know that's precisely why. People like me can't be honest about who we are. There's too much risk. My humiliation morphs into anger, like some shape-shifting monster from an Arthurian legend.

"I'm just imagining things? Is that what you're going to say?" I narrow my eyes at him, trying to keep any hint of tears inside. He looks up.

"No, that's not—"

"You've flirted with me this entire trip. Been Mr. Perfect and acted like you care or something. And now you're insinuating I'm some silly girl with a crush because I kissed you? I have a boyfriend, Henry!" The guilt of that last thing occurs to me for the first time.

"—not it at all..."

Henry's aura darkens as he stands. He rubs his hands on the hips of his jeans, less composed than usual. "I do care."

I stand and brush the grass off my dress, trying not to cry. "All these years since my father died, I've taken people for granted. I would've traded my connections with all of them for even one more conversation with Pop. Dylan. Lexie and Maddie. Maybe even my mom. But this?" I point between Henry and me. "This connection felt like something different. Am I wrong?"

"It's just that I don't want you to do something you'll regret later," Henry says quietly. Notably not answering my question. He's pushing me away the way I've pushed away everyone else. Poetic justice, perhaps. His expression is clouded, his forehead tensed.

"What does it matter? I regret everything I do, eventually. What's one more thing? Everything I touch, I ruin. Every relationship in my life. It's what I do."

"Don't say that." He sighs and steps closer to me. "It isn't true."

I take a step back, eyes stinging. "It is true! The only person I've even tried to repair my relationship with is my father. *After* he was dead. And I ruined that, too! I dropped his urn in the Thames."

Henry opens his mouth to say something, but it just hangs there in shock.

I laugh as a tear rolls down my cheek. "Yep. I sure did. That night in the alley? When I was soaking wet and wrapped in a towel? I accidentally dropped it in the river near Tower Bridge. I tried to jump in after it and almost drowned. It's gone now."

He stares at me helplessly as I zip my backpack and throw it over my shoulders.

I know better than to do the things I do sometimes, but I can't seem to stop myself. Ever since Pop died, I've made one bad decision after the next. I think maybe I've been waiting for him to come back and save me. But now I know he isn't going to.

"Forget it," I say, brushing past him. "Let's go."

CHAPTER
THIRTY-SEVEN

: Get Back :

WE SIT TOGETHER on the bus back to London, but Henry keeps his AirPods in and doesn't speak.

I power on my phone for a distraction. I was able to charge it at the bus station for half an hour before we boarded: 23% probably won't last until we get back. As soon as the home screen appears, the notifications start. It's an unending series of dings that makes Henry stir and look over.

Fifty-one missed texts, most of them from Dylan—all some variation of *I'm worried about you* and *Why won't you talk to me*. I can't process my feelings about it because my guilt is mudding it up. As I scroll, the phone rings in my hand. I jump and try to silence it, but accidentally answer instead. I hang up as soon as I realize what I've done.

It rings again immediately. But I send it to voicemail and turn the ringer off.

What?!

I switch to Instagram and search for Henry's page, careful not to let him see my screen. Not that he's paying attention. He fixes his stare out the window. I didn't follow him before because I didn't want him to know I was looking at his page.

I click on it, and there they are: pictures of the trip. I scroll. There's a picture of the Eleanor Rigby headstone in the dark. The Paul McCartney mural on the bus station wall that I sent to him. Storm clouds sitting over the city of Liverpool like a shelf. But then there are three pictures with me in them.

First is the picture of us that we took when we left The Dovey. We're smiling from ear to ear, like we're not pretending to be friends at all. We're actually friends.

The next is of us at Strawberry Field. Dylan doesn't know we almost kissed there, but I do, and it's written on both of our faces in the picture. Under the umbrella with the rain misting around us.

The post is only an hour old, according to the time stamp. He must've posted it while we waited at the bus station.

I wasn't wrong. He feels it, too. But for whatever reason, he's resisting.

The last picture is the one of me on my knees in the grass at Glastonbury. My hands are entrenched in the flowers, my hair flyaways are blowing in the breeze, and the sunlight illuminates a telling smile. My stomach twists.

I have a secret hate for selfies, because they never look like the me I see inside my head. I have to edit them like the rough drafts they are with whatever editing software I have before I find them remotely acceptable. This picture, though—the one Henry took—is me.

She's a girl who is sad. She's been weighed down so excruciatingly that she's lost her way, forgotten who she is. In this moment, though, she's beginning to remember. The light in her eyes and the expression on her face indicate obvious things, things she's known a long time but hasn't acknowledged until this trip.

Her father is dead.

Her determination is alive.

And her relationship with her boyfriend is over.

CHAPTER

THIRTY-EIGHT

: Run for Your Life :

THE SUN HIDES like a sulking child when our bus stops on
Blackfriar Road.

I've had three hours to think about what I would say to
Henry when he removed the AirPods from his ears, but I aban-
don all the planned rehearsals in my head and go for a safer, "I
guess it's been raining here."

Nothing like breaking your own small talk rules. He nods
his head and gives me a half-hearted *yeah* in response. We walk
toward the side street of Fox Den, feet tapping the puddles as we
go. I stand back as he unlocks the alley-entrance door and we
step into the quiet. Felix rouses from the landing on the stairs as
we pass him, and he follows behind Henry's feet. We part ways
in the hallway outside our rooms with mumbled *see you laters*.

I close myself into the solitude of Patrick's room.

On the bed, a cherry-apple red Samsonite covered in sewn-
on patches awaits. It smells like an airport. I open my texts.
There are messages from Lexie and Maddie waiting, but none
from Dylan. It gives me a cold feeling, like I'm already sensing
the void where he won't be soon.

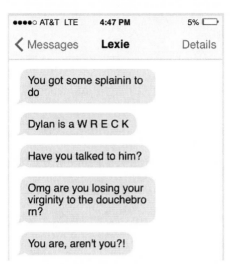

I feel guilty every time she makes some reference to virginity. I'm not sure why I didn't tell her about Dylan and me. She'd be so upset if she knew I kept that from her. But when I think about telling someone, all I feel is shame. I flip over and read Maddie's texts.

I don't answer either of them, because what can I say? Neither of them know even the most basic details about my relationship with Dylan. Instead of keeping them in the loop, I shut them out, even when I was home. Dylan talks to them more than I do now. They hear his side before they hear mine. Who knows if my life at home will even look the same when I get back.

I switch over to another text thread and send one of my own.

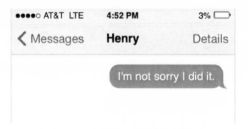

●●●●○ AT&T LTE   4:52 PM   3% ⬜

❮ Messages   **Henry**   Details

I'm not sorry I did it.

I'm tired of dancing around things. Maybe I can do things the right way with him, the way I failed to do with everyone else. Maybe if I'm honest, things will be okay. I stare at the screen for a long while, heart in my throat, but Henry doesn't respond.

To kill time, I unzip and unpack my vagabond suitcase. It spent weeks traveling to exotic destinations without me. Once it's empty of my clothes and shoes, I put the plastic bag of my medication on the dresser and then unzip the last inside pouch. One glance at the contents makes my body go cold.

There, in a small pink box, are the tampons I should've needed a while ago. Warm saliva pools in my mouth. Math has never been my strong suit, but I do it furiously in my head now. I count on my trembling fingers. I'm not just a little bit late.

I'm a lot late.

The last time Dylan and I were together was the Sunday before I left for London. We were in his room on his tidy bed that his mother still makes for him every morning. His parents were golfing with friends, so we had the house to ourselves. I was trying to take a nap, exhausted from a morning hike in Pisgah, but he was interested in other things. He took my shoes and socks off, then moved up to my waist and undressed me.

I let it happen more than anything, because sometimes that's easier. He didn't seem to care that I was on the edge of sleep the whole time. I think he used protection. I think. Sometimes I have to remind him, but he's usually pretty responsible. Thinking back on it now, though, I can't be sure.

Dread bubbles up at the back of my throat. I run for the bathroom and fall on my knees in front of the toilet.

I barely make it in time.

CHAPTER

THIRTY-NINE

: I'll Cry Instead :

I GET UP early Monday morning and go for a walk through the quiet pre-dawn streets, three blocks over to the drug store.

Do I feel different? I slip a hand over my stomach and press down. Is there a bump? I don't think so, but I've never been pregnant before, so I have no idea how it's supposed to feel. Other than the fibers of my shirt, I feel nothing.

On aisle 13 (of course it's aisle 13), I find what I'm looking for. The box is oblong and hot pink, about as subtle as a car horn. They're buy one, get one free. Why not, I guess.

The cashier eyeballs me, judgy-pants as hell, while she rings it up.

Before I make it back to the Fox Den, a light rain begins. I think back to that line in Pop's letter. *We'll forget our umbrellas on purpose.* It was a stupid line and it makes me angry. There's nothing special about rain. It's a scientific process. Henry could explain it in lofty terms that might make it sound magical, but it isn't. It's just recycled water.

I sneak inside the alley door, after struggling with the handle again. George steps out into the hallway as I start up the stairs. His eyes widen. I tuck the bag under my arms so he doesn't see the bright pink box.

"Are you all right, love?"

I shake my head and avoid eye contact. "I'm not feeling well. Girl stuff."

He shifts uneasily. That's the quickest way to get a man to stop asking you questions.

"Why don't you skip your shift today and rest, then?"

I give him a grateful nod and move past him. "Thanks."

It's chicken, I know. But I might finally lose it completely if I have to address this complicated situation with Henry today. Or not address it—which is how things tend to go with us. He never even responded to my text.

· · ·

I stare at the box for a long time before I get the nerve to open it.

One line is negative. Two is positive.

I follow the directions and then sink to the sterile chill of the bathroom floor. I stare a laser beam into the results window, waiting. One little pink line begins to populate the tiny square. I hold my breath. Suddenly a blast of music roars in my back pocket.

I grab the phone and silence Dylan's call. What would he do if he knew what I was doing at this very moment?

Just the thought of him sitting at home in his comfortable little world, with two parents who are present, completely oblivious to the hell I'm in right now—it makes me churn with rage. If there's a baby in there, it's a rage baby. How could he have been so reckless? And then it hits me... how could *I* have been?

If I'd told him how he was making me feel when I first started feeling that way, that last time would've never even happened. I should've had the guts to be honest and break up with him. What's more, I should've had the guts to tell him the first time was the only time instead of allowing myself to be guilt-tripped into a physical relationship I didn't want and wasn't ready for in the first place. Maybe we would've had a chance if I'd just found the courage to be honest.

I go into settings and change his ringtone to *Nowhere Man* while I wait on results.

One line is clearly visible now. I don't know how long it's been, but I stare at it, praying a second line doesn't appear. I'm frozen, just watching.

The second line never appears.

Relief washes over me, but I can't stop shaking. I start to cry. I cry when I'm happy, I cry when I'm sad. I cry when I'm angry. Maybe this is my default now. Another seal broken.

Google says that it's likely the sudden discontinuation of medication—and the weight loss coinciding with it—that sent my cycle haywire. Once again, my meds are to blame for my psychological spiral.

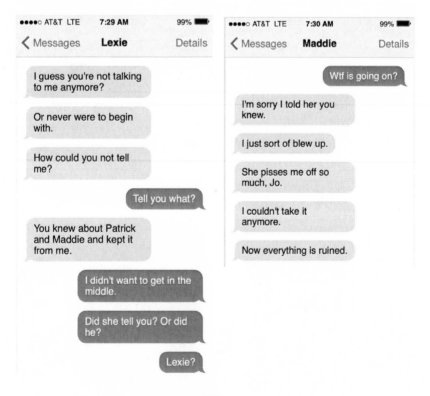

Any chance you'd want to come home early? I've done something rather despicable and might have to cut my trip short.

I don't even know what to say right now.

I'm really sorry.

CHAPTER

FORTY

: Nowhere Man :

IT'S MIDNIGHT BEFORE I get the courage to call Dylan.

He answers on the first ring, but he doesn't say hello. Just, "What?"

Well then. "Hey."

"Do you want to FaceTime?"

"Not really."

He stays quiet for a moment. "Okay."

"Things haven't been the best lately," I finally say.

"Understatement." Hurt quivers in his voice and it almost makes me chicken out. Almost.

"I think we should break up."

His breath whooshes into the speaker. "What?"

"You're surprised?"

"Don't make this decision right now. You aren't yourself."

I start to argue with him, but then stop. Am I myself? I can't tell anymore.

"You were off your meds. Give it time to feel like yourself again and—"

"That's just it, Dylan. You don't get to say when I am or am not myself." And I'm still off my meds, for his information. Or rather, *not* for his information.

"Why don't I? I know you better than anyone." The assumption in his tone rings haughty. Controlling. But above all, misinformed. Somewhere deep inside, something snaps.

"You don't know me as well as you think you do."

"Don't do this over the phone."

My voice cracks. "It can't wait. I hate the way you've been since I got here."

"Oh, you hate that I miss talking to you? You hate that it upsets me when you don't have any time for me? You hate that I don't like to see you with some other dude? I see all these pictures show up on his social media of you. What am I supposed to think? You think it's unreasonable for me to be upset?"

I swallow. He's right. "It isn't unreasonable. But it's not that. I can't confide in you. When I try, you tell me that my feelings are wrong."

He breathes on the line for a minute. "Well then give me a chance to be better. I'll try harder."

I pick a spot on the ceiling and stare at it, gathering my wits to tell him about the pregnancy scare. That's all it took, really, for me to know this is the right thing to do. The thought of being permanently attached to him in that way made me realize I don't want to be attached to him at all.

"We're being tested. Long distance is hard."

"But long distance isn't the reason—"

"Trust me," he interrupts. "You'll be glad we gave it another chance when you're feeling like yourself again."

This. This is why I know I won't be glad. Maybe it's cruel, but I know what will change his mind for good.

"I kissed him."

He doesn't say anything for a long time. I barely hear him breathing.

"The guy you told me you don't even like?"

We are silent for a few long moments.

"You're going to need me. You'll wish I was still here." There's a long pause and then a click. The line goes dead.

I toss my phone on the desk and flip the light out. *No, Dylan. I won't.*

· · ·

My eyes are wet.

I clutch a blue notebook binder against my chest, heart thudding against the smooth surface. Henry towers over me. There's a fading yellow bruise around his left eye.

"Will you come some place with me?" It sounds far away, even though the vibrations of his words swim through my veins like a tranquilizer.

"Two hours. That's it."

My fingers uncurl around the binder in slow motion. Before I can look down and see what's inside, my eyes snap open in the dark.

Rain putters against the window in Patrick's room. Henry isn't here. It's just me.

Alone.

CHAPTER

FORTY-ONE

: I Want to Tell You :

ON TUESDAY MORNING, I take the other test. It's negative.

It gives me a sense of finality and relief, so I put on my big girl pants and head down to the store for my shift. I'm surprised to find that Henry isn't there. George is sitting behind the counter.

"Where's Henry?"

He smiles. "Moping."

"Moping?"

"Yes, well. Technically he's off mudlarking with Sanjay, but I suspect he's still moping."

I don't ask why he's moping, and I refuse to let myself hope it's because of me. Before I can ask what mudlarking is, George sidetracks me.

"Do you think you can handle helping him open and close the store for the rest of the week? I have to go away and sort some things out for our vendor spot at the Boomtown Festival in the fall. I'll be back this weekend."

I stare at him. What am I supposed to say? *No, please don't leave me here alone with him?*

"Of course we can handle it." I give him my best smile. I guess we'll do what we've been doing: ignoring each other.

He beams. "I have some things to take care of in the office this afternoon. I won't leave until he gets back."

I nod as he stands from his spot and goes into his office.

Instead of obsessing about the coming forced proximity, I spend the day helping customers and doing whatever busy work will distract me. Today, that means being extremely creative since the inventory crew left things pristine. Once I've cleaned the glass on the listening stations, swept the floor, and pounced on every customer in an overzealous car salesman way, I go in search of more busy work.

I'm re-sorting albums when Henry jogs down the stairs. I never even heard him come in.

My heart plunks down, through my feet, through the floor, all the way to the earth's mantle at the sight of him. Dark jeans. Blue Henley. His hair is damp as if he's just showered. He pulls out the counter stool and plops down, flipping through the pages of the inventory report. I'm halfway across the store, but I swear I smell his soap. He glances up at me over the rim of his glasses. I look away quickly and stumble into an endcap.

How did I ever function around him before?

A few minutes later, as I'm dusting shelves for the hundredth time, George emerges from his office with a rolling suitcase.

"I'll have my cell if you need anything," he tells us. "Behave yourselves." He points at Henry when he says this, but Henry ignores him. I wave to him as he disappears into the hallway. The back door shuts behind him with a thud that shakes the building.

After that, the quiet becomes deafening.

I spend the rest of the afternoon re-alphabetizing the punk rock section. It's already pretty alphabetized, though, so that only consists of me finding a misplaced Gorillas album between The Chefs and Chaotic Discord, and putting it back in the correct section.

Ten minutes before close, I'm out of things to do, so I close myself inside a listening station at the front of the store. I pull the folded green flyer from Saint Catherine's out of my back pocket, where it's been since I put it there.

I haven't been able to stop thinking about what it would be like to take a photography class and extend my time in London for the remainder of the summer. Not that everything is going swimmingly here or anything, but I'm also in no hurry to get home. Nothing waits for me there but drama.

I google neighborhoods near Saint Catherine's and think about where I'd even stay if I did the workshop. With Patrick ready to come home now, it's not like I can ask him to come back to London and sleep on the couch in his own house. I'd have to find someplace else. I could use the rest of my cash to stay in a hostel, maybe. Or a cheap hotel.

As I'm checking the area for accommodations, a text dings in my hand. My heart skips a beat when I read it.

The ludicrousness of texting him from the same room—the empty room we're alone in—isn't lost on me. But he's talking to me again, so I'm not complaining.

I open the door to the listening station and walk over to him. His expression loosens with every step I take towards him. I stop on the opposite side of the sales counter. We stare for a moment. He doesn't say *I'm a dick for not responding to your text the other day*. And I don't say *Yes, you sure are*. Not out loud, anyway.

I hand him the flyer. My heart won't stop beating itself bloody in my chest. If I can barely get through wordless conversations like this, we can never, ever speak of what happened at Glastonbury.

He peers at me through his lashes. "This is a good opportunity."

"I have to leave before it starts, though. My mom probably wouldn't let me stay longer. And Patrick will be home by then, anyway, so I won't have a place—"

He cuts me off. "You could stay in my room."

My eyebrows shoot into orbit.

"I won't be here then," he quickly adds. "I'm moving back to Bristol after Patrick gets back. My classes start in a couple of weeks."

Though I'm floored by his offer, I'm still a little doubtful I could make it work.

"I only have my cell phone camera," I say. "So I'd have to buy a camera. And I wouldn't really even know what I'm doing."

He smiles. "That's the point of taking a class, love. To learn."

I balk at the softness in his voice. *Love?*

"I guess I just hate being the only person in the room with no talent."

"You have talent. I've seen your shots."

I shrug. He studies me for a moment, like he's deciding something. "I have an extra camera. Let's close up shop here and go shoot some stuff. If you want to."

All the moisture in my mouth evaporates. "Actually, I was going to check in with Nigel this evening and see if he and Walter can meet."

"Oh." Henry's face falls.

I weigh my options. Which would I rather do? Take pictures with Henry? Or go sit in a puddle of my own snot and tears and talk about my dead dad? It's not like Nigel ever bothered to call me back.

"You know what?" I amend. "That can wait until tomorrow."

A smile dawns over his face. "Brilliant. I know exactly where we can go."

CHAPTER

FORTY-TWO

: What You're Doing :

THE FANCY NIKON hanging on a strap around my neck swings back and forth as I leave my bus seat.

I grab it and press it against my middle as I move. It's pre-loaded with 35mm film and a bulky zoom lens. When the bus doors swish open and I see our destination, in all its legendary glory, my eyes well up with tears.

Abbey Road Studios sits in an unassuming white building, trimmed in gray. Just down the street from it, the zebra-like crosswalk where the famous album cover was taken winks at me through beams of sunlight. Tourists take turns walking the length of the crosswalk, snapping photos of each other with their cell phones.

We disembark and I glance up at Henry. "Why here?"

He grins like he's very proud of himself. "Two reasons, really. First, because look at how perfect the evening light is here. And second, because there's an abundance of people. Watch and learn." With that, he saunters over to the crosswalk and gets the attention of a lady who is just about to snap a picture of her husband.

"Pardon me, ma'am." He gives her his dimpled, winning smile—the one that could hush crying babies and usher in world peace. "My friend and I are taking photographs for a project. Would it be all right if we took yours crossing the street here? We'd be happy to give you a print once the film is developed."

"Oh," she giggles, a little flustered. "That's so nice of you! Did you hear that, honey? This nice young man wants to take our picture." Her deep south accent gives her away. Georgia. Maybe Alabama.

"Actually" —Henry points over his shoulder at me— "she's going to take it."

On the bus ride over, he gave me a crash course in how to use the older camera, along with the science behind how it works. There's no digital screen preview, only a viewfinder where I'll snap the photo once I'm satisfied with what I see.

Henry makes suggestions for where they should stand, and I pull the camera to my eye and move quickly to get an angle that's similar to the album cover. I snap a few pictures, rewinding the film after each click.

"Slow it down," Henry says over his shoulder. "I won't let any cars bowl you over."

I laugh a little and take a deep breath, watching the way the older couple interacts. He's doing it all for her benefit. If I had to guess, based on his protruding gut and orthopedic shoes, he'd much rather be sitting at home in his recliner watching Antiques Roadshow. The lady is giddy, though. Full of herself. This trip was clearly her idea.

Some of the people on the surrounding sidewalks stop to watch.

When I'm satisfied that at least one picture will be acceptable, Henry motions them over and writes something on a Fox Den business card from his wallet. "Come by tomorrow and pick up your photo," he says.

"You sure there's no charge?" the husband asks, crotchety as I suspected.

"None at all." Henry smiles again to reassure him.

Our evening proceeds this way, recruiting willing volunteers. Some uni students give us enthusiastic poses. A family visiting from Japan does, too. On this goes until the street grows too dim under the shadow of the trees to take any more satisfactory photos without a flash. (Flash photography is a lesson for another day, Henry tells me.)

While we wait for the bus, we stroll back down Abbey Road together, where the last sliver of daylight is projected on the front steps of the old studio. The angle of light is so beautiful that I don't want to miss an opportunity to capture it.

"Sit on the steps," I say. "Let me get a shot while the light is good."

He hesitates at first, but then concedes without a word.

"Move to the left a little. Okay, closer to the middle. Lean forward a bit. Tilt your chin up. There." I peer through the viewfinder and click, click, click away. Forgetting everything he told me about what to look for.

I can only see him.

Before I get to the end of the roll, the bus pulls up to the stop on the sidewalk. We both scramble towards it before we get left behind. When we take our seats inside, I hand him his camera back. "That was fun. Thank you."

"Look, there's one picture left." He points to the counter on the top. He leans over the armrest, into my personal space, then turns the camera backwards and points the lens at us. I guess this is how they did selfies in the old days. "Smile," he says.

I do. And I mean it.

CHAPTER

FORTY-THREE

: I Want You (She's so Heavy) :

EMPTY PIZZA BOXES pile on the table in the darkroom.

We've spent the evening bingeing on junk food and developing the fruits of our labor. Film developer, agitator, enlarger, projection onto photo paper, developer again, stop bath, fixer.

"This is an oddly satisfying process," I say, taking a swig of Vimto, a weird soft drink that Henry swore was delicious. The jury is still out. It tastes like a raspberry burp.

Henry nods as he pulls the last photo out of the chemical fixer and hangs it on the line to dry. He mouths the words to *Octopus's Garden* as it plays from my phone on the counter.

Abbey Road is on its second rotation. Playing the album while we developed the photos from Abbey Road was 100% my idea, but he didn't exactly protest. I'm starting to think he's full of shit about not liking the Beatles. One can hope.

"So what's mudlarking?" I ask him. He looks up from where he's hanging the photos to dry. "Your dad said you were mudlarking earlier today."

He smiles. "History nerds digging through the mud."

"Oh?"

"There are lots of buried artifacts on the city's riverbanks. Sanjay started doing it because the group guide is a classmate of his." He smiles. "A girl he's keen on."

Did he also go for a girl, I wonder, or was he just there to be the wing man? I decide I don't want to know, so I focus on helping him hang photos on the line.

The first few of the older couple have a giant shadow over one side. That turned out to be my thumb. Thankfully, I moved it at some point and got one really good shot of them. Her silver hair is blowing in the breeze and she's smiling so big that it confirms her teeth are real—false ones would fall out of her mouth. Her husband is looking off to the side, bored. Fake smile. But at least he's smiling, even if his heart isn't in it.

Henry moves slowly down the line and inspects them one by one. "You really are great at capturing light," he says. "Have I told you that before?"

I grin at him through the dim red haze of the room. "You might have mentioned it."

The picture of him on the steps is my favorite. But I don't want to lurk around that one too long and give myself away. As I inspect the others, I notice a trend. In each group we photographed, for every three people looking directly at the camera, there's at least one who's looking away. Isolated. Alone. I wonder aloud to Henry why that is.

He glances sideways at me. Our elbows touch. "The short answer is that it's difficult to get people to do things in unison at precisely the same millisecond."

"And the long answer?" I don't move my arm, even though we're standing very close. To an unnecessary degree, even.

"The long answer is that we're all on different wavelengths for much of the time. Which is lonely business. If you start paying attention, you can spot it in people, but it's easier to pick out in photos."

I move down to the last photo hanging on the line.

"What about this one?" I point to the one he took of us on the bus. We're both looking directly at the camera. "Which person in this photo is lonely?"

The song changes to *I Want You (She's so Heavy)*.

His throat moves as he swallows. He glances at the photo, and then back at me. "I think you already know it's both."

The way he lowers his voice to say it rattles me.

I clear my throat. "Well, that's grim."

"Is it, though?" He turns his body to face me. "I think it's the thing that connects people. It's what makes us find comfort in each other."

A palpable tension invades our airspace. I am acutely aware of every breath I take.

The song drags its mouth over our ears.

I twirl the end of my hair in a figure eight between my fingers. His eyes follow the movement. Behind him, the usually violet aura has shifted. To lavender, then amethyst, and now— just around the edges—it's red.

It could be the red lighting of the room, but...

"I think it's why you kissed me." The words are barely audible over the electric guitar riffs swimming through the room, but I hear it loud and clear. I guess I was wrong about our unspoken agreement never to mention this. I exhale a shaky breath and roll my eyes.

"You say that like you didn't kiss me ba—"

"I did kiss you back," he interrupts, stepping closer to me. "I never claimed I didn't. That's my point."

For once, I'm speechless. My thumping heart does all the talking. We're very still. Deadlocked. Inches apart. I could kiss him right here, right now if he'd just meet me in the middle. But I don't move even a fraction of an inch, a mental chorus of *don't do it* holding me back. I don't want to be wrong about his cues again.

"But it was a mistake." No matter how hard I try to punctuate with a period, it still sounds like a question mark.

"It's just that there's a lot you don't know."

I recoil. "About kissing?"

He laughs then: a hearty, chest-deep rumble. "No, no. The kissing was…" His eyes trace an invisible line from my lashes to my lips. "The kissing was lovely. I mean there's a lot you don't know about *me*."

What an eager student I would be, though, in the classroom of Henry.

"And you have a boyfriend," he adds.

"Yeah." I peel my gaze away, wishing I could tell him I broke up with Dylan.

But I don't. For two reasons.

1. The red notes of his aura—brilliant vermillion—are multiplying by the minute (and denote romantic interest), and

2. We are in extremely close proximity. In a darkroom. With this sexy song playing like some kind of get-naked-and-make-bad-choices anthem. And I'm off my meds, so. Not a good combination.

When I look back up at him, the red halo in his aura has spilled over the violet.

This *should* make me feel happy. But instead, it makes me anxious. There's always the possibility that I'm wrong. That the darkroom lights are fooling me. That my own emotions are fooling me. That we're on different wavelengths and I'm too clueless to see it.

I won't take the risk of another first move. He's going to have do it this time.

But we stand stock still for such a long time, it becomes clear he isn't going to.

"I think I need to take a break from this." I pick up my phone and silence the music. And then slip out of the darkroom.

He doesn't stop me.

CHAPTER

FORTY-FOUR

: All Things Must Pass :

READING MY MORNING text messages gives me an anxiety jolt stronger than coffee.

●●●●○ AT&T LTE   8:09 AM   100% ▮▮▮▸

‹ Messages   **Lexie**   Details

So let me get this straight: you don't just keep secrets about my sister from me.

You also didn't bother to tell me that you and Dylan have been sleeping together?

Oh, and you broke up with him. Which you also didn't tell me.

But maybe you're telling Maddie all about it.

She has an opening for a new sister, so have at it. You two are perfect for each other.

My bottom lip splits under my teeth. I absentmindedly stroke Felix's head with one hand as I scroll through my phone with the other, tasting the metallic tang of blood. I cross and then uncross my legs, scooting against a display of records at the front of the store.

The only person who could've told her any of this is Dylan. I've never met the vindictive side of him but somehow always knew it was there. Does he get to keep my friends in this break up? I exhale in a whoosh. Mad at Patrick for coming in between my two best friends. Mad at Dylan for telling Lexie things I should've told her myself. Mad at Maddie for asking me to keep a secret and then selling me out. Mad at Lexie for not loving her sister when some people don't get to ever experience the love between siblings. Mad at Henry for having such a kissable, out-of-reach mouth. But most of all, mad at Pop. For dying and putting me in all those other situations to begin with.

"Something wrong?"

I look up. Henry eagle-eyes me from his perch behind the register.

"Yeah. Lots of drama going on back at home."

The front door opens, sweeping in a roar of street noise. I climb to my feet and join Henry behind the service counter. A group of customers enters the store and files into the classic rock section. Felix trots away to the stairs and curls into his favorite spot on the landing.

"Want to talk about it?" He leans forward onto the counter and props his chin in his hand.

I don't, but things have been weird between us since that night in the darkroom, so I'm okay with faking normalcy.

"My two best friends hate each other's guts now. Over your brother."

Henry's eyebrows shoot skyward. "Seriously?"

"They're sisters."

His eyes grow wider still. "I'm sure he's enjoying himself."

"I don't think he is."

"Oh please," says Henry. "Patrick loves being the center of attention. At any cost."

"I told him he should leave them both alone, and according to them, he has."

"Hmm." He crosses his arms. "Perhaps he's miraculously turned into somebody else, then."

I give him a look and open my mouth to ask him why he's so harsh about Patrick, but a lady steps up to the counter to check out.

"Goodness. It's so quiet in here," she says. "Don't music stores usually play music?"

Henry points to the listening stations. "You can listen to anything you like as long as it isn't cellophane-sealed."

"Oh, I know, I meant for background noise. Feels like a library."

Henry gives her a tight smile as he hands her a receipt. "Have a nice day."

"She has a point," I say as we watch her exit the store. He glances sideways at me. "I wondered the same thing when I first got here."

"Mum always said we shouldn't force our musical tastes on patrons. They should be able to listen to what they like."

I shrug. "Maybe they don't know what's good."

Henry grins.

"Kind of like you," I add.

"What, because I'm not a Beatles superfan, I have no taste?"

"Other than the offhand comment about being more of a Stones kind of guy, you've never mentioned what music you like."

"Other than the Beatles, neither have you."

"Fine, but I asked you first," I challenge.

"I never heard a question."

I roll my eyes. "Henry, what's the last song you listened to on purpose?"

"The eye roll was a nice touch." He laughs. "Really convinced me of your sincerity."

"Fine." I round the counter to the used section and thumb through a few albums. "I'll go first."

When I find the record I'm searching for, I take it to the listening station adjacent to the cash register. The record swishes as I pull it from its sleeve. I drop the needle onto the vinyl, unplug the headphones, and leave the door open.

The opening chords from *Memory Lane* play.

"This is the last song I listened to before falling asleep last night."

He rubs his jaw. "You like Elliott Smith?"

I shrug. "Sometimes."

He nods like he knows exactly what I mean. We listen to the melody, the tortured lyrics, in silent reverence. When the song ends and I lift the needle from the vinyl, Henry finally speaks.

"Such a shame somebody killed that guy."

I squint at him, puzzled. "He killed himself."

Henry shakes his head. "No, I don't think so."

"Um, yes. He stabbed himself in the heart."

This seems to ruffle him. "I know the story, thanks. But I don't believe that's what happened."

I point behind me at the stopped record. "Did we listen to the same song? The guy who wrote that song wanted to die."

Henry starts to pace behind the counter. "You don't find the whole thing is suspicious? People don't stab themselves in the heart."

"He talked about killing himself constantly."

He rounds the counter, on some kind of mission now, and changes the song to *Twilight*. It plays for a moment and he sticks a finger up in the air. "This." He points. "He was working on this album when he died. Why would he be so optimistic if he was thinking of stabbing himself—arguably one of the most painful ways to go?"

"Is it optimistic, though?" I cross my arms. "I always thought that line meant he'd rather die than lose the things he loves."

"Dying means losing those things anyway, though."

"Maybe he didn't see it that way."

Henry changes the song again, a little frustrated. "What about this last one?" When we're halfway through the song, Henry adds, "He's self-aware. He has willpower."

My neck gets hot. I'm defensive for an artist who was dead before I was even born. "I've read the articles, Henry. He had no illegal drugs in his system when he died. All prescription ones. Doctors think antidepressants are some kind of magic cure all, but they're not. So maybe he *was* murdered. By his prescriptions."

Henry stares at me like he's deciding what to say next. Finally he says, "You think his antidepressants made him do it?"

I nod. "Maybe he wanted to feel something. Maybe shoving a blade through his chest felt better than walking around numb all the time, either from the heroin or the pharmaceuticals."

"He loved heroin, though." Henry cocks his head to the side. "Referred to it as his friend."

I shrug. "Maybe he wasn't afraid of pain or numbness he thought he could control."

"I could see that." There's a subtle shift in Henry's voice. From speculation to a hollow understanding. His throat moves as defeat settles over his face. "That's how I felt when I took antidepressants. Or didn't feel, I should say. I felt nothing. But that didn't make me want to shove a blade into my chest. Twice."

The vulnerability of that statement floors me. Maybe that's what forces me to admit something aloud that I've never even admitted to myself.

"They made me feel that way, too. For a while, death seemed like it would be a relief."

His face falls and he goes silent for a moment.

"Then that wasn't the right medication for you. Just like it wasn't for me. But that doesn't mean all medication is bad, Jo."

I sense it coming: the spiel I've been hearing from Dylan and my mom for ages.

"It's cowardly," I say, flexing my jaw. "Trying to control yourself with chemicals. Prescription or otherwise."

Henry shakes his head. "Cowardice is knowing you need help, yet refusing it."

A chill spreads over me, ceiling to floor. The unspoken statement hangs between us, ugly and obvious. It's what Pop did. And maybe he's suggesting that by not taking my meds, it's what I'm also doing. Tears flare.

"Not all depression looks the same, Henry."

He flexes his jaw. "That's exactly my point."

A shrill ring makes me jump—his phone. I give myself a minute to recover from our conversation while he answers it. I reach under the cash register and slide the stack of photos we developed out and thumb through them on the counter. Most of the folks from Abbey Road came by this week to pick up their prints. Not the older couple, though. I stare at the picture and try to escape from the remnants of our conversation; half rattled, half listening to Henry's conversation.

"I can't leave this week because Dad is gone... yes... he says he has a vendor meeting." He laughs. "Yes. *Allegedly.*" He laughs again. "Sure, Saturday night. I'll be there. Of course. See you then."

My ears perk up. When he hangs up, I ask him, "You don't think George is really at a vendor meeting?"

"Uh—"

"Sorry to eavesdrop."

"Yeah. Pretty sure he's seeing the festival organizer. He doesn't want me to know about it. Thinks I can't handle him replacing my mother." As he says this, he steps over to the used records and searches till he finds one. "Now where were we? My turn, yes?" He selects one and walks it to the turntable. A guitar and piano harmony begins to play. We listen together. *It Takes A Lot to Know a Man* fills the store with its cautiously optimistic melody.

"Damien Rice?"

He nods.

I wonder if he's trying to send some sort of message with this song choice, but I just keep sorting through the photos on the counter as it plays. He steps over beside me and studies them over my shoulder.

"This one," he says, pointing to the picture of the older couple. "The light is perfect." He stares a while longer. "Only people who spend a lot of time in darkness can truly appreciate light."

I try not to read into it too much, but reading into things is one of my specialties.

"Register for the workshop," he says.

I look up at him. "I don't know if I can make it work."

He shakes his head. "Don't give me that. With a little formal training you'll be incredible. Stop putting your life on hold."

It's like he's giving me permission to pursue something I want. Shoving me in the direction I already want to go.

"Henry?"

He looks at me. "Hmm?"

"I appreciate that you don't treat me like a wilting flower."

He nods and fixes his gaze on the picture again. "Why would I? You're anything but."

I pull up my phone browser and fill out the registration form online. A few minutes later, a confirmation appears in my inbox.

CHAPTER

FORTY-FIVE

: Two of Us :

WE STEP INTO Blackfriar's Crow a little after six on Friday night.

It's a relative ghost town—only two people sit at the bar. I'd planned to come here alone, but when I told Henry where I was going, he asked if he could tag along. I didn't have the heart to tell him no. Every night this week, I've passed the time playing with a roll of practice film and doing photoshoots with Felix while Henry was off with Sanjay.

It's nice that he wants to hang out with me, and not because he's being forced to do it for work. The whole week has been a careful balancing act of working together and being friendly without crossing lines.

"What can I get you?" The bartender asks.

"We're actually here to see Nigel," Henry says. At that moment, Nigel exits the kitchen and does a double take when he sees us there.

"Oh," he says. "Hello there. So good to see you again." He smiles, but it's distant.

"Hi. You, uh—couple of weeks ago. You said to drop by, but I missed you last time."

His forehead scrunches, then relaxes as he remembers. "Of course," he says, wiping his brow with the back of his forearm. "Come on back." He heads back through the kitchen doors, a little hurriedly. I'm not sure at first that I'm supposed to follow him, but Henry nudges me forward.

"Nigel, listen, if it's not a good time…"

"Oh, nonsense." He smiles over his shoulder at me. "Just a little forgetful sometimes is all."

We meander through the kitchen, which is a buzz of movement and energy. It's a stark contrast from the deserted pub. Henry and I follow Nigel around stainless steel tables and through employee conversations as they chop vegetables and prep dough. They follow us with their stares. Nigel leads us into a small windowless room at the back of the building.

A desk piled high in disorganized paperwork sits directly across from a sofa with pillows and blankets. The space feels like a vacuum. Hollow. Devoid of joy. Once the three of us have stuffed ourselves inside, he gathers up the pillows and blankets, tosses them in the corner, and invites us to sit on the sofa.

"Sorry, I don't actually live here, though I know it looks that way. I just sleep here sometimes. Especially since I lost my wife. Don't much like going home to an empty flat." He paints on a smile. The first time I noticed Nigel's aura, it was an unassuming blue. Like the sky. Peaceful. But now it has tones of brown. Muddy. Dirtied up. Guarded. Maybe Henry was right— everyone really is lonely in some way.

He glances back and forth between Henry and me. "What can I do for you?"

I glance over at Henry. "You said we could talk."

He nods a little and leans back, crossing his arms over his chest. "Sure, sure."

"Do you know if Walter Kingsley could meet us? If not tonight, then sometime later?"

"Oh," he sighs and wrings his hands. "Oh, I'm terribly sorry, dear, but I don't know. It could be difficult to coordinate on short notice."

Sweat prickles the back of my neck, and I try not to seem too disappointed.

"What can you tell me about my pop?" I clear my throat. "Nate Bryant," I add, in case he's forgotten.

"Well," Nigel says, looking at Henry but talking to me, "Walrus Gumboot kind of put us on the map. The locals heard about them and started showing up every night they'd play. They became a real sensation in a short period of time. Tourists loved it. If they'd come up with their own stuff, they would've been bigger than Oasis. It was the early nineties, you see."

I nod along, waiting for new information, but Nigel stops there. Smiles. Almost... dismissive. I shift in my seat.

"I guess I was hoping you could tell me something about him that I don't already know? If that makes sense."

Nigel sits up straighter in his chair, uncrosses his arms, and leans forward on his desk. "I don't know what you do or don't know about him already, my dear. But I can tell you this: he loved his family. Especially you. Talked about you all the time."

It's sweet the way he says it, but it also feels like a canned response. I glance up at the walls behind him. Framed pictures make a geometric pattern around file cabinets with drawers ajar. Groups of people, some with guitars, some crowded around the bar. I squint my eyes and look for familiar faces. My heart beats a little faster as I study them.

"Is he in any of those pictures?" I point.

Nigel shakes his head. "No, I'm sorry. I don't think so. Those are fairly new."

My heart sinks. I get the feeling he doesn't want to be having this conversation with me. Maybe he's too busy to be bothered right now. Someone calls his name from the kitchen.

He stands abruptly. "Excuse me for a moment."

I stand, too. "No, look, I'm sorry. We won't keep you."

Nigel's face relaxes. His aura morphs and lightens. "So sorry, dear. Busy Friday night ahead. Come back one day next week, perhaps? We can talk then. I'll ring Walter and see when he's free."

I nod as he shows us out.

When Henry and I are on the street in front of the pub, I turn to him.

"Is it just me or was that—"

"Terribly awkward?" he finishes the thought, squinting into the sunlight.

I laugh. "Right? And he kept looking at you instead of me. Is that some kind of misogynistic English thing?"

Henry smiles, but it's tight. "I think we caught him at a bad time."

"Maybe." I shrug.

A few blocks down, we pass an ice cream shop. Henry points. "Hot day. You wanna?"

I laugh at his sarcasm as I follow him inside. "Oh yeah, practically sweltering."

July in London feels like April in Asheville.

We each order a scoop—him a cone and me a cup—and he pays for both, despite my protests. It makes me feel weird. Like this is a date or something. But it can't be. Right?

We take our ice cream to a wrought iron table outside. I sit down and he sits across from me. Two other couples sit nearby, glued together on the same side of the table.

It's settled, then. This isn't a date. We aren't sitting close enough.

"So listen," he says between licks. "There's this thing tomorrow night. For Zara's birthday. At a dance club." He rolls his eyes. "She chose the place. Anyway." He looks up at me. "Would you like to come?"

I shove a spoonful of ice cream in my face to give myself time to think. There's a definite possibility that I'm misreading this, but it feels like he's asking me out.

He clears his throat. "With me, I mean."

I swallow and give myself brain freeze. "Oh." I wince. "Sure." I try not to overthink it but *my God I am overthinking it.*

"Brilliant." He smiles. "Dance clubs are a bit miserable, so I thought it might be nice to have someone to, you know, be miserable with." He licks the cone again and leaves a little chocolate blob on his upper lip. For the briefest moment of insanity, I consider reaching over and swiping it off with my finger.

"You have some—" I point to his lip.

Redness crawls over his cheeks, and I think it's the first time I've ever seen him blush. He sticks his tongue out and licks the ice cream off his upper lip. "Did I get it?"

I nod. And giggle. God help me.

"So your boyfriend" —he wipes his mouth with a napkin for good measure— "he isn't going to have a stroke over it?"

I clear my throat. "Well, no. Because he isn't my boyfriend anymore."

Henry's eyes widen momentarily, but he recovers. "Oh? New development?"

I drag a spoon through my ice cream and draw little swirls. "Since Monday."

Behind his narrowed eyes, I imagine him mentally cataloguing our week together, counting how many times I've had the opportunity to tell him this but didn't.

"Wow," he finally says.

"Yeah. I didn't want to talk about it before."

"But you want to talk about it now?"

"Not really? I don't know." I stare down into my melting ice cream. "I made some mistakes with him that I can't take back. Everything is kind of a disaster. My friends are mad at me for it. I keep ignoring the situation, hoping it'll go away."

"That generally doesn't work."

I chuckle. "So I'm learning."

"Well if you decide you want to talk about it, I've been known to listen. Once or twice."

I risk a glance at him. "Noted."

· · ·

Later, when I fall asleep for the night, I dream again of Pop. A fond memory, rather than a premonition.

The autumn mountain sunshine turns everything golden. Though it's cool outside, sweat rolls down my forehead from the exertion. I swipe it away before it can drip into my eyes and burn them.

"Here," Pop says, handing me an extra bandana from his backpack. It's rusty red, the exact color of the leaves flaming the mountainside.

"Thanks." I tie it around my hair.

We hike through the tall brown grasses of Graveyard Fields, over manmade boardwalks covering uneven areas of the ground.

Pop points at a narrow brown trail marker ahead. "To Old Butt Knob." He snickers.

I'm almost fourteen at this point, so I'm not a little kid anymore. I'd never laugh at that in front of my friends. But out here in the wilderness with Pop, it's funny. It's okay to laugh. I giggle along with him.

I anticipate his words before he says them, because I've thought of this hike a million times since. It's our last hike together. The weekend before he leaves for London.

"I'm sorry I didn't tell you," he says.

Wait.

I stop in the shade of a twisted pine, next to the river crossing. "Sorry you didn't tell me what?"

But he keeps talking like he doesn't hear me. "I was so afraid I'd lose you. Your mother, too."

The memory bends and distorts, fiction merging with fact. I shake my head, trying to get it right in my mind. This is not how it went. He's supposed to bend down, pick up a pebble, and say *How many times do you think I can make this skip?* And I say *Definitely no more than three.* Then he laughs and yells, *You underestimate me!* And he throws it and gets an impressive five skips out of it.

But none of that happens. He grabs me by the arms, looks me dead in the eye, watery blue brimming over. The river rushes on behind him. The stone he's supposed to skip lies at his feet, untouched.

"We could've been a family, Jojo. But I fucked it up."

Everything vanishes to blackness.

I slingshot back into my skin like a crazed phantom. My eyes open to Patrick's room.

Outside, the London rain batters the window. I grab my phone off the nightstand. 3:33 a.m.

What was that? Pop didn't talk like that in front of me. Ever. Mama would've smacked him for using the f-word. I don't understand. Sorry he didn't tell me he was doing drugs again? Sorry he didn't tell me he was depressed? Sorry he couldn't feel anything, couldn't love me enough to stay? He messed it all up. That part does make sense. But the rest of it doesn't, because we were a family. Nothing can change that. I say it out loud as I close my eyes again.

"Nothing can change that, Pop. Nothing."

CHAPTER

FORTY-SIX

: Birthday :

CLUB 27 SITS across the highway from Saint Catherine's University.

When Henry and I arrive, the moon hangs above the building full and bright. A group of university students gather in a semi-circle in the front courtyard by the door, smoking cigarettes. All the girls are wearing bodycon dresses with booties or heels. Every single one.

"I'm underdressed."

"You aren't. I promise," Henry says. Easy to say when you look as dapper as he does at all times. Striped oxford, dark jeans, black peacoat. Hair tussled just so.

I shove my hands into the pockets of my blue plaid flannel dress with the sweetheart neckline—the one Mama calls my grunge gown. I always pair it with black tights and Doc Martens (all thrift store finds for under thirty bucks, thankyouverymuch). It's the warmest outfit I packed. Henry warned me that the building is an old warehouse and might be chilly.

I suffer through the introductions at the door. Henry seems to know everyone, and I hadn't considered that I would have to actually talk to other people. He introduces me as *my friend, Jo.* When we get to the guy sitting on a stool at the door, he digs into his pocket and takes out two five pound notes with Queen Elizabeth's young face on them. The door guy puts them in a little metal cash tray. I dig in my purse for my own cover fee, but Henry laughs and takes my hand. "I got yours, come on."

He pulls me in the door of the building, which is a big dark box with laser beams of light flying around the room. And it's loud.

"I'll pay you back," I sputter, not sure if he can even hear me over the thump of the music.

Henry swings around in front of me and walks backwards without letting go of my hand. The warmth and the closeness set me off-balance. He leans in close so I can hear him. "If at any point you're not having a good time, we can go. Okay?"

We can go. As in, we're here together. A unit.

I nod, unable to shake the queasiness. Dylan always paid for me when we went places together, but we were dating. Henry and I aren't—I look down at our joined hands. Oh God. This is a date.

"Look who's here!" Mons shouts as he approaches us through a stream of blue flashing light. "And holding hands!" he adds.

"Ignore him," Henry says directly into my ear as Mons arrives. He lets my hand go to give Mons a fist bump. Behind me, someone nudges my shoulder. I turn. Zara grins at me.

"Nice outfit," she shouts, pointing at my boots.

"Th-thanks." It feels weird to get a fashion compliment from someone wearing an ink-black jumpsuit and red t-strap heels. "Happy birthday!"

She leans in and hugs me. For once, it's not awkward.

"Thank you! I'm so glad you came!"

Henry turns from his conversation with Mons. He flashes Zara a grin and she steps forward and wraps her long arms around the back of his neck. I watch as he hugs her, his hands meeting along the small of her back—it's friendly, respectful.

But a zap of envy charges through me. I want to be able to hug him like that.

"I have a present for you later," Henry tells her. It's meant for only her ears, but he has to say it over the music. It feels like I'm intruding so I glance over to Mons, who is one giant eyeball focused on Zara. He watches her as she laughs with Henry. Mons doesn't just look at her. He examines her, like he's doing it for a thesis.

"Come dance with me." Zara grabs my hands. "I want to introduce you to some of my other friends."

It takes a moment to realize she's talking to me, but once I do, my body locks up and I assume cat-on-a-bathtub-ledge posture.

"No." I shake my head vigorously. "Nuh uh, no way, nope, no—"

"Oh, come on." She pokes out her bottom lip. "Don't be like Henry. Please? It's my birthday!"

"Maybe later," I lie.

Mons steps up and breaks her hold of my hand. "I'll dance with you, lovey."

She wiggles her fingers out of his grasp and waves at him. "You wish. Way too early in the night for that." She dances away, laughing, into the sea of swaying bodies.

Mons raises a highball glass to his lips and takes the last swig. "Always watching her walk away," he mumbles. "She would've said yes to you, though." And he lightly nudges Henry with his elbow.

Henry gives him a tight smile. "How's work?"

"Oh, you know." He laughs. "I'm running Dad's business into the ground."

"Come on, mate." Henry cocks his head to the side.

"It's true." Mons stands up straighter, taut as a stretched rubber band. "Lot to learn yet. He can't do as much anymore."

Henry either doesn't know what to say or chooses not to say anything. I don't ask what they're talking about, either, because my anxiety is through the roof.

"I'm off for another scotch. Be back." Mons stalks away to the bar.

"Is he still that pissy about the photoshoot?"

He shrugs. "He's still pissed that Zara and I dated for a bit. The photoshoot was just insult to injury."

I focus on the dance floor instead of what he said, pretending Zara didn't already share this information with me. Pretending I'm not standing here deciphering what *dated for a bit* really means. A few months down the road, will Henry tell people that he and I dated for a bit? Dated for one night? Made out on a grassy hill in the English countryside and then bumbled around each other for the next couple of weeks?

He leans in again, so close the words vibrate on my ear. "I'm going to get us a drink. What do you want?"

"Just water," I say, like the most boring person ever. But hey, boring people don't puke in trashcans. Or do all the stupid things that flash through my mind when his lips are that close to my ear.

"I'll be right back," he says.

I nod and search the dance floor until I see Zara again. When she makes eye contact with me, she smiles, teeth megawatt bright. Her friends dance around her in a circle, but she outshines them all. She could be a runway model—grace and poise and confidence and beauty. And I know it deep in my bones when I look at her. I can never compete.

Henry returns with my water a moment later. "How are you holding up?"

Oh, you know, just sitting here being despicably jealous of your lovely friend.

"I'm fine."

We watch the people on the dance floor for a few minutes, shoulder to shoulder. When I see the way some of them move together, I get a little shiver imagining what it would be like to dance with Henry like that.

"You know," he says. "It's not that we can't dance. It's that we choose not to."

I swallow, a little freaked out by the way he says things that seem to answer my thoughts sometimes. I smile without looking at him. Maybe this telepathy thing is working between us, after all. "Exactly."

When Sanjay arrives, an entourage accompanies him. He introduces the beautiful girl standing closest to him as Aditi.

Once we've all exchanged pleasantries, I lean over to Henry and whisper, "The mudlarking girl?"

He smiles and nods.

When Zara finally leaves the dance floor with her uni friends, she gets hugs from Sanjay and his friends. "Let's go up to the roof." She points. "We can sit down before it gets too crowded."

We make our way as a group to the brick stairwell at the back of the building and follow single file to a door at the top of two flights of stairs. Henry places his hand on the small of my back. Acutely, I feel every point of contact between his fingers and my spine.

When we emerge on the roof, my ears are cottony from the loud music downstairs. It's faint and faraway below, but the damage to my eardrums has already been done. I glance around at the London skyline and try to ward off the dizziness. People sit at the rooftop bar, but there are empty tables everywhere. We push a few together so we can sit as a group. Henry and I sit across from Zara.

"This seat taken?" Mons gives each word an extra syllable as he takes the chair on the other side of me. I clear my throat and shift away.

Henry gives him a look, but his phone rings. He stands up and steps away to answer it. Mons moves closer, eyeballing my water glass. "Not the usual whiskey on the rocks kind of night for you, eh?" He chuckles.

I swallow back the bile of the memory. "I'm never drinking again."

"Bollocks. I always say that, too." He holds up his drink. "But here we are!"

I glance up at Henry, who's speaking animatedly in his phone. "Wonderful. Thank you so much. I'll stop by tomorrow." He and Sanjay exchange a glance and he nods at him. Sanjay smiles, then leans over and whispers something to Aditi.

Mons offers me his drink. "Have a sip."

I decline, but he commandeers a few more inches of my personal space and offers again. "Oh, come on. You'll loosen up a bit. Single malt scotch. Tastes much better than Jameson's." Up close like this, his eyes look even more bloodshot. His breath curls hot and sour.

"No thanks." I scoot my chair backwards.

He fixes his gaze on my mouth for a moment, then nods and looks away. "Suit yourself."

"What were you saying to Henry earlier? About your dad? Is he sick?"

Mons looks at me again, this time less predatory. "He has Parkinson's," he says. "Hard for a man who works with his hands. He can't complete jobs as fast as he used to, so he's losing business."

This new information gives me a twinge of guilt for disliking him so much. Maybe people who seem horrible are really just going through something that makes them seem horrible. Maybe Mons is just lonely, too.

"That sucks," I finally say.

"Yeah, well. We do what we have to for our families, don't we? No matter that I'm shite at fixing cars. I'll live on my father's reputation for a while until everyone figures it out."

He wraps an arm around my shoulders and pulls me into a side hug. In that instant, I catch Henry's eye as he hangs up the phone.

"He's keen on you, you know," Mons says, tongue thick with scotch. "Shame, really."

I turn to Mons, sliding out from under his arm. "A shame?"

But he doesn't answer; he's watching Henry.

Suddenly Henry's hand is in mine. He's helping me to my feet. "Are you all right, love?"

I am a little taken aback, but I nod. "Of course."

Mons jumps up and slams his drink on the table. "Yes, she's all right, Henry, for fuck's sake!" His outburst draws the attention of everyone around us. "You're such a bloody tight ass."

"Shall we mingle?" Henry doesn't acknowledge the dig. He leads me in the opposite direction. He's trying to be light, to pretend this isn't a big deal, but I feel the storm brewing.

To our backs, Mons shouts, "Always the white knight, aren't you, mate? Saving ladies from the villain!"

"Just ignore him," Henry says for the second time tonight. We make our way to the other side of the table where Zara is sitting. "He's been itching for a fight for ages, and it gets worse when he drinks."

Henry's body jerks—so abruptly I have to let go of his hand. His glass clatters to the ground with a bursting tinkle. I sidestep to avoid the sudden explosion of shards.

Mons grabs Henry by the lapels of his coat. He's shorter than him by several inches, so it looks a little cartoonish.

"Mons, stop it right now!" Zara yells at him.

"You're pissed, mate. Don't do this," Henry warns, stern and calm.

"Tell me, then, why is it that you think you're the hero?"

"Mons," Sanjay warns, stepping up behind him.

Henry glares at Mons, stone-faced. "You can stop being the villain any time you want."

Mons laughs then, looks around at his audience, because everyone is watching. Exactly how he likes it. My pulse throbs so hard in my throat I feel like I might choke on it.

"We're not talking about me." He lets go of Henry's lapels and brushes them off. "We're talking about you."

"Let's just go, Henry." It comes out as a whisper. A plea.

Mons turns his head my way, and a smile slithers its way from his left ear to his right. He looks back at Henry and stabs a thumb in my direction.

"She thinks you're the hero, too, then. That's quite rich, don't you think?"

"Mons," I say, thinking maybe he'll listen to me. "Everything's fine, okay?"

"You think so?" He puts his hands on his hips and smiles, showing teeth. "Wait till you hear all of this one's secrets." He pats Henry on the chest. Hard. "Do let me know how fine you are after that. I don't believe you'll like him very bloody much then."

"You're a pathetic little man," Henry says, stepping back. But before he can turn, Mons lunges at him—a barrel of snarls and fists and knees. He makes surprise contact and Henry's head stutters backwards. Just once. Then all hell breaks loose.

CHAPTER

FORTY-SEVEN

: With a Little Help from My Friends :

HENRY SLOUCHES IN a rolling desk chair, pressing an ice pack against his left eye.

I stoop down in front of the bathroom sink and sort through spray bottles of cleaner and trash bags and hand soap until I find the first aid kit: a hard green box with a red cross and a fancy snap-latch. The English are so *extra* about everything.

"I'm fine," Henry says as I set it on the desk by his bed. "Really."

I give him a look he can't even see because one eye is closed and the other's swollen shut. There's a spray of blood down the front of his half-unbuttoned shirt. I make a pact with myself to keep my eyes above his neck at all times.

"The cut looks pretty nasty. He must've got you with his ring." I stall while I come up with a plan. My fingers separate the bandages from the antiseptic wipes, the antibiotic ointment from the alcohol pads. I have literally no clue what I'm doing.

Eeny-meenie-miney-mo. I settle on the antiseptic wipe and tear the package open. When I remove the ice pack from his face, he lets go and opens his good eye. Him watching me blunder around incompetently makes me eleventy billion times more nervous than I already was.

"I can't believe that tosser broke my glasses. I bloody liked those glasses."

"Be still," I command, and with a shaking hand, I dab the cut above his left eye with the wipe. He hisses through his teeth in response. "Oh, don't be such a baby."

"I'd like to see a baby take a punch like that," he mutters. "Or not hit the guy back. I could have, you know. I wanted to."

"Yes, you are a big strong man, and everyone was very impressed by your self-control."

A smirk spreads between his dimples. "Even you?"

"Especially me." I push his forehead back until his neck rests on the back of the chair. With a Q-tip, I dab some of the antibiotic ointment and paint it delicately over the wound. Even with one of his eyes all busted up in ten shades of maroon, his face may as well be a gallery exhibit. Chiseled cheekbones. Delicious dimples. Boy band hair. I paint on an extra coat of ointment, just to buy myself twenty more seconds to look at him up close. I could be an A-list romance heroine, objectifying him like this.

"Will you two be able to get past this?"

Henry closes his right eye again as I work. He chuckles. "This isn't a new thing for Mons and me."

"Because of Zara? Or…"

"That started it, yes."

I wait for him to go on. When he doesn't, I ask, "What happened?"

"One night Zara and I hung out alone. We drank too much and we kissed."

As I watch his mouth form the words *we kissed*, my stomach twists. I instantly regret asking.

"It felt right at the time," Henry says. "As drunken decisions tend to. It's easy to confuse levels of relationships."

"What do you mean?" I blot away the excess ointment with gauze.

"Being close friends with someone can make you sort of thirsty for more. You think, wow, I wouldn't even have to do the work of getting to know someone if I fancy this person here, who already knows I'm a bloody asshole sometimes but cares for me just the same."

I swallow. *Oh.* So maybe that's what this is. With me and him.

"But the truth of the matter is, we got things confused for a bit. It was convenient."

"So Mons decided he liked her after this?"

Henry shifts in his chair. "Not exactly."

I wait.

"He always had a thing for her."

"Oh." One at a time, I put small butterfly bandages over the cut.

"You're judging me."

"I'm not."

"You are. I see it in your face."

"Well, if he liked her first and you knew... Never mind. Finish the story."

"I'd been telling him all along that he shouldn't ruin their friendship, it wasn't worth it. But he made his move anyway. She shut him down by using us as an example. Told him we'd been seeing each other but decided to split, and that she knew from experience dating friends complicates things. He lost his mind because we'd kept it from him. It took us all a while to recover and go back to being friends."

"Based on your busted eye, Henry, I don't think Mons has recovered."

"Fair point. Everything I do now pisses him off."

I take a deep breath, admiring my improv handiwork.

The image plays back in my head: of Henry holding Mons down on the ground, eyebrow dripping blood, refusing to let him up until he calmed down. He could've beaten the ever-loving hell out of him, but he didn't. He used his head instead of getting revenge for the cheap shot. It was maybe the most evolved thing I've ever seen a guy do. The bouncers still kicked them both out, though.

"So why didn't you hit him back tonight?"

His jaw tenses.

"I care about the guy. Anyway, I hit him enough the night he came on to Zara." He opens his eye again. "I hit him more than a few times."

I grimace.

"Don't look at me like that. It wasn't a possessive thing." He shakes his head. "He shoved his tongue down her throat and groped her. *After* she said no. That's assault." He takes a deep breath. "I saw him with you and…" He clenches his fists at his sides. "Let's just say I wouldn't have been so charitable if he'd tried anything like that tonight."

I go a little wobbly. Mons was right about one thing: Henry is the hero. Normally I'd reject this kind of bravado, but he gets away with it. Somehow I know, beyond any shadow of doubt, that Henry would never be the guy who'd send me pictures of his limp, bread dough junk and expect me to swoon. He'd never tell me that the seal is broken just because we had sex once, and expect it to continue despite my weak protests. He'd never drive himself into my stupefied-with-depression body while his parents were out golfing.

Henry is a different breed of boy.

The kind of boy I might *willingly* be with. Not out of obligation or habit.

I try not to let this scroll over my face like a message from the emergency broadcast system. We're still for a few moments, even though I'm out of reasons to stand in his space like this, sharing his oxygen, his knee touching my leg, my hand on his shoulder. His bed inches away. I think about how his mouth felt. In real life. In the dream. How I could lean down a tiny bit and melt right into it. My phone buzzes on the desk and my soul startles right out of my body.

I take a step back and grab my phone.

Long before you.

Every syllable is an air-horn reminder that I am a temporary blip on this radar. That workshop or not, I'll be an ocean away soon.

"Is that Zara?"

I nod.

"Shit!" he yells, and I jump.

"What?"

"I still have her birthday present. Tell her I'll bring it to her later."

I relay this to her via text, and then set my phone down on the nightstand. I hand him two pain relievers from the first aid kit. He takes them and washes them down with a glass of water.

"So what'd you get her?"

"Tarot cards," he says as he slinks out of his blood-spattered shirt and tosses it at the hamper.

My knees liquefy. I freeze and try not to look at all the bare skin.

He reaches into his coat pocket where it hangs on the back of the chair and pulls out a deck of cards with a red ribbon tied on them. Before I see the deck, I already know it's solid black with music notes of golden filigree. He hands it to me and dives into his bed.

"Scoot over," he says to Felix, who's been sleeping on his pillow ever since we got back. Felix stands, stretches, and growl-yawns, then trots to the bottom of the bed where he collapses into a furry pile and goes back to sleep. "Look at them," he says. "The artwork is nice. I think she'll like them."

I nod and swallow. This would be a terrible time to draw a Lovers card.

"What is it?" He squints at me with his good eye. "Tarot cards freak you out or something?"

"No, it's not that." I hand him the deck. "I'm just tired." I take the first aid kit to the bathroom and put it back under the sink cabinet.

He flips his TV on and scrolls the channels with the remote. I glance up as he stretches out.

"Goodnight," I say from the doorway and give him a little wave.

He lifts his head a little, and I can't tell if he's giving me a weird look since only half of his face is readable, but it feels like he's giving me a weird look.

I can never seem to stop myself from running, even if I want to be caught.

"Thanks for everything," he says. He looks like he might say more, but I leave before he has the chance.

CHAPTER

FORTY-EIGHT

: Do You Want to Know a Secret :

IN PATRICK'S ROOM, I crawl out of my dress and tights and shoes.

I allowed things to happen with Dylan. Never really because I wanted to. Even the night we met—at Mom's work Christmas party—he talked me into sneaking outside when I didn't really want to. But he had a nice smile and he gave me attention and I was sick of pretending to have a good time. I never analyzed his glances, his words, the way his body moved.

Not like this.

I crawl into bed, hair and teeth brushed, face washed, and night shirt on, and then reach for my phone to check my texts. But it isn't there. And then I remember.

I left it on Henry's nightstand.

An inordinate amount of time—read: obsessive, ridiculous, absurd—is spent debating on whether to go into his room through the bathroom or the hallway. Hallway seems less personal, somehow. So I go that way, and stare at his open door while my muscles remain at maximum clench. Light from the TV flashes shadows on the walls outside his room. Faint music plays. As I get closer, I recognize the tune.

I peek in the door. A Beatles movie is playing on the screen. It's at the part in *Let it Be* where Yoko has asserted herself in the studio and the guys are emitting their bugger-off beams.

Henry turns his head and looks up at me then. Bare from the waist up, under the covers from the waist down.

"I left my phone." I don't know why I whisper it.

He points at the TV. "The BBC is having a Beatles marathon."

I smile. "I haven't seen this one in forever."

He lifts the covers beside him and glances down at the empty spot on the bed. A wordless invitation. My cheeks flame. Saying no is the right thing to do.

"I'll keep my hands to myself, if you want," he says. "I kept that promise once before, if you remember."

If you want? I swallow. "I do remember."

I only think about it for another half a second before I crawl in, enveloping my chilled legs in the warmth of the covers. His bed smells like him. I settle in under the blanket, stiff as a studio with Yoko in it, and fold my hands awkwardly over my stomach. Like a corpse. He looks sideways at me.

"There you are." He smiles.

A nervous laugh bubbles up. "Here I am."

He doesn't touch me; he doesn't scoot closer. He looks back at the TV and I clear my throat.

"So why are you, the non-fan, watching a Beatles movie marathon?"

"I'm not so much watching it as listening to it since I'm working with one near-sighted eye at the moment."

"Don't you have a back-up pair of glasses?"

"Yes. In the darkroom somewhere." He turns to look at me. "But everything I need to see right now is already up close."

Oh God. Was that a line? I fix my eyes on the movie and pretend not to catch it.

"So why are you listening to the Beatles, exactly?"

He shifts in the bed until he's on his side, facing me. The same way he did at Glastonbury. "Can I tell you a secret?"

"Uh, sure." I gulp and keep my eyes deadlocked on Paul at the piano. His gaze heats the side of my face while I wait.

"I actually really bloody love The Beatles."

My mouth falls open with a little pop. I cave and look at him.

"I thought you'd like to know." He grins. "Your theory was correct. Liar or asshole. I'm a liar. Also sometimes an asshole."

I think back to that day. The smarmy look, the whistled Rolling Stones song.

"That's a pretty stupid thing to lie about. I at least try to ration my untruths."

He laughs. "I had my reasons."

"Oh yeah?"

"When you first arrived, my daily goal was to irritate you."

On some level, I already knew this, but I have to ask. "Why?"

He touches the end of my nose with his index finger. "You do this thing when you're flustered where your nose draws up just here, and…" He drops his hand, trailing off as he meets my eyes. "It's adorable."

Inevitability is sometimes a feeling, like letting go at the top of a slide. You know the moment you release your grip, you're going to zoom—exhilarated, amused, alive. But then you hit bottom and it's over. It isn't the slide I'm afraid of. It's the bottom. And right now, I don't trust myself not to let go. It's easier to watch Paul and George argue about simplifying guitar rhythms, so I look back at the TV.

"This is my least favorite of all their movies, if I'm being honest," I finally say.

"Bittersweet," he agrees.

"And it's the end," I add. "I hate endings."

"Me, too."

We're quiet for a few minutes.

"So tell me about these untruths you've been rationing," he says.

It feels like a nudge. To get me to admit things he already knows.

"You'll have to wonder." I flash him a flirty grin.

His dimples wink. "Truth or lie: my aura is purple."

"Truth."

"Truth or lie: my eye doesn't look that bad."

"Trick question," I say. "It didn't look that bad in the tube when you asked. It looks terrible now."

He chuckles. "I appreciate your honesty."

I turn on my side to face him and prop my head up with my hand. My heartbeat makes my entire body vibrate. "Can I ask you one?"

He nods.

"Truth or lie: What Mons said tonight."

A shadow crosses his face. "Which part?"

"The part about how your secrets will make me not like you."

He hesitates. His eyes wander down to my mouth and pause on my lips. Sometimes when Henry and I talk, I think maybe we're both just lips and eyes and eyes and lips, thinking about kissing all the time. Ever since that one time we did.

The Beatles begin their studio version of *Don't Let Me Down* in the background.

"Truth," he finally says.

Our bodies mirror each other in the dark. A few heartbeats of space separate us. I want to beg him to tell me those secrets, the way I've been telling him all of mine.

"Somehow I doubt I could ever not like you."

"Truth or lie," he whispers. "You want me to kiss you right now."

My heart trips over itself. "Truth."

He leans in and presses his lips against mine. Warmth, pressure, and electricity simultaneous. I get lost. For once, I don't think about the past, or the future, or meds or pain or drama, or who I am or who I'm not or what the hell I'm even doing on this planet besides wasting space and oxygen. Every particle that makes me who I am lives in my lips while Henry is kissing me.

He tastes like peppermint, always peppermint, and it's my new favorite flavor. His big, warm hands skate gently across the skin on my hips, beneath my nightshirt, pulling me close. I melt into him.

At some point, minutes or days later, I remember how very temporary this all is.

The slide is amazing, but the ground is coming. I pull away and sit up.

Henry opens his eyes. "I'm sorry, did I—"

I shake my head. "No," I barely manage.

"We can stop." He searches my face. "I didn't plan that."

"I know." I run a fingertip over his swollen cheek.

"Stay," he says, withdrawing his hands. "I'll keep my promise. Let's watch the movie."

I nod and slide into his shoulder, resting my head in the nook between his neck and collarbone. He laces an arm around my back and I hug his waist, and we watch the Apple rooftop concert until we both fall asleep.

∶ ∶ ∶

A series of dings wake me up. My eyes flutter open. Henry's warm body is pressed against my back. His breath is slow and steady on my neck, and his legs are tangled with mine. A solid blue light from the TV casts a hazy glow over the room. I pick up my phone and glance at the time, then text Patrick back, wondering what he'd think if he knew where I am right now.

I'm sorry I messed things up so spectacularly with your friends.

Truly I care for them both, but I really liked Maddie.

I should've been up front with Lexie instead of relishing in the attention.

Sometimes it's hard to do the right thing. I get it.

Henry shifts in his sleep and turns over, so I roll onto my back and peek over at him. The light from the TV glows around his face. It's a photogenic face. One that I'll miss terribly. A sad sort of restlessness breaks loose and swims through me. I'm not looking forward to saying goodbye to him. I grab my phone and snap a picture of him sleeping.

Caption: too good to be true

Things might look different to him in the light of day. I have very little time left with him, and I'm afraid of what will happen if I'm still here when he wakes up.

But I can at least get his spare glasses for him.

Slowly and quietly, I stand up and tiptoe out of his room.

* * *

In the dark room, I rummage around, trying my best not to make noise.

Some drawers are filled with chemicals, others with old film canisters. I stoop down and open a drawer beneath the negative processor and—aha!—finally spot them on top of a mountain of pictures. When I grab them, some of the pictures fall to the floor.

As I clean up the mess I made, I notice a photo of Henry and Patrick together. From a few years ago, it looks like. Patrick's in a soccer uniform. Henry's wearing a Radiohead tee. They're huddled together smiling from ear to ear. They look nothing like a couple of brothers who don't get along.

The next one on the stack is another of Henry and Patrick—this time younger. Both laughing, draped in towels at the beach.

I sink to the cold floor and sit cross-legged, then lift a stack of photos out of the drawer. As I flip through, I watch them age backwards. Each picture with both of them tells the same story: brothers and friends.

I wonder how they could've let family drama tear something so obvious apart.

But of course, as Lexie and Maddie have both separately pointed out, I don't have siblings. So maybe I know nothing.

About halfway down the stack, I find one with old tape on it, like it was once in an album. Or hanging on the wall. It's Patrick holding Felix when he was a tiny little kit. Felix has a gauze wrap around half of his face, and two bandaged paws. As I put it down, though, something niggles at the back of my mind. Something off. I pull the photo closer to my face in the subdued light of the room. It isn't Patrick holding Felix, because he would've been 12 years old when the little fox was rescued. This is a man, not a teenager. He's looking down, so I can't see his face. Only the top of his red hair is visible. I study the slope of his neck and shoulders, the way his freckled arms cradle the little fox and disappear beneath his fur. There's something familiar about him, so it was easy to assume it was Patrick. This must be John. Patrick's real dad.

I set the picture down and pick up another. The next one, though, has the same man in it. My hands start to shake. All of a sudden, I'm thrashing in the Thames again, frozen and unable to breathe.

This picture isn't of the top of his head.

A cold sweat starts at the top of my head and moves to my feet like a dynamite fuse.

This picture has a full body view.

Henry and Patrick huddle under each of the man's arms. I see the similarities between Patrick and his father as they stand side by side. They have the same eye color. The same nose. The same cinnamon freckles on their faces and arms. My eyes blur as they stop on the man's forearm, just above the wrist, where there's a loopy tattoo.

It says Jojo.

The current swallows me whole.

CHAPTER

FORTY-NINE

: I Just Don't Understand :

I SHOVE THE proof in my backpack but leave the rest of the photos scattered on the darkroom floor.

Puzzle pieces snap together in my brain.

I can't feel my fingers.

He called me Jojo at the airport, for God's sake! He gave himself away first thing and I didn't see it. All this time... *All this time!* I thought he was the one person I could trust.

Bile rises in the back of my throat.

The festival poster... George's insistence that they'd never heard of Walrus Gumboot. All lies.

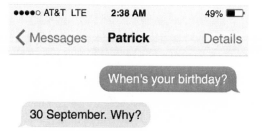

He's younger than me, but in my grade. I was born January 11th of the same year. I do the math. My mother was at the end of her pregnancy with me when Patrick was conceived.

I remember the story Mama once told me, about how Pop almost didn't make it home in time for my birth. He'd left for London the day after Christmas to play a few holiday shows, and he made it back the day she went into labor.

Back in Patrick's room, I start pulling open drawers, looking for more evidence. Anything. I pull books off shelves and flip through them. I dig inside album sleeves. But I find nothing else. There's not an ounce of clutter, no shoeboxes under the bed, no hidden answers in his pristine closet.

I pull out the stack of photos I swiped from the darkroom. Handfuls of photos of Pop—with the boys. With Henry and Patrick's mother, Julia. With people I don't know and have never met. He had a longstanding relationship with this family, but he never told me?

Worse still, *they* never told me.

My stomach plummets. I close my eyes. This is just a dream. A really weird dream. I'm going to wake up and everything will be fine. There will be no pictures of Pop in this place. *1, 2, 3, 4, 5. Exhale.*

I open my eyes again, very much present in the nightmare.

Then I remember Nigel's strange behavior. The way he wouldn't give me anything but vague answers I already had. The way he looked at Henry instead of me. The way he ushered Walter away before he told me anything of substance that night at the Crow. And I know, all at once, that Nigel was in on this secret, too. And I'm going to make him tell me why.

I grab my bag and dart out the door, taking the steps two at a time all the way to the ground floor. I swing around into the hallway toward the back door as I hear footsteps above. My heart speeds up triple time. I pull on the door and meet resistance, stuck as always. My whole body tears at the knob, the latches, the chain. My breaths quake as I struggle and pull. Above me, footsteps move louder, closer together.

"Jo?"

Finally I lift the knob and put my hip into it. The door opens and I dash outside into the moonlit street. I don't look back to see if he's behind me. I just run.

Through the alley, around the corner, down the street. I keep running, past the sparse cars on the otherwise empty street. My breath puffs in little white clouds in front of my face. My legs ache and my lungs burn. I sprint in and out of side streets, convinced that Henry is right behind me the whole time. I don't look back.

When I get to Blackfriar's Crow, the building is locked and the lights are out. I bang on the glass until my hand stings, but nobody comes to the door.

I collapse onto the sidewalk in front of the Crow. Tears stream down my face. Henry will probably know to look here. Or maybe he won't look for me at all.

I'm startled to realize that scares me more.

I pull out the stack of pictures and go through them again, trying to decipher their ages, do the math. They're all taken at different places, different stages of his life. The short hair phase, the leather jacket phase, those awful cowboy boots that Mama hated. Every picture tells a different story—the only thing they have in common is that I don't know the man in them.

I never really knew him.

Then there's one of Pop and Julia, sitting on the stairs at the Fox Den. Felix is propped on his lap. Julia's legs are kicked up against the wall. She's smiling so genuinely. She has the same dimples as Henry. She's beautiful. And I hate her.

Was he always coming here for her? Did he want to be here instead?

Did they get to see his body when I didn't? Were they all there? Are they the people who were called when he was found by a hotel maid? How much of the story I've been told about his death is even true? The numbness gives way to boiling jealousy. Then anger.

Were they having an affair the whole time?

Suddenly nothing makes sense. Everything I ever thought my life was has been disproven by one big destructive lie. The emptiness I once felt—the one I felt at my lowest—slides over my bones and paralyzes me where I sit. And it's not the meds this time. It's me. It was always me.

Hands shaking, I reach into my backpack and pull out the bag of pill bottles. I take one of the blue ones. For panic. I sit there for a long time, waiting for it to kick in. Shivering in the cold drizzle, but not caring if I freeze. When the bad feelings don't dissipate, I take another one. And another.

Then get paranoid I took too much.

I quickly google the medication side effects on my phone.

Drowsiness. Lightheadedness. Slurred speech. Auditory hallucinations.

Maybe hearing Pops' voice was never real to start with. I stopped hearing it when I quit the meds. My phone rings. I click the green button with a numb finger, press the phone to my ear, but don't say anything.

"Please hear me out," Henry begins.

"So this was your big secret?" I don't recognize the sound of my own voice. It's raspy, tear-drenched.

Silence on the line for a moment. "Yes. And I wanted to tell you. So many times, I almost—"

"Oh, bullshit. You've had a month!"

"Where are you right now? Let's have this conversation face-to-face."

I choke on a sob. "You let me trek all over the country, trying to contact his spirit or some shit, for answers you already had."

"Please listen to me. He was like family to us. Before. Patrick didn't know the truth until after he was already gone. We knew about you. He talked about you all the time, Jo."

Tears sting my eyes.

"I knew this wasn't the best way. But it's how he wanted us to tell you."

"Did you see his body?"

Henry sighs. "Jo…"

"So you did."

Massive sigh. "Yes."

I hang up on him and dial Mama's number. She answers on the second ring.

"I need you to tell me the truth." My voice cracks as a lone car roars past.

"Josephine? What is that racket? It's late there… What's going on?"

"Tell me the truth about the Pembertons." A terror-filled silence stretches between us. "Mama?"

"Where are you right now?"

And that's how I know.

Telling me the truth in my fragile mental state will surely break me, she assumes, and she needs to make sure I'm not standing on a ledge.

"Honey, it's a very complicated situation and there are lots of things—"

"A complicated situation?" I scream. Anger completely possesses me; I'm no longer in control. "You are a liar and I hate you!"

"Josephine—"

My other line beeps. Henry. On the other end of the phone, wire hangers clang against the rod in her closet. Zippers move up and down furiously. Then Patrick's voice in the background—*Is everything okay?*

"I'm coming there," she says to me.

I hang up on her. Turn off the phone. Behind me, the lock on the door snaps open. I look up. Nigel studies me for a moment through the darkness before he opens the door.

"My dear, why are you yelling on my doorstep at three in the morning?"

I wipe my face and clamber to my feet. I open my mouth to tell him I hate him, too. For lying. For knowing Pop better than I did. For being selfish and keeping him from me. But the sadness on his face weakens my resolve and only a whimper squeaks out.

"Come inside. Let's have a chat." He hooks an arm around my shoulder and scoops me inside, twisting the lock behind us.

CHAPTER

FIFTY

: Yesterday :

I OPEN MY eyes on the tweed sofa in Nigel's office.

Sitting up, I rub the sleepy, medicinal feeling away from my eyes and push the stale blankets off me. Last night comes back in blips.

Yesterday, I didn't know that everyone I care about is untrustworthy.

I didn't know my father was an adulterer, my mother was a liar, and the people I've grown to care about this summer were hiding significant pieces of my father's identity from me. What a difference a day makes.

"Good morning," Nigel says to me from the other side of his desk. He pours water from a steaming kettle into a teacup and pushes it across the desk to me.

I can't remember our entire conversation, only that I cried a lot. And that he apologized a lot. And made a pallet for himself behind the bar so I could sleep on the sofa in his office.

The letter Pop wrote me is open on the desk next to my teacup. I pick it up, remembering how we read it last night, how I tried to find clues while I fought against the current of exhaustion and drowsiness from the anxiety medication.

"I want to show you something." He opens a drawer and pulls out a leather-bound book and hands it to me. "I wanted to show it to you last night, but you were already so upset."

I take it from him.

"It's a scrapbook my wife made, from the early days of the Crow."

There's at least one picture of Pop on every other page. With the band. With Nigel. With George. With people I've never seen before. Sitting at the bar. He's so alive in every photo. So saturated with happiness. As I reach the end of the album, there's one of Pop pointing at an audience member with a face-splitting smile. Julia. They're so young. The picture tells a story that couldn't be summarized with a caption. Worth a thousand words and all that.

"This is why you didn't show me this when I asked you about pictures before?"

He nods.

"Why did everyone lie to me? Didn't they know I'd find out eventually?"

Nigel nods. "Of course, my dear. It was always the plan to tell you."

My brows pull and it makes my whole face feel weird, being so taut from crying. "When?"

He clears his throat. "I believe you'd better let George or Henry or your mother tell you that."

I stiffen. "I don't want to talk to anyone else. I've read this same letter over and over. For years, Nigel."

His face is solemn, drawn downward.

"None of it sounds like some grand plan to introduce me to his other family. Henry's lying. I need someone to tell me the truth. Someone. Anyone. You."

He drags his hands over his face.

"Your father was very ill for most of his life. I remember the first time I met him—he'd come into the bar with Julia and some of her other friends—and I could see it in his eyes. He was haunted."

"Who are all these people?" I ask, turning the album around to face him. "These people who loved him? All this time I could've been talking to them. Finding out about him."

A loud banging echoes through the building and familiar voice calls, "Nigel? Open up!"

My heart starts pounding and I glare at Nigel. "You told him I was here?"

"I'm sorry, dear." His eyes soften. "He was very worried about you."

"I don't want to talk to him right now. I mean it."

He swallows and nods. "Okay. I'll let him know."

A few moments later, Nigel returns to the office with Henry on his heels. He gives me an apologetic shrug. I spring to my feet, shocked by how strangely unfamiliar Henry looks to me now.

He's wearing the rimless glasses I found in the darkroom. A deep bruise blossoms around his left eye. Dark shadows circle the other like he hasn't slept in days. His aura hangs around him like an inky cloak. His hair is sleep-matted to his head, clothes are wrinkled and disheveled. He clutches something in his hands. My eyes fix on it, taking in the shape, the size, the details.

Beneath a layer of caked dirt, a bright *Yellow Submarine* sticker peeks through. Next to it, an *All You Need is Love* sticker. I can just make out the words through the river sediment.

I blink and tears roll down my face. "How did you…?"

He extends the urn to me and I take it. My hands tremble as I do.

"I had help." His voice is strained like he's avoiding tears of his own. "From Sanjay's mudlarking group. We've been looking for days. Got the Port Authority involved. The harbor master called me last night when they found it. I picked it up this morning. I'm sorry I haven't had time to clean it up yet."

I remember the call he took at the club as I turn the urn over and over in my hand, examining its weight, sick with worry about the integrity of the ashes inside. My swollen eyes burn.

"When you told me…" His voice trembles. He takes a moment and regroups. "I knew I had to get it back for you."

"I'll give you two a moment," Nigel says. He closes the door of his office behind him as he exits into the bar.

Henry and I bathe in the uncomfortable silence until I can't take it anymore. I look up at him.

"There was never a John, was there?" Sadness and anger war in the pit of my stomach. "You just made that up. Gave him a fake name."

"No." He shakes his head. "No, it's not like that. When he met my mother, he told her that was his name. His role in the band. She never stopped calling him that. We knew his real name, but we never called him by it."

I stare daggers at him. "Which makes your mother Yoko. Fitting."

Henry winces. "You don't think I know that? I was hurt by all of this, too. I lost them both."

It's hard to process. To relive the summer backwards in this new context.

"Shortly after he died," Henry continues, "I had to watch my family fall apart, and then lose my mother to cancer in the space of a year."

It's all too much. A choking sensation lodges in the back of my throat; it's like drowning on dry land. The room shrinks by degrees and I *have* to get out. I shove the urn into my backpack, retrieve the letter on Nigel's desk and put it back in my wallet, then shuffle the backpack onto my shoulders.

"Please wait." Henry catches me by the arm as I walk past him. I yank against his icy grip and he lets go. "Your mother's on her way in. She and Patrick land this afternoon."

My throat closes up. I shake my head, waiting, trying to find the strength to say something without sobbing.

"Coming here was a mistake."

I try again to slide past him but he steps in front of the door.

"I know how much it hurts, and I'm sorry. I told them this would happen. I knew it would turn out like this and they wouldn't listen."

I think back on the night I heard him talking on the phone in the darkroom, when I was eavesdropping outside the door. *I know, I tried to tell him.* Then I remember what he said about the mugwort tea, that he'd given it to me because he was trying to communicate with me. *I want to help you find your father.*

"I'm so sorry." His voice cracks and his eyes fill with tears. "I wanted to tell you. I swear to God I did!"

We are both still for a very long time, no sounds but sniffles.

"Then why didn't you?"

His lip trembles. "I gave Patrick my word. Your father made some very specific requests when he found out she was dying, and before she died, my mum told us she wanted us to honor them. Patrick gave her his word, and I gave him mine, even though I didn't want to do it this way."

"What requests?"

Henry lets out a chest-deflating sigh. "There are letters. You can read them all. Just come back home with me."

I stare at him a long moment.

"Please, Jo." He steps closer to me, but I move away. His face falls. "Let me fill in all the gaps for you. Answer any questions you have. Let me try to make this right. Or at least bearable."

Tears stream steadily down my cheeks, burning the skin on my face.

I nod once.

CHAPTER

FIFTY-ONE

: In My Life :

AS WE ENTER through the alley door, Henry's phone rings.

I hear George's voice, *yelling*, before he even says hello.

Henry sighs. "I know, and I'm sorry. I'm—yes. Okay."

The quiet reverberation of Henry's *bye* reaches me as he hangs up.

My eyes must ask the question, because when Henry looks at me, he says, "Dad's on his way home."

I don't respond. We climb the stairs. My body is reluctant and my legs are numb. I'm only here because I want to see this thing Henry claims Pop wrote. I want to hear Pop's side of this story.

I slide down onto the floor next to the bed in Patrick's room. Henry goes to his room and returns a few moments later with a shoebox and a piece of paper. It's folded and tattered on the edges, like it's been read as many times as the one in my wallet. He extends it to me. Tears prick the corners of my eyes when I see the handwriting. Julia's name. The address for the Fox Den.

I steel myself and open it up.

October 9, 2018

Dearest Julia,

I understand why you'd prefer to keep the pact we made when we were young and foolish. But the easy thing isn't always the right thing. I'm hiding the truth from my children. Jojo has a brother she'll never know if we don't change course. Family is important. Take it from a man who never had one until now. I don't want to have to tell them alone. I want us to do this together, while we still have time.

Jojo has been begging me for years to bring her here, to show her what my life looked like before I woke up in that emergency room and looked into her mother's eyes. I'm running out of reasons to deny her that. I need her to know she has family here. I need her to know how much I love you and Patrick, and that her mother wasn't the only person who saved my life.

I'll give you time to get used to the idea, but soon, I'm coming back. I'm bringing Kristina and Jojo. Once they know your family, they'll love them. Henry and Patrick and hell, maybe even George. We'll give them time to get close, then we'll tell them all the truth. Believe me when I say it'll only work if we do it this way. Jojo is stubborn. She'll never be open to it otherwise. She's that much like her old man.

Please meet me in the middle on this. If you deny me everything else for the rest of my life, don't deny me this. I'm already going mad with heartache because you won't just see me and let me say this to you instead of writing it. You'd think I'd be used to you choosing him over me since you've done it all along. It never gets easier. I keep losing you, over and over. But it doesn't have to be like this. We can be our own kind of family. We can be here for you as you fight this illness. I need you to be honest. I need my son to know who I am. I need my daughter to get to know you all. Really know you.

All my love.

I'm tumbling, rolling underwater, holding my breath. Scanning back to the top, I read it again. And again. And again. Henry slumps over beside me, defeated look on his face.

I clear my throat. "We thought he was on tour. When it happened."

Henry shakes his head. "He came here in a manic daze, thinking Mum would be fine with him showing up and telling Patrick the truth. She told him on the phone that he shouldn't come, that it was a bad idea. They'd agreed long ago that they'd take the secret to their graves, but Mum said he changed his mind when she told him she had cancer. Which is sort of understandable. He knew she wasn't going to live." His voice cracks. "The unfair thing, though, was that he wanted to ease you and your mother into the truth, but he wanted to spring the whole ugly thing on my family first, with no preparation. While she was undergoing chemotherapy."

I shudder at the thought. "Do you think he wanted to leave my mother for her?"

He drops his head and stares at a spot on the floor between us. "I don't know. They had a long history, but we only ever knew they were friends. It never seemed like anything else, especially to my father."

"How did they meet?"

"At a pub. While Mum was at university. He was a homeless musician. She gave him a place to stay."

I inhale, surprised. "She was the uni girl."

His eyebrows crease.

"Remember, in the letter he sent me... He said a uni girl gave him a place to stay." I continue, tears rolling down my face and into my mouth.

Henry looks at me through haunted eyes. "She kept all the letters she wrote him. They were all returned to sender. I kind of wonder if he did that to keep your mom from seeing them, or in hopes of my dad finding them."

He flips open the shoebox he set on the floor earlier. "Would you like to read them?"

I stare at the box. It takes me a minute to find the strength to answer. "I don't know if I can."

He nods. "Is there anything I can do?"

I sniffle and shake my head. I wish I could tell him to promise me that the empty feeling will go away. But I know that he has no control over that.

"I think I just want to be alone."

With this, Henry gives me a solemn nod and leaves the room. I listen to his footsteps in the hall, down the stairs, until they've faded to silence.

Then I begin to read.

The letters aren't really in order, so I have to piece things together as I go.

Dear John,

George has been fired from Leeds, so we don't have to hide that we're together now. He's secured another job at the community college. Really, you should come out and visit us soon. I think you'd like him a lot...

Dear John,

I'm in love with George. I know it's inappropriate because he's my professor. But you can't possibly understand what we have. I care about you, but it's more for you than it is for me...

Dear John,

We've decided to name him Henry... George sends his love. He says you must come back to visit again soon.

Dear John,

Thank you for coming by to visit. Henry loved the Christmas presents you gave him. If he were old enough to talk, I'm sure he'd say thank you himself. George says he's sorry he missed you. I suppose he'd be even sorrier if he knew what happened.

    The truth is, I regret it horribly. We made a bad choice. We've been friends all these years, we just have to forget that it happened. Promise?...

Dear John,

Patrick was born on Tuesday. He has red hair and blue eyes...

Dear John,

We must take this to our graves...

Dear John,

Little Felix the fox is doing remarkably well now. You should come and visit soon. George would love to see you!...

Dear John,

You understand me in a way that George doesn't, but I can never give you what you want. I'm so sorry...

CHAPTER FIFTY-TWO

: Within You Without You :

ONCE I'VE READ all I can process, I pack the rest of my things.

I don't leave Patrick's room. I drift in and out of sleep. Though it's only a matter of hours, it feels like days.

So much for the workshop at Saint Catherine's. I don't know if it's the thought of losing that opportunity or losing the people here that makes me feel worse. Leaving this place feels like another death. The sadness crawls into all my corners and makes me want to hibernate.

"Josephine." My mother's voice shakes me awake. She opens the door to Patrick's room and crouches next to the bed, eye level with me. Her clothes are wrinkled and her face is splotchy from crying. If she's brushed her hair, it isn't immediately evident.

I haven't seen her in a month. I've barely spoken to her. But it isn't the time away that makes her look like a stranger to me now. I stare at her through blurry tears.

"I'm so sorry." She leans over to hug me, but I sit up and scoot back. She rises and sits on the edge of the bed. Folds her arms over her chest in a way that makes me think she'd crumble if she let go.

"When did you find out?" My voice scratches against my throat.

She shrugs, looking sideways out the window, where a line of blackbirds preen on the roofline across the street. "I always sort of knew."

I narrow my eyes. "You knew? Before he...?"

She nods. "I didn't know who. I just knew that he wasn't always coming here for the band."

I can't wrap my head around how she tolerated this. "You didn't care?"

"Of course I cared! But I didn't think it was this kind of situation. I didn't think there was a Patrick." She laughs grimly. "I gave him room to be himself. He came home alive. That's all I cared bout."

"Except that last time, you mean."

Her lip quivers. "Except the last time."

I scrub my face with my hands and take a deep breath.

"George reached out to me on Facebook about a year after he passed. It was so hard to keep it from you, but you were finally getting better. I couldn't tell you and ruin all that progress."

I sniffle. "You have no idea about my progress. But I'm sorry you got hurt."

Her face crumples. "Oh, honey. Not as sorry as I am that you did. I knew what I was getting myself into. He was a drug addict that came to me half dead to start with."

My stomach rolls. It destroys me to hear her talk about him like that—with this tone of acknowledgement that he ruined her life. Does she regret having me? Did Julia regret having Patrick?

"He was this completely other person." I stand and pick up the urn off the desk where I set it, turn it over in my hands. It's still covered in river sediment. "Someone I didn't even know."

"He didn't even know himself." Mama steps beside me and drapes an arm around my shoulders. I don't want it there, but I don't shake it off. "But I knew him. And you are all the best parts of him."

I put the urn in my suitcase and zip it. Mama stands there as I finish packing, make the bed, and tidy up. I look around at Patrick's room when I finish. It seems empty without my things in it.

"Henry told me he showed you the letter," she says.

"Yeah."

"He sent that to her the day he passed." She clears her throat. "He was devastated about her illness."

"Is that why he started doing drugs again? He'd been clean."

She touches my arm. "He thought he was going to dull his pain. But you have to understand, honey, that once an addict has been clean for so long, their body can't tolerate the same amount of drugs they took before. He made a terrible mistake. The overdose was an accident."

I give in and hug her. She feels so small and frail in my arms. She's been carrying this secret around for a long time. Missing her husband, worried about her daughter. She's just as lonely as I've been.

"I got us a hotel room," she says, once the sniffling has subsided.

Inhale. Exhale. "Okay."

"Patrick wants to see you. I think you should talk to him before we go."

I'd rather claw my way through the brick of this building's third story. But I know she's right. I have a brother, and we have a lot to talk about. I pick at my fingernails.

"Is Henry down there?"

She shakes her head. "He left when I got here."

. . .

Patrick sits across from me at the table in George's kitchen.

It's like seeing Pop looking back at me. So weird. And so obvious. I don't know how I didn't see it the moment I met him. Each time I start to talk, my eyes well up. I glance over at Mama and George in the lounge, where they sit ramrod straight, having tea and stilted conversation. They're pretending not to listen to us.

"You—eh." Patrick's voice shakes a little. "You want to go for a walk?"

I nod.

In the alley behind the Fox Den, we walk side by side. Maybe it'll be easier this way, to talk without having to look one another in the eyes. Before we get to the end of the alley, Patrick speaks up.

"I'm sorry."

I look over at him. "Why are you sorry?"

He shrugs. "For not telling you straightaway? For going along with this charade because I thought honoring his last wish was the right thing to do? And, you know, for existing." And then he laughs, but not because there's anything funny about this. "I am the thing that ruined two families."

I stop at the edge of the sidewalk. In all the time I've spent feeling sorry for myself—before this trip, before I knew, and since I found out—I never once considered that someone might have it worse than me. Patrick does, though. He is a living reminder of a mistake his mother tried to hide. And he didn't lose one parent. He lost both.

As terrible as I feel, I can't imagine how awful that burden would be on top of everything else. I shake my head at him. "Don't say that. You didn't ruin anything. Everyone loves you."

"That's debatable." He leans against the side of the building. "Henry and I stopped getting along. He took up for Mum, because she was dying. I took up for Dad, but Dad couldn't even look at me. I threw myself headlong into football for a distraction. Helped my game a bit, at least." He half smiles.

I half smile back at him. We stand in silence for a few moments until someone turns the corner of the alley. Henry stops for a moment when he sees us there, then speeds past us toward the back door.

I want to tell him not to go, but I don't say a word.

Patrick whispers, "Jesus, did you hit him?"

"What?" I turn to Patrick's shocked expression. "No. Mons hit him."

"Again?"

I nod.

When he gets to the back door and puts his key in, he glances over at me. His expression is loaded with longing. My heart squeezes and I take a mental snapshot.

Caption: why does it have to be this way

He disappears inside the building.

"What was that look? Is there... bloody hell. This is awkward. You aren't related to him, but it's weird, okay?" Patrick props his hands on his hips. I tear my eyes away from the closed back door. "I mean, if you two got married someday..."

Behind all the pain on Patrick's face, there's a hint of humor. Of teasing.

"We aren't getting married." I giggle. "We aren't even speaking."

"You said a lot with your eyes just now."

"Yeah, we do that. It's kind of our thing."

I glance at the back door again, willing it to open. But it doesn't.

"He fought us, you know."

I look over at Patrick.

"On this whole thing. He said John was gone and we should do what's best for you, and that the truth is always best served cold and up front."

I swallow. "That sounds suspiciously like something he would say."

"He stomped around yelling, threatening to tell you everything the moment you got here. Dad had to beg him. He finally agreed but said he wouldn't lie to you if you came right out and asked."

I think back on all the opportunities he had to come clean but didn't.

"I was furious with him. This was a man's final wish, and our mother's final request, and he couldn't honor it because it wasn't convenient for him?" Patrick glances at the back door like he's expecting him to come back, too. "We were going to tell you when I got back to London, just before you left to go home. He said that was manipulative, to wait until the last minute like that. I suppose I see his point now. Even though I worried he'd blow the whole thing before I got a chance to get to know you myself."

When he looks back at me, his eyes are glassed over. My breath catches. They're undeniably Pop's eyes.

"Is that why you told me to avoid conversation with him?" I ask.

"Kinda, yeah. But also because he's a bloody wanker."

We both smile.

I lost my father. But maybe I gained a brother.

CHAPTER

FIFTY-THREE

: Misery :

I THOUGHT IT'D be a relief to get away from the Fox Den.

But after spending time with Patrick, I feel lost. Listening to him talk about my hometown, my best friends—it made me want to hear more. I'm somehow homesick for both North Carolina *and* London, even though I haven't left yet.

I pull my phone out of my suitcase and power it on for the first time in almost two days.

When neither of them replies, I refold the contents of my suitcase and spread it all out over the floral hotel bedspread. For the third time. It's a nervous habit. Something I'm doing to keep my hands busy as the truth of what I'm feeling settles in.

Mama looks up from her phone. "Are you okay?"

I miss my best friends, but I'm not ready to go home yet. I can't leave. Not yet.

"I registered for a photography workshop at Saint Catherine's University." I sink to the mattress and face her on the other bed. "And I still want to go."

She raises her eyebrows. "Oh?"

"I'd planned to ask you if I could stay longer, but I hadn't gotten around to it when everything happened. It starts in ten days."

"Josephine." She sets her phone down on the night table and sits up. "I think it's best if you come home."

I tense my jaw and shake my head. "I think we have some pretty definitive proof that you don't always know what's best for me, Mama. You don't even know what's best for you."

She draws back like I've slapped her. The truth hurts sometimes. I'm feeling bold, so I ask her something I've always wanted to know. I clench my hands together in my lap and conjure all my strength.

"Why did you erase all those emails he sent me?"

She opens her mouth to respond, then closes it again. Regroups. "I was worried about how much you were reading them. You were so stuck in denial."

"You had no right—"

"I printed them all out for you, honey. I have them. Every last one. They're in a folder in my desk and I'll give them to you when we get home."

I swallow the shock. I can't find the right words to express my relief, because *thank you* doesn't feel appropriate. I wait a beat.

"I really want to stay here and do the workshop."

She takes a deep breath and her eyes grow wide with the beginnings of defeat.

"And where will you stay?"

It isn't a no. I sit up straighter.

"I made a friend here who goes to Saint Catherine's. I'll ask her. Or I'll stay in a hotel—maybe even this one. I've been thrifty all summer. I can probably swing it."

"But what about your appointments with Dr. Robert?"

"I'm not going to see Dr. Robert anymore. I'll try someone new, but I don't want to go back to him."

Her mouth hangs slack, but she doesn't say a word. I keep the confessions coming.

"I quit taking my medications. Things were better, at first. Now I'm not so sure. I think I may need different ones."

She takes a deep breath and twists the ring on her left hand—the one Pop gave her, the one she never stopped wearing.

"You are old enough to make informed choices about your health. I can't force pills down your throat every day. I tried that, and you told me what I wanted to hear so you could spit them back out."

I move over to sit next to her on the bed. "They didn't fix me."

She nods. "You're right. There's no magic pill for grief or sadness or depression. But sometimes they do help."

I think about what Henry said to me a few days ago.

"Pop depended on substances to mute his pain. I don't want to be like that. I'm already genetically predisposed to using it as a crutch." I take a deep breath and look up at her. "But I also don't want to refuse help when I know I need it. I'll see another doctor. One here, even, if George has recommendations."

She wrings her hands, blinking more than necessary. "How long does the workshop last?"

My heart stutters. I stand up and dig in my bag for the green flyer, then hand it to her. She unfolds it and stares at the dates and information for a long time.

"Okay."

"Okay?" I suppress the urge to smile. Smiling doesn't feel right. Not yet.

She nods. "We'll figure out all the details tomorrow."

∴

Once I'm settled in bed, I text Zara.

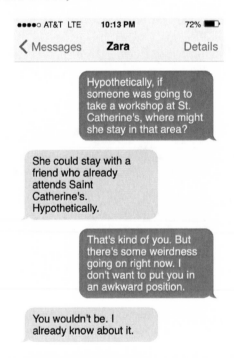

I can't let myself think about what he might've told her right now. When I don't reply, she sends me a string of additional texts.

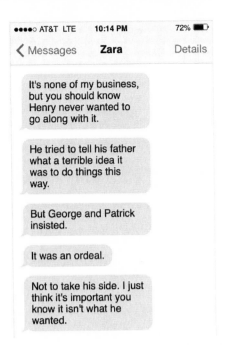

I squeeze my eyes shut, but my phone dings again.

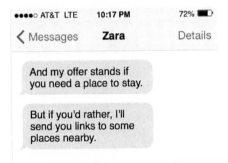

I type about twelve different variations of a response but settle on this.

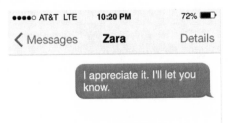

When I'm sure Mama is asleep, I get dressed in the dark, slide my shoes on, and slip out of our hotel room. The only thing that has made me feel better since Pop died was being able to talk about it with Henry. The thought of losing that is gutting, even if I am mad at him.

Everything feels messy and broken, but not ruined. I rehearse my speech as I make my way to the tenth-floor elevator.

I'm really mad at you for keeping this secret, but I forgive you.

On the descent to the lobby, I hover near the back of the elevator.

You were just doing what you were asked, what you thought was right.

The elevator dings at each floor.

But I'm still mad.

People crowd in and file out. I lean against the back wall and wait.

But I can forgive you. Because all summer, you listened to me. You were there for me. Above all, you respected me. You didn't take advantage of me when it would've been really easy for you to. I would've let you.

The elevator doors open to the lobby.

And I'd still like to stay in London and take the workshop and learn more about photography. Because you helped me discover that I like it. That maybe I'm a little bit good at it. And I'll always be grateful to you for that.

The crowd disperses as I step off and continue my epic silent speech. But when I look up, he's there.

Henry. Is. There.

He paces beside the elevator bank. Mumbling to himself. The bruise on his eye has morphed into shades of purple.

I stop walking and somebody bumps into me from behind. The muttered apology is barely audible because at that moment, Henry's eyes meet mine.

I'm not sure who's more surprised. He walks toward me.

"What are you doing here?" I breathe.

"I was going to text you." His voice is cautious. "But I figured you wouldn't answer." He stops in front of me, a safe distance away.

My throat aches to cry again, but I swallow it. "I might have answered."

He risks a grin. "Yeah?"

I shrug. "I said *might*."

He smooths away his smile.

"I came here to tell you that Nigel and I put something together. If you okay it, of course. At the Crow." When I don't say anything, he keeps talking, crossing and uncrossing his arms. Then fiddling with the ring on his thumb. "We invited some of your pop's old friends. I thought—" He hesitates. "I thought maybe you'd like to meet them. Since you didn't have the opportunity to give him a proper sendoff." He shifts his weight from foot to foot and waits. "None of us gave him a proper sendoff."

Tears well up in my eyes.

"Yes, I'd like that." I nod.

He looks like he wants to hug me, but he doesn't. He takes a few steps backwards.

"Monday. Seven o'clock."

I nod again.

He points at me. "You'll be there?"

"I'll be there." I watch him leave, feeling my carefully planned speech evaporate.

I'm sorry, too.

I'm texting you separately because I'm not ready to make nice with my sister yet.

Your mom filled me in on everything.

God, no wonder you've been struggling.

I love you. We'll figure it all out when you get back.

I just saw your text.

You don't have to apologize. I'm the asshole here.

I should've never dragged you between Lexie and me.

If I had known all this stuff was going on...

I'm sorry.

I'm here for you whenever you're ready to talk.

CHAPTER

FIFTY-FOUR

: All Together Now :

THE SIGN ON the door reads *Closed for a private party*.

A huge crowd is gathered inside.

"You ready?" Mama asks as we stare into the plate glass windows of the Crow.

I nod, even though I can't stop trembling. This is what I wanted all along, but now that it's right in front of me, I'm petrified.

Nigel opens the door for us with a toothy smile. Laughter and conversation roar as we step inside. Nearly every table and booth is filled.

I spot Patrick in a big round corner booth next to George. They both wave to us. I scan the crowd. No Henry. Mama hooks her arm into mine and leads me over to join them. A waitress brings us a pitcher of water and glasses. Patrick studies me as I scoot in next to him.

"You good?" he asks me with a nudge.

I nod and take inventory of the room. "I can't believe how many people are here."

Patrick says, "Here comes another."

I meet Henry's eyes as he approaches our table, carrying Patrick's guitar.

"Room for one more?" He looks directly at me. I nod. I barely slept the other night after our conversation in the lobby. Beating myself up for all the things I didn't say. He pulls up a chair at the end of the table and passes the guitar to his brother.

I glance over at Patrick as he props it on the floor between him and George. "Are you planning to play?"

He shrugs, impish grin spreading over his face. "Never know. I'm full of surprises."

We all turn to the stage as Nigel does a mic check.

"Thank you all for being here tonight on such short notice," he says. "Nate meant a lot to all of us, and of course it only made sense to have a bit of an informal memorial for him while his family is in town." He motions toward where Mama and I sit.

"I know some of you have prepared some words about Nate, but you don't have to have a perfect speech planned. If you'd like to say a few words—"

Several hands go up at once.

And that's how it starts.

They line up to share memories. The first is Walter Kingsley. He was the former drummer of Walrus Gumboot, who quit—long before I was born—to start a family. He talks about the camaraderie of the guys in the band, the way Pop was the leader and the glue that kept them all together.

It doesn't go unnoticed that none of those other members are here, which kind of reinforces his point. Without him, they all drifted away.

Friends of Julia's from university get up then, one by one. The last of them tells the story about how the resident advisor found Pop in the girl's dorm. As it turns out, he was naked and playing his guitar in the showers on their floor. The story draws hearty laughs from the crowd.

Then there's the man who grew up in the boys' home with Pop at Strawberry Field. Then a bar owner who took him to rehab. Friends who let him sleep on their couches when he was homeless. A former manager for the band, who quit to chase his own sobriety—at Pop's suggestion.

One after the next they go to the microphone to talk about what Pop meant to them. With each story it becomes clearer. Pop brought joy to these people's lives.

I glance over at Mama through my tears. I could pick her apart. I could stay mad at her. But I think about how she forgave Pop, forgave him before she even knew all the details. How she's forgiven a dead woman, enough to welcome her son—the very proof of a heartbreaking betrayal—into our home with open arms and treat him like family.

She lost more than I did. She lost her husband, her partner in parenting. But she forgave everyone who played a part in her loss. No questions asked.

Mama and I are different in a lot of ways, but this is one way I could stand to be more like her. More forgiving.

When everyone has shared, Nigel takes the microphone again.

"Anyone else?"

The room goes quiet. I only have to think about it for a second, before an invisible nudge makes me raise my hand.

Mama's eyes widen.

"Are you sure?" she mouths. Everyone at the table stares at me. Even Nigel's eyebrows rise as he calls on me. As I approach the stage this time, it isn't like the night I got up to sing. It's better and worse. Better because it doesn't matter now if my delivery is imperfect or choked with tears; people will expect that. It's worse, though, because the hope of him magically appearing is gone now.

I step up to the microphone and face the crowd. Every face is a blur, but it doesn't matter. There's a kaleidoscope of auras and I feel the warmth emanating from each of them.

"Thank you all for being here," I tell them. "It means a lot to my family and me." I glance up at Patrick when I say it. He smiles. "Though I've learned a lot about my father's life during the time I've been in London, I'm still filling in a lot of blanks from the years he spent here before I was born. And maybe even after I was born. Hearing you all share your stories about him tonight is the most comforted I've felt since we lost him."

They all clap. Tears burn my eyes and I ask Pop for one last favor. Please, help me keep it together for this. I reach into my back pocket.

"I'm going to read you a letter he sent me just before he died. Until this moment, only one other person knew about it. I kept it to myself for a long time because I didn't want to share. I wanted it to be all mine. I realize now how selfish that was. So I want to share it all with you."

I read the letter. The room is dead silent, save for a few sniffles.

When I glance up, I catch Mama's expression. She's crying.

"Just so you all know, I've done everything he suggested we'd do here, except dance on the glass floor at the bridge." Everyone laughs. "Heights kind of terrify me."

Henry's eyes meet mine through the crowd. He's smiling that smile.

I tried for a long time to handle my grief on my own. That's my biggest regret.

Everyone here lost him, just like I did.

"We all loved him," I say. "Thank you for being here."

The room becomes a hug fest when I leave the microphone. As I descend the steps and return to my table, I'm stopped over and over by people who want to tell me something about Pop. How he helped them in some way, how he gave them his last dollar for cigarettes or pushed their car out of a ditch. He was a flawed man, but he left a mark on every life he touched.

When I make it back to our corner booth, everyone is standing. Mama grabs me and hugs me for the longest time. "I'm so proud of you," she whispers.

"I need to give you something," Patrick says. He reaches into the booth and picks up the guitar by the neck and outstretches it toward me.

"Wait, what?" I take it, confused.

"It's yours," he says, shoving his hands in his pockets.

"I don't understand." I glance at each face staring back at me, then to Patrick again. "That's your guitar."

He shakes his head. "It's yours."

Mama looks at me like she was expecting this. Like it was previously discussed.

"He bought it the day he died," George says. "And we are certain now that it was for you. It was in his hotel. Tags still on it."

"But…" I glance down and feel the warmth in the wood as I turn it over in my hands.

Then I remember. *PS - I picked up a little something for you today.*

"He told us for years that he wanted to buy you a Lennon replica." George smiles.

I blink away tears and glance at Henry, remembering the night he refused to let me ruin it in the rain. "You knew?"

He nods.

My hands trace the pickups. I stare at my reflection in the shiny finish. A tear splashes beside it and I wipe it away.

I look up at them. "Thank you."

Patrick steps toward me and wraps me up in a hug. Mama drapes her arms around us both. Then George does the same. Henry places a hand on my back. He squeezes us into the most epic group hug I've ever felt.

As we stand there, one big dysfunctional family, a warm sensation shivers over me and a familiar voice whispers in my ear.

We're finally together.

CHAPTER

FIFTY-FIVE

: Ob-La-Di, Ob-La-Da :

HENRY'S ROOM IS unusually tidy.

I am certain that he's cleaned it up for my benefit. The bed is made. Sheets are fresh. Books and papers and records are organized and stored in a way that makes me think Patrick supervised the cleaning. The blanket he bought in Liverpool is folded across the bottom of the bed.

"Oooh! I've got it!" Zara flips her phone screen around. I lean in from my spot on the (vacuumed!) rug and look at the map. "There's a place in Newbury. About halfway between."

She's planning ways for us all to hang out after Henry leaves tomorrow. There's a two- hour commute between Bristol and Saint Catherine's, but if we all get on a train and meet in the middle, it'll only take an hour. I look up at him.

He's wearing a new pair of glasses that look like his old ones, and his bruise has faded to palest yellow. He leans on his dresser and grins at me. I still haven't told him I forgive him. Not aloud, anyway.

"Some of us prefer verbal communication," Patrick says, spinning in circles in the desk chair, balancing a soccer ball between his knees. "Is that a yes? To Newbury?"

I laugh. "It's a yes."

"Brilliant." Patrick stands and smooths his uniform. He has his first game today since he got back. He points at his brother. "If I don't see you before you head out, be safe."

Henry leans in and gives him a fist bump.

"I've got to go, too." Zara stands up from the bed and stretches her legs. "Rehearsals in an hour."

I hop up and give her a hug.

"You sure you don't want to stay with me?" she asks. "We can fit a foldaway in my dorm."

I shake my head. "I'll be good here, I think. It'll give me more time to hang out with Patrick."

It's still weird every single time I remember I have a brother.

"Okay. Call me tomorrow."

I nod as she steps over and gives Henry a hug. "Don't become too important for your friends once you're back at Bristol."

"Never." He grins.

As Zara waves and heads out the door, I move to follow her.

"You're leaving, too, Jo?" Henry says to my back.

I look over my shoulder at him. It isn't that I want to leave. It's just that I haven't been alone with him since that night before everything happened. It's easier to be near him when other people are around. Makes things less complicated. Doesn't affect my heart rate the way this does.

"Hang on a sec, okay?" He goes over to his closet and opens the door. A few things fall over and spill out onto the floor. Which explains how he cleaned his room. I chuckle to myself as he stands on his toes and pulls something off the top shelf.

When he turns to me, the déjà vu shimmies through the room to meet me where I stand.

It's a blue notebook binder.

He outstretches his arm and I take it from him. My fingers trace the smooth outside edge as I flip it open. Inside, there are plastic sleeves with photos. Some are from our trip to Liverpool. Ones that I took, ones that he took. I sink to the bed and flip through without saying anything. There's the one of him sitting on the steps at Abbey Road. The one of me in the grass at Glastonbury. Closer to the back, there's a full-on photoshoot I did with Felix when I was bored.

I blink up at him.

He shrugs. "I developed the roll that was in the camera. Maybe you can compare those to what you learn at the workshop. Use some of them for your school credit, too."

It's a great idea, but I don't think I want to skip photography my senior year now.

I stand up and hug him. No warning. No thinking. I just do it.

"Oh," he laughs, and slips his arms around my back. "Hey."

"Hey," I say into his chest. He's warm and smells good. I get a lump in my throat when I think about going home after the workshop. Facing an entire senior year with an ocean between us. While he dates college girls and maybe forgets about me altogether.

"I'll miss you, Henry."

He draws a little circle on my back with his fingertip. "Two hours. That's it."

"Actually, one hour, if we stick to Zara's plan." I don't mention what happens after the workshop. The ocean-between-us part.

He loosens his grip and pulls back a little. I don't focus on the relative proximity of our faces. How easily I could kiss him with a tippy-toe climb. No, I don't think about that at all.

"I ought to tell you I'm sorry," he says. I start to interrupt but he shakes his head. "No, let me finish. I ought to have told you as soon as you arrived in London. Barefoot in the airport. I should've come clean right then. But one thing bothers me about that. If I had, would any of the good things have happened?"

I stare up at him, watch his eyes switch channels between my eyes and my lips. Back and forth. "I don't think they would have."

I swallow. "Somebody once told me it's foolish to imagine an alternative present. We can only live in one reality at a time, right?"

A smile dawns over his face. "Right." He looks down at the bed beside us, where the blanket is folded. "That night with the mugwort tea? I was trying to tell you the truth through a dream. I thought if I communicated it that way, I wouldn't be breaking my word."

My lips part. "Oh."

"But it didn't quite go as planned." His cheeks flush and he glances at my lips.

Heat crawls up my neck and I smile. "No. Not quite. But I forgive you, anyway."

He leans down and kisses me. It's fast, but then slow. It burns away my will to live anywhere but the present. This present.

When it's over, he smiles against my mouth. "Would you come someplace with me?"

I can't remember how to speak, so I nod.

．．．

The big red double decker drops us off at the Tower Bridge stop.

He takes my hand, and I don't question it. An invisible barrier has been lodged between us for too long. I'm so happy it's finally gone that I don't focus on the fact that he'll be at Bristol by this time tomorrow.

It doesn't occur to me where we're going until we get to the elevator that will take us there.

"Last list item." He grins. I tilt my head all the way back and look up at the glass-bottomed bridge. My heart aches in my chest. At the thoughtfulness. I know I'll compare every boy I ever meet to him for the rest of my life.

"Henry, we don't have to do this."

Traffic and wind roar in our ears as we wait. He cups a hand around his ear.

"Sorry," he yells around a smile. "I can't hear you!"

Tourists crowd into the elevator with us, and then onto the bridge when we get to the top. The panoramic view takes my breath away.

Tiny cars pass below. The mighty Thames sloshes beneath them. The memory of how cold that water is will never leave me. I stay close to the side and hold on to the railing, even as the guide tells us how many tons of weight this many layers of reinforced glass will hold.

Henry steps out into the middle of the bridge. Over the wide empty nothing. And jumps up and down. He wears his trademark mischievous grin. "Don't be scared!"

Pop loved him. He would still love him.

Maybe I even love him.

He reaches into his pocket and pulls out his phone. After a second of scrolling, *Ob-la-di, Ob-la-da* starts playing and he drops the phone back in his pocket. He holds out a hand.

I give him a look "Henry."

"Come here."

I shake my head. "I think we've already established that we can't dance."

"No," he says, stepping closer. "It's not that we can't dance. It's that we've chosen not to, remember? We can always change our minds."

I take his hand. Because how can I say no to that?

He pulls me to his chest. Neither of us know where to put our feet. I laugh as he steps on my toe. "That was clearly your fault," he says.

And then I trip over his feet, but he catches me around the waist.

"That was *your* fault," I say, a little giddy.

Right there on the glass bridge, we dance. It's awkward and silly, and it's in front of God and everybody. But it's the most perfect thing that's ever happened to me.

A little seed of happiness sprouts in my heart.

He twirls me around and I spin into his chest. We stumble and nearly fall over.

"I have to leave tomorrow," he says. "But are you free to-night, by chance?"

I grin up at him. In the worst fake accent possible, I say, "If it pleases his majesty."

And just like the song, life goes on.

∴ ∴ ∴ ∴

Read more from bestselling author
Jen Marie Hawkins.

"A luminous YA love story with magnetic characters and
literary flair." —Kirkus Reviews (starred review)

ACKNOWLEDGEMENTS

All the Lonely People would still be a messy first draft without my agent, Hilary Harwell. Thank you, Hilary, for your guidance over many iterations of this book. I am eternally grateful for your wisdom, partnership, and unwavering support. You are my life raft in this business.

To Emma Nelson, my publisher, you have made my dreams a reality. Thank you for taking a chance on my work, and for championing it so generously, and for being the reason the world can read my words. I'm so glad to call you friend. Olivia Swenson, my editor and collaborator, you make my books better and encourage me at the same time. Thank you for re-teaching me the same concepts over and over again. You have the patience of a saint. Hannah Smith and Carrie Geslison, thank you for being such an enthusiastic, cheerful-hearted team. Owl Hollow is truly a parliament of dream makers and I am so lucky to work with all of you.

To Jennifer Schildmeier, my sister by marriage but friend by choice, thank you for being my number six. Go ahead and count. You've been there for me through the highest highs and the lowest lows. You're an annoyingly perfect name-doppelgänger who never stops challenging me to be better in every aspect of my life. I want to be like you when I grow up, as long as I can still drive like me.

To Dawn Mahaffey Gramling: you are the main reason I fell in love with the Beatles as a kid. Every time I hear *I Saw Her Standing There*, I'm transported to a dance party in your bedroom in that house on Rainbow Drive. Thank you for your steadfast friendship (and side-splitting voice recordings) even all these decades later.

Sonia Hartl, my OG CP, thank you for reading this book like seventeen times and finding reassuring things to say every single time (though the hairless cat comment is still my favorite). You truly saved me from that Full House moment. Sometimes I think I only write books for your inevitable comment bubble jokes. I couldn't do this without you.

Kes Trester, thank you for taking time out of your vacation and walking the streets of Southwark to give me live-action updates as I drafted. Your serendipitous presence in London was the perfect failsafe for my imagination. I am so grateful to still be your padawan, long after your commitment expired. I can't wait to watch a West Coast beach sunset with you one day very soon.

To my writing den—thank you for adding so much to my everyday life. Summer Spence, I can't wait until the world gets to read your beautiful words. Thank you for always offering an inspiring word or an inappropriate joke, whatever the situation requires, no matter how busy you are. Elly Blake, your encouragement, example, and gentle-but-tough love make me a better writer (and a better human). Thank you for always making me feel seen and validated. Kristin Wright, you are always the first to volunteer to read for me, and then you give me the most insightful, game-changing notes, even on the draftiest of drafts. Thank you for being my steady voice of reason, in writing and in life. Mary Ann Marlowe, you are my go-to on all things music and tech and will be forever, whether you like it or not. Thank you for so unselfishly sharing your infinite savvy. Kelly Siskind, thank you for always being willing to brainstorm or offer resources. You make my kissy scenes kissier. Ron Walters, your work ethic and determination are a perpetual source of motivation (okay, and maybe shame, stop making me look so bad!)—yet you still find time to be supportive to a group of strong-willed women. Thank you for making us laugh and keeping us sane. Every single one of you is simultaneously so talented and humble. You each bring something uniquely valuable to our little group. I love you all madly. Never leave me—you know too much!

April Simmons, my soul sister and unpaid therapist: how dare you move to Hawaii and limit the number of waking hours I can call or text you. I forgive you, though, because you are the best friend a girl could ever have. Thank you for holding my hand as I turn my messy ideas into readable things. I'm glad we are close, no matter how many miles separate us.

I am so grateful to Kristin Reynolds, Shawna Parker, and Sarah Reid for early reads and insight on all things UK, The Beatles, and witchy woo. Someday soon, when this stupid pandemic is over, I am going to press you each to my heaving bosom and cry happy tears that you're in my life.

Janet Wrenn and Kristy Wyatt, thank you for always being there with a shoulder or discerning eye to help me overcome whatever obstacle lies in my path. I adore you both.

I offer my most heartfelt thanks to the writers who have helped me countless times along the way and made me feel welcome in this community: Carrie Brown-Wolf, Claire Campbell, Roselle Lim, Heather Truett, Kellye Garrett, Rachel Lynn Solomon, Rebecca Maziel Sullivan, Tracie Martin, Carlee Caranovic, Margarita Montimore, Jennie Nash, Brenda Drake, The 2014 Pitch Wars Mentee Group, Bethany Hegedus, the staff at The Writing Barn, and so many more.

All the incredible women in my life—sisters and moms and nieces and friends—who continue to love me unconditionally: Becky Blanton, Julie Machin, Jamie Gordon, Gwen Hayden, Rebecca Yates, Gracie Schildmeier, Caitlin Gordon Clark, Jane Blanton, Faye Chapman, Joan Hawkins, Julie Walsh, Crystal Morris, Hailey Moore, Kim Collins, Rima Cerone, Angie Holliday, Tamara McGuire-Hall, Robyn Sanders Bivens, LeAnn Carver, Julie Carter, Joanna Diamond, Melissa Vickery Embler, Joy Stringfield, Melissa Speary, Teka Siebenaler, Amanda Wick, and Gwen Whitaker…thank you for reading my books. I would love you even if you didn't, but your support means everything.

My father-in-law, Michael Hawkins, who we lost in 2016, was the biggest Beatles fan I've ever known. If he were here now, I'd insist we watch *A Concert for George*, even though I've already seen it at least a thousand times at approximately one hundred decibels because of him. I miss you, Pops.

To my husband, Jeremy: I stopped being lonely the day I met you. For more than eighteen years, you have been my true north. I don't have the cerebral grasp of physics principles that you do, but I think I understand quantum entanglement because it exists in us. You are an inextricable part of me. No matter what storms life has thrown our way, we've weathered it together. I am so grateful our boys have a dad like you. Thank you for making me laugh through my tears, for tolerating my bright screen when you're trying to sleep, and for making me lattes with little hearts in them when I'm tired but have to press on. You've been a relentless supporter of my dreams and a partner in every sense of the word. My love for you exceeds the space-time continuum.

And lastly, to my boys...

Jonathan: thank you for all the late-night philosophical discussions. Your brain amazes me. Those conversations have given me so many epiphanies on character motivation throughout the development of this story and others, too. Your insight on human nature, and your optimism despite that understanding, make me so proud to be your mom. The only thing I love more than talking to you about music is listening to you play it and sing. I admire the brilliant, hilarious, talented man you are becoming. Jackson: thank you for being my dancing buddy and my constant source of comedy. You have the biggest heart of anyone I've ever known. Your sweet little laugh and your squishy mean-it hugs are a bright spot in every day of my life. I'm so proud of your endless sense of compassion. And I love your unique artistic perspective on everything. I'll never understand why *Taxman* is your favorite Beatles song, but you do you, ya little weirdo. Watching you both grow up is one of my life's greatest privileges.

This book is for you two. Not because it has anything to do with us (other than our love for the Beatles), but because no matter what I write, you are the muses that get me through every strug-

: 309 :

gle. You remind me what's good about the world, and why life, with its pools of sorrow and waves of joy, is always worth it.

JEN MARIE HAWKINS

is a nurse-turned-writer. She writes books for young adults and the young at heart. She is a creative writing coach for Author Accelerator, and her short works can be found in literary magazines including the *Decameron Journal*. Two of her novel-length manuscripts have been finalists  for the YARWA Rosemary Award and the RWA Maggie Award, and her debut novel, *The Language of Cherries*, was named a Kirkus Indie Romance Book of the Year (starred review).

Originally from South Carolina, she now resides in the Houston, Texas area with her husband, two sons, and enough animals to qualify her home as a wildlife center. When she isn't reading or writing stories sprinkled with magic, you can find her cuddling her boys and daydreaming about traveling the world.

Jen is represented by Hilary Harwell of KT Literary Agency.

Find Jen online at jenmariehawkins.com

#AlltheLonelyPeople

Made in United States
North Haven, CT
25 October 2021

10573977R00182